FOR DWARF'S SAKE

FOR DWARF'S SAKE

DWARF BOUNTY HUNTER™ BOOK EIGHT

MARTHA CARR

MICHAEL ANDERLE

Copyright © LMBPN Publishing
Cover Art by Jake @ J Caleb Design
http://jcalebdesign.com / jcalebdesign@gmail.com
Cover copyright © LMBPN Publishing
A Michael Anderle Production

LMBPN Publishing
PMB 196, 2540 South Maryland Pkwy
Las Vegas, NV 89109

First Version, May 2021
Version 1.01, May 2021
ebook ISBN: 978-1-64971-724-5
Paperback ISBN: 978-1-64971-725-2

Johnny Walker's rental SUV rolled to a stop in front of a pair of massive gates. He glanced in the rearview mirror as Lisa pulled up behind him in the second rental before he nodded and leaned through the open driver's window to look into the tiny eye of the video camera mounted on the gate tower.

A light buzz issued from the structure, followed by a heavy metallic click before the detailed iron gates swung open slowly on their mechanized hinges.

Beside the bounty hunter in the front passenger seat, Leroy lowered his cyborg head to peer through the windshield. "I don't like it when you don't tell us what's going on, boss."

The dwarf sniffed and rolled the window up against the February chill before he accelerated. "You might not have hopped on the jet if I told you ahead of time."

Lisa eased her SUV in behind his and the gates creaked slightly when they drew together again to block out the rest of the world.

"See, that doesn't make me feel any better." Leroy turned to look into the back seat at June, who sat in the middle—without a seatbelt—her arms folded beneath her perpetual scowl.

"It ain't supposed to." The SUV rumbled along the worn dirt track that cut across the massive expanse of the ranch in Cody, Wyoming.

"Did we do something wrong, boss?"

Apart from take over my property, destroy my yard and the boathouse, and save my ass a few too many times to count?

"Naw." He spared the cyborg shifter a sideways glance. "But I didn't wanna color your thoughts about anythin' before we roll into this."

"Huh." Leroy scratched his head. "You mean you didn't want us to argue with you."

June scoffed. "He didn't want us to fight back 'cause he knows we'd kick his ass."

Johnny shook his head and forced himself to not glare at the Crystal borg in the back seat. "I ain't tryin' to fight anyone. Y'all sit tight and watch the cards get dealt, huh?"

"That's kinda hard to do when you won't tell us what cards we're looking for," the shifter muttered.

With nothing to say to that, the bounty hunter focused on driving across the rolling hills of the ranch. He'd stayed away from it for over fifteen years and now, he was returning for the second time in less than six months.

This time, I have a plan. And if the borgs ain't up for it, I ain't gonna force 'em. Probably.

They crested the rise of the final gentle slope in the brown grass dusted with light snow from that morning and stopped in front of the low, squat building positioned in the middle of nowhere.

That's what ranches are, ain't they? All this space out in the middle of nowhere, and if there ain't livestock roamin' around, there's a buildin' that looks like the end of the road.

Lisa's SUV stopped beside his and he felt Leroy's gaze on the side of his face almost like a slap.

"You're seriously not gonna tell us?"

"Nope. Come on." Johnny turned the engine off and hopped out of the rental. The icy wind gusted across the field but he headed into it toward the building. The borgs would follow. They always did.

As I see it, this is their chance to quit followin' someone else and do what needs doin' for themselves.

Multiple vehicle doors opened and shut again quickly as Leroy and June emerged from the first SUV, followed closely by Lisa, Brandon, and Clint. The hounds bounded out of the second vehicle. He didn't turn to make sure the others were coming or to stop for any explanations. Heading into this wasn't nearly as bad as gearing up for a goodbye the first time he had dropped Amanda off at the academy but it was a damn close second.

Luther raced after his master with a low whine. "What's going on, Johnny?"

"Yeah, are we here to chase some cows?" Rex added and trotted along dutifully with his nose pressed to the frosted ground.

"We have a meetin', boys." He stopped at the steel door that marked the building's only entrance and looked into the shiny black orb of the security camera mounted below the awning. "Y'all settle now and let this happen the way it's meant to."

"Yeah, sure, Johnny." Luther sat at his master's heels when the door buzzed and a green light blinked above the handle.

"Do they know what's gonna happen?" Rex asked and licked his muzzle.

The door opened with an audible click and the dwarf made no effort to answer his hounds.

The borgs gotta go in blind. They gotta make their own decisions without me tellin' 'em what to do.

He stepped into the dimly lit room that took up the front half of the building and stopped to hold the door open for everyone else. Leroy darted him a curious frown but entered without a word. June didn't look at him. The twins glanced at each other as they passed him and Clint shrugged. When Lisa brought up the rear to step out of the cold and into their next meeting place, she met Johnny's gaze with raised eyebrows.

"Ready?" she asked.

"I can't read their minds, darlin'." He let the door close behind her and turned to face the long table stretched across the center of the room.

Lisa stopped him with a hand on his shoulder and leaned in closer to mutter, "I was talking about you, Johnny."

"Me?" He sniffed and she removed her hand when he shrugged. "This ain't about me."

She shook her head but fortunately didn't say anything else.

I couldn't lie to her if some asshole put a gun to my head and told me to.

When he met her gaze again, he scratched the side of his face through his wiry red beard. "Hell. It is what it is. We simply gotta let it play out."

"Okay."

The borgs had spread out around the room to study their new meeting place. It was empty—of other purely biological life forms, of course—and Leroy turned toward Johnny with his regular eye wide. His mechanical eye swiveled and spun and the shutter opened and closed. "It looks like we got stood up, boss."

"Naw. We're early—"

A row of blue track lighting lit up with a hum along the walls directly below the ceiling, and the overhead lights flickered before they brightened.

"Welcome, Johnny Walker and team." The mechanical male voice filled the room and almost drowned out the click and droning whine of other tech moving behind the walls. *"Please take a seat and make yourselves at home. Your host will be with you momentarily."*

The borgs froze and gazed intently at the pieces of installed tech that blinked to life around them—the flashing blue and green lights along panels in the walls, the track lighting, and the four cameras mounted high in each corner. Clint nudged his brother's shoulder with a fist and nodded at one of those cameras on the far side.

Brandon tilted his head. "Make ourselves at home? It looks like an interrogation room to me."

"It ain't. Not as long as we sit and wait patiently." Johnny gestured toward the chairs surrounding the long table and headed toward one in the center to take a seat.

Lisa sat beside him but the borgs remained where they were and scrutinized the room none of them knew anything about. "He won't make an appearance for this, will he?" she whispered.

"Naw. I think he'll send one of his crew instead. It makes it seem more natural."

"Based on what you told me about him, I'd say anyone is more natural."

"Yeah."

June turned from where she'd squared off in a staring contest with the left-hand wall and scowled at them. "What are we doing here?"

"I told y'all to wait and let it work itself out," Johnny muttered without looking at her. "You heard the man. Take a seat."

"That wasn't a man," Leroy said. "That was a machine."

"Same thing."

"What?" Brandon frowned at Johnny. "That only applies to us."

"Most of the time, I'd say you're right." The dwarf leaned back in his chair, folded his arms, and stretched both legs out in front of him before he crossed one ankle over the other.

Leroy and June exchanged a nervous glance before the shifter borg strode toward Johnny and Lisa. "What is that supposed to mean?"

"It means things are a little different here, is all. Now y'all better sit your asses down and wait for—"

A low hum came from the other steel door at the far end of

the room, which didn't have any handles or even a panel to punch in a code to open and close it. It swung into the room all the same and a man in his late sixties stepped out. His hair was bone-white with age and hung in thin strands down to his shoulders. He wore a thick tan Carhartt jacket over matching overalls and heavy work boots. As soon as he entered the room, the door closed behind him on its own with a hydraulic hiss and he focused on the four borgs who stared at him in skeptical surprise.

"I hope I didn't make you wait too long." He approached the table and leaned across it to extend a rough, work-worn hand toward the bounty hunter. "Emmet."

"Johnny." He took the proffered hand with a firm nod, surprised by the strength in the man's grip. "This here's my partner, Lisa Breyer."

"A pleasure." Emmet grinned as he shook her hand next, then straightened and glanced at the borgs again. "And while there's little I like more than meeting a beautiful woman when times are good, I have to say it's even more of a pleasure to see the four of you standing here on the Flatstone Ranch."

They gave him matching stares of disapproval.

Johnny grunted. "The big guy over there is Leroy. The twins are Brandon and Clint. And that's—"

"Fuck the introductions," the Crystal muttered.

"June."

"It's nice to meet you all," Emmet said, still grinning.

"Johnny. Hey, Johnny." Luther's tail thumped on the concrete floor as he panted beside his master. "What about us?"

"Yeah, don't forget about the hounds," Rex added. "We're people too."

The bounty hunter ignored them and waited for their high-stakes meeting to begin.

The silence in the room finally grew thick enough to make Brandon uncomfortable. He cleared his throat and stepped closer to the table to extend a partially metallic hand toward their host. "Same."

Emmet stared at the thin silver rod that ran down the center of the cyborg's hand toward his middle finger. "You're not gonna break my hand with that, are you?"

"Not if you don't give me a reason too."

The white-haired man laughed and bravely risked a handshake with the cyborg.

"Seriously?" June stepped toward them and glared at Brandon. "Some moron smiles and holds his hand out and you're suddenly best friends?"

Brandon and Clint gave her matching frowns as the borg released Emmet's hand. "It's called being polite. What's the big deal?"

"I don't trust him." She folded her arms again and studied the newcomer with a sneer. After a moment, she turned her gaze to Johnny. "But he wants us to."

"This feels like the time for an explanation," Leroy added.

Emmet turned his smile onto the dwarf. "You haven't told them."

"No." He ignored the borgs' stares and shrugged. "I thought they'd take it a little easier hearin' it from you for the first time."

"Sure. That makes sense." The man lowered himself into the single chair on his side of the table, then gestured toward the others. "Please. Have a seat."

The four didn't move.

Lisa slid her foot toward Johnny's until their calves touched, which made him turn to look at her. Her concerned frown told him everything he needed to know, which was that they were both on the same page here.

Either they take to it the way I thought they would or this whole thing goes to hell and we're startin' all over again.

He tried to give her a reassuring nod but it felt more like an uncontrolled twitch.

"If you're worried about breaking the chairs," Emmet added with a chuckle, "don't. They don't look like much but trust me. A few hundred extra pounds won't make a dent."

Clint was the only one who moved. He grasped the closest chair, gave it a little jiggle, then clicked his tongue and dropped into the seat. Leroy and Brandon followed suit, albeit with reluctance. June remained where she was on the side of the room and squinted at the white-haired man who'd come to meet with them.

"That's close enough, I guess." The old man shrugged. "I have an offer for you. Johnny said he thought you'd be open to it, so here we are. It's time to hear it straight from the cyborgs' mouths, right?"

"Wait." Brandon leaned forward so he could peer around his brother to stare at the dwarf. "I thought we were on a job."

Leroy looked sharply at the bounty hunter. "You brought us out here so you could hear an offer?"

"I lied." Johnny shrugged.

"Johnny's only the facilitator in this case," Emmet added and nodded calmly. "Whatever decision you make after this is entirely your own."

"Decision about what?" Leroy's voice bordered on a growl.

"A big move." The man on the other side of the table grinned and gazed slowly from one cyborg face to the other. "Or, if you prefer, call it a change of employment."

CHAPTER TWO

"Johnny, what's he talking about?" Leroy muttered.

Brandon shook his head. "Yeah, this is—"

"It's not a change of employment," June said from the corner. "He doesn't pay us shit."

"Now hold on a minute." Johnny pointed at her. "Y'all ain't even let the man say his piece yet."

"Don't get me wrong." Emmet folded his hands on the table and looked entirely unfazed by the growing confusion and anger among four cyborgs who could blast this entire ranch and everyone on it completely off the map if they wanted to badly enough. "Mr. Vester isn't technically offering a steady paycheck, either. At least not as far as traditional salaries and benefits are concerned."

"We already tried the cyborg-slave situation." June hissed her indignation. "I'm not interested."

"My employer is not Dr. Monroe." The old man's smile disappeared in an instant and erased every trace of his friendly demeanor as he focused all his attention on the Crystal. "And I can assure you that nothing awaits you on the other end of this deal that even remotely resembles what the four of you endured in that woman's lab. So instead of being insulted by that premature accusation, I'll keep talking. And I'd appreciate it if everyone held their questions and comments until the end. Understand?"

Johnny snorted and immediately wiped the smirk off his lips when Lisa glanced warningly at him. *The man ain't beatin' around the bush. And he listened when I said they're like a huddle of teenagers with mood swings.*

"Now...I work for a magical named Grady Vester. The Flat-Stone Ranch is only one of his many properties but the one he prefers to call home because he doesn't leave much." Emmet caught the amused glance shared by the twins and chuckled. "And no, it's not because he doesn't exist or because he's on his deathbed. Mr. Vester is in perfect health—all things considered. Johnny can attest to that."

"Uh..." The dwarf rubbed his mouth vigorously. "I...if we're talkin' about his mental capacity, sure."

"There is no point in splitting hairs." Emmet stared at the bounty hunter for an uncomfortably long time and a knowing smile spread slowly across his lips. "Mr. Vester wants the four of you to come work for him here at the ranch. And while you won't receive monetary compensation or employee benefits— which I can't imagine any of you need in the traditional sense— there are benefits. There is more than enough space for you out here away from most of civilization. It would be much better than being cooped up in a little boat in the Everglades—"

"Houseboat." Johnny pointed at the man. "And it ain't little."

"Of course."

"So you're looking for free labor," Leroy said.

"No." Emmet's eyes widened when he fixed his gaze on the shifter borg. "Mr. Vester has studied bio-tech for decades and specifically, the marriage of magical organisms with technology far more advanced than anything out there on the market right now. Or anything that will be out on the market in the next fifty years. Similar to the enhancements the four of you now call part of yourselves."

"No way." Brandon shoved away from the table, which fortunately had been bolted to the floor. "I don't care how much space there is. I will not sign up to be a lab rat. Not again."

"This isn't about experimentation."

"I don't care."

"Brandon, right?" The old man nodded and the borg paused in his attempt to get up from his chair. "I knew it would be tricky to get all the right information out on the table, but I honestly didn't think it would be this hard to convince you. My employer isn't looking for hired muscle, per se. He isn't a scientist and he doesn't want to dissect you."

"Then what does he want?" June muttered.

"Well…" The man sighed. "If I had to guess, I'd say he's excited about the idea of not being alone."

"You're here." Brandon eased warily into his chair again. "Who wants cyborgs for company? Besides Johnny, of course. He's the only one who ever did anything to help us."

The dwarf cleared his throat and could only stare at the table. *This ain't goin' anythin' like I thought it would.*

"Mr. Vester understands what it's like to be in your shoes," Emmet added. "Which is why there's an offer at all."

"I think I've heard enough." Leroy stood. "I'm not sure what we were supposed to get out of this meeting, but that right there gave it away."

"And why's that?"

"No one knows what it's like to be us." The shifter thumped a fist against his chest with a metallic clang. "Except for us. And anyone who thinks they know is either way too full of themselves or a complete idiot—"

"You were right, Emmet." The same robotic male voice echoed through the small room. *"I underestimated their dedication."*

The old man winked at Johnny but responded to the seemingly disembodied voice. "I'll get it resolved, sir."

"There is no need. I'll take it from here, thank you."

The borgs scowled at the white-haired man. "Who was that?" Leroy asked.

"Dedication to what?" Brandon asked at the same time.

"See for yourself." Emmet stood and stepped sideways down the table to give everyone a clear view of the automatic door with no handle behind him.

Lisa leaned slightly toward Johnny and whispered, "Was that him?"

The bounty hunter inclined his head in the affirmative and watched Emmet while the borgs all watched the door open slowly with another hydraulic hiss.

Johnny was surprised to see his old friend Grady up and moving around again, especially after the last time he'd come to pay the gnome a visit on the ranch. Of course, Grady Vester was in no condition to move anywhere on his own. The guy hung from a heavy metal stand on wheels, suspended by wires and cables and with tubes of organic material that twisted around and through his body to keep him alive.

He looks like a damn IV bag.

Then again, he had connected himself body and mind to some of the most advanced technology on either planet, which meant he could, in fact, get around on his own. It was simply that the machines were all a part of him and had been for quite some time.

"Whoa, whoa, whoa, Johnny." Rex uttered a low whine and crouched low on the floor as he stared at the newest magical to join their meeting. "That guy's got serious problems."

"It smells like mud and fried wires," Luther added and crawled slowly on his belly under the table to get a closer look. "Want us to get rid of it?"

The dwarf snapped his fingers and both hounds stopped moving.

Leroy stood and glared at Emmet. "What is this?"

"This is someone else who completely understands what it's like to be in your shoes." The robotic voice came from all around them through the speakers hidden in the walls, although the speech clearly now came from the gnome who was more machine than organic material. Despite this, his brain was as keen as it had always been. *"Unless, of course, you still think I'm either way too full of myself or a complete idiot."*

Johnny snorted. The shifter cleared his throat and glanced at the other borgs.

"You're Grady?" Brandon asked as he and Clint pushed from their chairs as well.

"Mr. Vester," Emmet clarified.

"That's all right, Emmet. They can call me whatever they like, before or after taking us up on the offer." A series of green strobing lights raced around the perimeter of the room, streaked to the ceiling and down to the floor, then moved in tandem until they illuminated the bounty hunter in a column of glowing green like a spotlight. *"It's good to see you again, Johnny."*

The dwarf nodded, ignored the light around him, and stared instead at the suspended, emaciated body of his old friend. "Yeah, you too."

In a second, the green lights winked out and a series of clicks came directly from Grady's mind-controlled suspension stand on wheels.

"This is my offer to the four cyborgs in this room. I want to help you learn more about yourselves. What you're capable of. What purpose you can and inevitably will serve now that you've evolved into something more than you ever could have been before your unique enhancements. I know what you need because as you can see, I've done much the same thing to myself."

Clint's jaw dropped and he growled harshly in protest before he muttered, "You did this to yourself?"

Everyone in the room stared at the usually speechless twin, even when Grady's creepily robotic laughter filled the room.

"I did. I still am. There are always improvements and upgrades to be made. It's a constant process. But I promise I won't do anything to you unless you want it."

June finally abandoned her surly position in the corner and stepped toward the table to study their highly augmented host. "What do you want from us?"

"Your company. And for the four of you to be my eyes and ears in the world outside FlatStone." Grady's metal stand lit up with a burst of bright-white lights that raced up the metal pole like a beacon. *"There's only so much I can do from here. The Internet's fun and all but being able to actively experience life through the perspective of a few friends is something I've always wanted to try."*

It seemed that was all the gnome had to say on the matter, and after another ten seconds of silence, Emmet shoved his hands into the pockets of his heavy Carhartt jacket and grinned at the borgs. "So, what do you say?"

Leroy's mechanical eye spun and whirred madly as it zoomed in and out again on the gnome attached to his odd set of wheels. The twins looked at each other and no one else.

"I'm in," June stated.

"Seriously?" The shifter borg stared at her. "Just like that?"

"Yep." She shrugged. "It sounds like a good deal to me. We start today, right?"

Emmet chuckled. "If that's what you want."

"And if Johnny agrees, of course," Grady added.

The dwarf raised an eyebrow at her. "I didn't think you'd set your heart on Wyoming so fast."

"You're cool and all," she said with a shrug and a smirk that might have been teasing, although with her habitual scowl behind it, that wasn't clear. "For a dwarf. But living on a houseboat in the swamp for the rest of my life wasn't exactly the best plan. And I don't even know how long the rest of my life will be now that I'm…you know." She spread her arms and shrugged. "This."

"It can be as long as you want," Grady interjected. *"At this point, nothing is stopping any of us."*

"Okay." Brandon clapped a hand on Clint's shoulder and nodded at Emmet and the gnome. "We're in too."

"Excellent." The old man grinned at Leroy. "And you?"

The shifter borg stepped away from the table to fix Johnny with a confused frown. "Are you trying to get rid of us, boss?"

"That ain't it and you know it." The bounty hunter gestured toward their hosts. "You know I ain't equipped to give y'all anythin' other than a cramped houseboat and the odd job here and there. Y'all have bigger things to take care of."

"Bigger things." Leroy shook his head. "This is nuts."

"The offer stands if you need some time to think about it."

"No. If June stays, so do I."

"Then that settles it." Emmet nodded toward the front door of the low building where Johnny and his soon-to-be ex-crew had entered. "We'll head out and I'll give you the grand tour."

"Of a ranch?" June snorted. "There's nothing out here."

"If you truly believe that, you're in for quite a surprise." With a broad grin, the man stepped around the table and headed to the door. "Whenever you're ready."

A burst of cold air wafted into the room when he stepped outside and the door swung shut behind him and left Johnny and his team in silence.

"I'm looking forward to this." Grady's robotic voice was quieter now through the hidden speakers as his metal stand rolled toward the open automatic door and the room beyond filled with blinking lights. *"Don't be a stranger, Johnny."*

"You'll find me whether I want you to or not."

"Just because I've left emotional attachment behind doesn't mean I

expect anyone else to. By the way, how did that device work out for you?"

Johnny stood and nodded at the gnome's receding form through the door. "It got me inside an armored worm's brain, so I have to say it's a win."

"Interesting." That was the last thing Grady said before his suspended body disappeared and the door closed.

June burst out laughing and trudged across the room to throw the entrance door open and step outside.

"So this is goodbye then, huh, boss?" Leroy scratched the side of his head with his segmented metal fingers.

"Naw. It's only a see ya later. Let's go outside." The bounty hunter stood, snapped his fingers for the hounds to follow, and held the door open for Lisa and the other three borgs.

"Are you in a hurry to get away from us?" Brandon asked with a smirk.

Johnny waited until the door shut completely and they'd moved a good twenty feet away from the squat building to return to the rental SUVs. "I merely thought that if y'all wanted to say anythin' you don't want overheard and cataloged in the tech brainiac's system, you oughtta say it outside. It might be the only privacy y'all get."

Leroy extended his metal hand toward the dwarf and nodded. "It's still better than a houseboat. No offense."

CHAPTER THREE

"That was one heck of a goodbye, huh?" Seated in one of the Adirondack chairs in Johnny's back yard in the Everglades, Lisa stretched her legs in front of her and zipped her light hoodie the rest of the way.

He sipped his glass of whiskey and watched the hounds race through the swamp after some creature. "It ain't a goodbye, darlin'."

"Oh, yeah? Because you plan to see them again soon? Maybe have them over for the holidays at the end of the year?"

The dwarf snorted and shook his head. "That's outta the question. Unless they wanna stop by, then I ain't tellin' 'em to turn around and get the hell off my property."

"Well, if you didn't do it while they were living here, why start now, right?"

"It's a good way to look at it." He swallowed another mouthful of Johnny Walker Black Label and drew a deep breath. "But damn, it's good to have the place to ourselves again."

"To ourselves. Not yourself." Lisa darted him an amused sideways glance.

"Sure, darlin'. The place is yours as much as it is mine at this point. You've been stayin' here with me long enough."

"Johnny, if that's the criteria you base this on, this property might as well belong to the borgs too."

"Don't even go there." Her laughter made him smirk before he buried the expression in his glass again. "It's gonna be nice and quiet around here now with more than enough space and peace to go with it. I get to work on my gear and program Margo however I want with no explosions and no attitude."

"Exactly what you've been pining for over the last three months."

He glanced and snorted. "I ain't pinin'."

"Well, not anymore."

"It's called lookin' to the future and likin' what I see a helluva lot more than the present. That was hard enough with the borgs here and now they're…gone."

"You don't sound all that happy about it."

"Maybe you ain't listenin' close enough, darlin'. 'Cause I tell you what. Now that we're on our own again, only the two of us and hounds, the list of problems got a hell of a lot shorter. No tryin' to convince rental agencies that their SUVs were already crooked and bent when we got 'em. No more buyin' giant-ass jars of pickles wholesale. And did you see the look on Felix's face when he hopped into the jet? The man looked like he'd been given a second chance at life."

Lisa laughed brightly. "That's what this is about? Making the pilot of your private jet happy because he doesn't have to worry about carrying four cyborgs' worth of extra weight?"

"Naw. It's about makin' me happy. Which I can do now that I don't have four annoyin', disrespectful, needy, ridiculously powerful, and effective cyborgs livin' on my property and callin' me boss. Askin' for the next job. Savin' our hides at the last minute."

Lisa straightened in her chair and turned toward him and a joking smile played on her lips. "You miss them already."

"What? No. That's not what I said."

"But it's what you're thinking."

"Lisa, that's the most ridiculous thing I've heard all day and we just flew home from an in-person meetin' with Grady. If you can even call that in-person."

Her mouth fell open as she stared at him with even more intensity. "You used my first name."

"So?"

"You only do that when you're pissed or when we're in the middle of a fight and something's about to explode. Or when you're hiding something. My gut and my brain tell me it's not the first two options."

Johnny grunted and muttered into his whiskey, "It's about to be the first one if you don't quit pushin' this."

"Ha! Fine. You don't have to talk about it and I won't bring up your sentimentality again for the rest of the day."

"Make it the rest of the week." He rested his head against the back of his Adirondack chair and let himself relax fully in his back yard.

Privacy, peace, and quiet. That's all I want. I have everythin' I need right here and it don't include the borgs. Right?

Lisa leaned back in her chair and sighed. "Fine. I won't bring it up again for the rest of the week. Besides, we have something else to look forward to at the end of the month."

"We do, huh?"

"Well, you don't strike me as someone who laments turning another year older and still looking fifty years younger." She chuckled and tried to cover it with a forced clearing of her throat. "Maybe forty."

"What are you goin' on about?"

"You know, the fact that most people usually look forward to their birthday."

"My—" Johnny's glass clinked on the armrest of his chair before he turned to fix her with a scowl. "How the hell did you find that out?"

Lisa grinned winningly and batted her eyelashes. "I think you're forgetting how much of your case file I read before we met."

"Christ." He downed the last of his whiskey in one gulp.

"And even if I hadn't read your file, I would still have pegged you for an Aquarius."

"A what now?"

"Aquarius, Johnny. Your astrological sign shared by everyone born between January twentieth and February eighteenth."

"Astrological sign?" He snorted. "That's a load of hooey."

"Did you say, 'hooey?'"

"You know it as well as I do, darlin'. There ain't nothin' in all that outer-space mumbo jumbo that means anythin'."

Lisa laughed and shook her head in mock defeat. "You truly don't believe in anything you can't see with your eyes, do you?"

"Or smell or touch. All this is folks lookin' for somethin' to bring 'em meanin' when they can't find it on their own. You already knew my birthday so you plugged that into whatever this Aquarius crap is and you pulled out whatever you wanted to see in there that makes me make more sense to ya."

"Oh, is that right?" She slid her hand into her back pocket and pulled her phone out. "You know, I would love to test this theory of yours."

"What are you doin'?"

"You have, based on what you've said, never looked your sign up, Johnny. So this is fun for both of us. You get to hear what I 'want to find meaning in,' and I get to watch you react to hearing yourself explained in detail by a complete stranger."

Johnny rubbed his mouth and red beard vigorously and stared directly ahead at the reeds and tall grasses that shivered in the cool breeze racing across the swamp. "This is stupid."

"Maybe. But listen to this first. Here we go. Aquarius." Lisa cleared her throat and tried to wipe the smile off her face to at least sound more serious. "Aquarius is an air sign. Supporting 'power to the people' and working to change the world through radical social progress."

"That ain't me."

"Rebels at heart, Aquarius signs despise authority and anything conventional. They're often identified by an offbeat fashion sense, unusual hobbies, and nonconformist attitude—"

Johnny snorted. "Come on. Anyone with a brain who ain't tryin' to be a sheep in this world would define themselves that way. And they wouldn't have to write about it on the damn Internet."

"The planet Uranus rules Aquarius and governs innovation, technology, and surprise events."

"Seriously—"

"Nontraditional nature, big thinkers, reputation for being aloof and distant in relationships. A stubborn streak and obstinacy that stem from a strong, righteous conviction. They need considerable space and alone time and value freedom above almost everything else. They thrive on shock value and view challenges to their independence as power-hungry attempts to control them and to keep them from flying their freak flag high."

"What the hell? I ain't got a goddamn freak flag." He reached for her phone but she jerked it away from him to keep reading.

"Aquarians will—" She laughed, glanced at him, then found her place again to continue reading. "Will find themselves moving with more ease in life when advocating empathy and compassion wherever possible, which can sometimes...sometimes be—"

She burst out laughing again and lowered her phone into her lap.

"What?" Johnny scowled at her. "Sometimes be what? Why's that so funny?"

"One of the most difficult things for an Aquarius sign to learn."

"Are you fuckin' kiddin' me?" He glared at her as she was consumed by laughter and tears formed in the corners of her eyes. "Gimme that."

Lisa didn't try to keep her phone away from him a second time, her fingers limp as she fought to catch her breath between shrieks of laughter.

The dwarf scrolled up and down through the astrological writeup, snarled, and tossed the device into the grass at their feet. "It's all bullshit."

"Oh, come on." She bent to retrieve it and wiped the tears from her cheeks. "That's you, Johnny. There isn't a single thing in there that doesn't apply directly to who you are. All the time."

"I betcha there's a next page that says all dwarves and all bounty hunters are like that too."

"What?"

"And what's your sign, huh? Annoyin'-As-Hellius?"

Her chuckles subsided and she looked at him in teasing exasperation. "See? That's what it said. You don't like being defined or squeezed into a box. Fly your freak flag, Johnny. Come on!"

"All right. We're done." He gave her his unamused look and turned quickly away to hide his smirk as he reached for the half-empty whiskey bottle in the grass beside him. "You already pinned me down without readin' some crackpot writeup, darlin'."

"Right. It merely reinforces what I already know." She watched him pour another four fingers and wondered why he didn't simply fill an entire glass. "You know, astrologically speaking, Aquarius and Cancer are considered one of the most volatile pairings."

"It's a good thing I only drink whiskey, then."

"For relationships."

The dwarf finally looked at her and allowed himself to smile. "Is that what you are?"

"Yep."

"See? It ain't nothin' but horseshit. Wait, when's your birthday?"

"Look it up, Johnny."

They sat together for a moment longer, enjoying the peace and quiet of their shared solitude at the edge of the swamp. Lisa leaned forward to slip the whiskey glass out of his hand and took a small sip before she returned it. "So what do you want for your birthday?"

"Aw, hell. I guess it's the same thing I always want—sit back, relax, and not do anythin' that ain't either one of those or huntin'."

"How exciting."

"Uh-huh. This year might be a little different."

She propped her elbow on the armrest and raised an eyebrow. "How so?"

"If you stick around darlin', we can call it my birthday present and leave it at that."

"Wow. That might be one of your better lines."

With a low chuckle, he inclined his head and raised the whiskey to his lips again. "It ain't a line."

"Well, we still have time to think about it."

CHAPTER FOUR

After an entire evening of sitting back, relaxing, and doing absolutely nothing—which was as satisfying as he'd expected after having his life in the swamp turned upside-down for the last ten months—Johnny put himself to work the next morning. He started with the houseboat.

"This is a goddamn mess." The bounty hunter walked through the lowest level of the massive vessel and scowled at the charred holes in the walls, the appliances ripped from their bolts, and the wooden floorboards torn up, shredded, and scattered in disarray. "That is the last time I let four cyborgs get comfy and settle into anythin' I own."

The hounds sniffed around the room, dug their snouts under piles of debris, and pawed through the wreckage. Luther caught a ripped piece of fabric between his jaws and tugged it out from under the table that lay on its side, its corners chipped in jagged edges. "Hey, Johnny. Looks like someone left their old t-shirt behind."

Rex approached his brother for a good sniff at the stained and tattered item. "Bro, I think that's underwear."

"Oh." The rag dropped to the floor again and his brother buried his nose in it. "That's why it smells so good."

Johnny snapped his fingers and both hounds whipped their heads up to look at him. "We're startin' with the big things first, boys. I gotta get all the furniture upright again and fix whatever's fixable. I need a damn clean-up crew."

"Don't worry about that, Johnny." Rex grasped an overturned chair by its bent metal leg and dragged it through the destruction. "You got us."

"Yeah, we're helpful." Luther snorted and began to dig through the pile of shredded metal and wooden wall paneling beneath one of the holes June had blasted into every level of the houseboat. "Anything you two-legs can do, we can do. Right, Rex?"

"And more." The larger hound sniffed the floor again and wove from one side to the other with his tail straight up in the air. "Like picking up a scent in here that isn't from the borgs."

"What's that?" The dwarf turned to watch his hounds as they converged on the trail only two coonhounds could find.

"Doesn't smell like metal."

"Nope. Smells like magic, though."

"You let someone else stay in here, Johnny?"

"Not knowingly." He headed after them but stopped when a small splash came from the outer deck, followed by a metallic thump and slow footsteps. He snapped his fingers but both hounds had already looked toward the source of the noise.

"Want us to check it out, Johnny?"

The footsteps drew closer.

"We'll catch him with his pants down," Luther added. "Assuming he has any."

The bounty hunter nodded toward the open doorway—the door to which had been ripped from its hinges and now lay in the pile of destroyed cabinets from the kitchen area—and fingered the utility knife strapped to his belt.

The hounds padded across the main room on the first floor. "Smells like someone we know."

"Smells like magic and fish."

"Bro, that's the swamp."

"Wait. Rex. The swamp is magic?"

Fighting to not call them back and take care of the intruder himself, Johnny stayed where he was and waited for the hounds to investigate their unknown visitor.

Any idiot who thinks he can walk onto my property now that the borgs are gone has another think comin'.

Rex's sharp bark blasted through the silence, joined quickly by his brother's. "Hey! It's you!"

"Why do you smell like fish?"

"I told you, it's from the swamp."

"That's not the swamp. It's—hey. Look at this!"

"That's mine. You can't—"

"Give it!"

"Johnny! Hurry! We found it!"

The hounds' low snarls and grunts rose with the scrabbling click of their claws on the deck. Johnny ran across the destroyed room as he drew his utility knife and flicked it open. He skidded through the open doorway, raced down the side of the deck, and reached the back of the houseboat. The first thing he saw was Rex and Luther playing Tug-O-War with a thick piece of ripped metal cable. They growled and jerked their heads from side to side.

"Hands up and don't—"

Lisa stepped around the corner and into view, both hands raised in front of her and a smirk playing on her lips. "You know, if you don't want my help to clean up here, all you have to do is say so."

With a growl either of his hounds would be proud of, Johnny flipped the blade shut and thrust it into his belt before he scowled at the playing hounds. "Y'all didn't think to tell me it was Lisa?"

"I'm gonna get it."

"No way." Rex shook his head vigorously and dragged his brother across the deck by a foot, the cable drawn taught between them. "I'm way stronger."

"No, you're only—"

"Hey!" Johnny uttered a piercing whistle. "Drop it!"

The cable thumped on the deck and both hounds sat to look obediently at their master.

"Y'all better say somethin' next time."

"We did, Johnny."

"Yeah." Luther's tail thumped against the metal deck, and he glanced down in longing at their abandoned toy. "Then we found this weird stick."

"Best coonhounds in the Glades." The dwarf shook his head. "Worst guard hounds on Earth."

Rex glanced from his master and the half-Light Elf who lowered her hands slowly with a chuckle. "What, you wanted us to attack her?"

"Hey, lady." Luther's tongue lolled from his mouth and he panted and his head raised and lowered repeatedly as he tried to watch Lisa and the torn cable at the same time. "You know how to play fetch, right?"

"Y'all ain't fetchin' hounds," Johnny interrupted.

"Yeah, but Leroy used to—"

"Leroy ain't here. Git on off this boat, boys. I got cleanin' up to do."

"Yeah, yeah. Sure, Johnny." Rex sniffed Lisa's shoes, took one tentative lick of the toe, then bounded off the back of the houseboat and into the swamp with a splash.

Luther crouched and tried to sneak toward the cable. "Let me—"

"Off!"

With a yelp, the hound skittered across the deck when Johnny shooed him away from what was certainly not a hound toy. "Hey, Rex! Wait for me!"

"I'll find us a better stick!"

They splashed through the water, shouted at each other, and bayed madly when they caught the scent of a critter before they raced after it.

Lisa picked the cable up and studied the stripped ends and the shredded wires dangling from both sides. "They seriously did a number on this boat, huh?"

"Uh-huh. I can't for the life of me think what for."

She tossed the cable aside and watched the bounty hunter scowl at the mess around them. "You truly thought I was an intruder?"

"When you sneak onto the houseboat like that? Sure."

"I didn't sneak."

"But you didn't think to correct the hounds, either. You can hear 'em, darlin', so you can't use that as an excuse."

Laughing, she followed him into the main room. "I came in halfway through their conversation. If you can even call it that. None of it made any sense."

He snorted. "It hardly ever does. Is everythin' all right?"

"Of course. I merely thought you might want some help with this mess."

"Naw. I'm sure you have better things to do with your day than go through all this." He righted the chipped table with a grunt. It stood for all of five seconds before one of the legs came free from its setting and it toppled to the floor in a puff of sawdust. A loosened screw and wing nut clinked before they disappeared under another pile of demolished furniture. "Damn."

"Yeah… I'll stay to help."

"Maybe only for the lower deck." Johnny scratched his cheek through his beard. "I'm sure things will get a little easier up top."

Lisa grimaced. "You mean on the level where June stayed and almost set off a forgotten cyborg bomb?"

"Shit. Yeah, all right. It's gonna be a long day."

"Well, it's a good thing we don't have any other distractions."

It took them two hours to sift through the wreckage of the lower deck's main room and separate the salvageable furniture and hardware from the piles of useless junk. Fortunately, the borgs hadn't bothered to mess with the bathroom under the stairs at the stern but they'd had their fun with everything else. As they headed up the back staircase toward the next level, Lisa pulled her phone out to check the time.

"Oh, hey. I wanted to talk to you about something."

"All right." Johnny strode toward the second-level deck without slowing or turning to look at her.

"So last night, you said this place is as much mine as it is yours."

"Uh-huh. 'Cause you've been here long enough to call it home. If that's what you want."

"Right."

They reached the top of the stairs and his upper lip twitched into a sneer as he scanned the main living area leading into the bedroom beyond. This level was as much of a mess if not more, but it had a larger number of smiley faces cauterized into the walls and the floors. "No, I ain't sayin' it to let you make up your mind on your own. And yeah, I might say I want the same thing."

Lisa chuckled. "Might?"

"What do you want me to say, darlin'?" He gestured toward the wreckage. "I already handed you a dog-translator in a black box and you freaked the hell out. I ain't about to get down on my knees and beg ya to move in with me."

"Well…I don't think that's something either of us wants."

He grunted as he kicked a fragment of splintered wood at the end of a trail of it that led into the back bedroom. "Nope. But if you ain't had enough of giant messes and explosions and not knowing who's gonna step onto the property next, then yeah. I want you here for good."

"Good." She sighed in relief. "Then I'm glad I brought this up."

Johnny froze. "What happened?"

"Nothing yet. Except that I bought a plane ticket to DC so I can clear my apartment and bring the rest of my belongings."

"It's been a while since I rented a place, darlin', but don't you have to give notice when you're movin' out?"

She tucked her dark hair behind her ear, shrugged, and fought to hold back a smile as she studied the mess in the short hall. "I gave my thirty days last month."

The bounty hunter turned to face her and leaned against the wall of the hallway with folded arms. "What if I'd said I wasn't ready for you to move in yet?"

"We'd already talked about it."

"I coulda changed my mind."

Lisa grinned. "I was banking on the fact that you wouldn't."

He sniggered. "I never pegged you for the bettin' type—"

The section of wall he was leaning against buckled with a sharp snap and fragments of wood paneling scattered around his feet. He reeled back toward the new hole in the wall before he staggered forward again and glared scathingly at the newest destruction.

"Are you okay?"

"For cryin' out loud. I can't trust a damn thing in this place to not fall apart like it's been rottin' away here for the last few decades." He kicked one of the largest boards aside and stormed into what had originally been an extra bedroom on the house-boat. Now, all that remained was the sliding door of the closet at the back. "So you gave your notice and aim to swing back to get your things."

"That's right." She pursed her lips to keep from laughing and followed him toward the open closet—which held all the evidence of June's almost-detonated energy bomb.

When he saw the burned hole in the back of the closet and the flare-marks of residual magic that charred the walls and the floor like the bomb had exploded, he inclined his head.

"There's no furniture."

"It makes sense. How many times did you see June use a piece of furniture?"

"I meant yours."

"What?"

He turned to point at her. "You collect your necessaries but I ain't makin' room in the cabin for extra furniture."

Lisa laughed. "Trust me, Johnny. I like your home the way it is. And I already found a storage unit in Richmond."

"They don't make 'em in DC?"

"Only the kind I'm not willing to dump money into on a monthly basis."

"Right. It sounds like you have it all resolved, then." He scowled and turned toward the burned remains of June's old closet. "Do you want me to come with you?"

"No. I'll only take a few days and I'm very sure you'll have your hands full here."

He frowned at her in confusion. "I sure as hell hope not. When is your flight?"

"Five o'clock."

"Tonight?"

"No. Tomorrow morning." She smiled sheepishly at him. "I expected you to sit around and enjoy your peace and quiet for a few more days before you tackled anything like this."

A low chuckle escaped him and he hooked his thumbs through his belt loops as it grew into a full laugh. "You thought you had me all figured out enough to plan this perfectly all the way through."

"Hey, I got three out of four covered."

Nodding slowly, Johnny let his laughter die down enough to add, "The only thing I can't stand more than not havin' my peace and quiet is havin' it while there's a mess needs tendin' to."

Lisa approached him and her footsteps crunched across broken glass, pieces of warped plastic, and chips of destroyed wood. "That's good to know. Next time, I won't leave you to clean a mess by yourself. You know, you could simply hire a cleaning crew."

"Naw, they take too long and I ain't about to pay someone for somethin' I can as easily do myself—and do better."

She ran her hand down his arm and leaned close to plant a quick kiss on his lips. "Well, I'm all yours for the rest of the day, as long as I get to bed at a decent time tonight. And you don't even have to pay me for the work."

Johnny growled and looked away to scan the wreckage. "You can't start kissin' a fella when he's tryin' to keep his mind on gettin' a thing done."

"Oh, yeah? I'm too much of a distraction?"

"If you keep lookin' at me like that, you are."

Lisa grinned and stepped away to begin to create a pile of everything that would later have to be hauled out of the houseboat, off the property, and onto a dump.

"Now what the hell happened here?" The bounty hunter scratched his head and turned to view the spray of burn marks that flared along the walls and left a much darker streak along the floor toward the front end of the main room. "This don't look like June's special brand of target practice."

"No… It was mine." Lisa pointed at the crater on the floor of the closet. "The hounds found her bomb in there a few seconds before I managed to keep it from sinking the houseboat."

"Ha. You said you disarmed it."

She wrinkled her nose, tossed a thick piece of broken wood onto the pile, and shrugged. "I guess sometimes, you have to blow something up to keep everything else from blowing up."

Johnny gave her a crooked grin. "You're a woman after my own heart, darlin'. It keeps gettin' better and better, don't it?"

"To be clear, what I said is different from your usual, 'blow up whatever you want to get something done' MO."

"Naw. It ain't that different. But now I gotta ask."

"What?"

"You know this ain't the last time we'll have to clean up after some boneheaded magicals who ain't thinkin' about what they're doin' before they do it, right?" He raised an eyebrow and pointed at the hole in the closet. "This seems to be a regular occurrence here now. So are you sure you can handle it happenin' in your back yard?"

"Of course I can handle it, Johnny." With a coy smile, she tossed her hair over her shoulder and spread her arms to include the whole houseboat in one gesture. "That's part of the charm."

CHAPTER FIVE

Johnny insisted on driving Lisa to the airport and made her promise to call him when she reached her apartment. "This isn't my first time flying, Johnny."

"I know that. I simply ain't a fan of you drivin' through rush hour when it ain't for a case."

"Which one of us has lived in DC?"

"That's the point. It takes a certain kinda crazy to wanna live there at all."

Laughing, she pulled him close for a kiss, opened Sheila's passenger door, and slung her purse over her shoulder. "I'll overlook the fact that you called me crazy—"

"That ain't what I said."

"And I promise to call you when I get to my apartment. Fair?"

He sniffed and gazed at the other early-morning travelers pulling up to the Miami airport for their departing flights. "Sure."

"It's only a few days. You and the hounds will have nothing to interrupt you until I come back. Enjoy it, huh?"

"Yeah, all right."

She flashed him a winning grin, shut the door, and disappeared through the airport doors.

Johnny stayed at the drop-off curb long enough to watch her through the front windows until she was lost in the crowds lining up at the check-in counters.

Enjoy it. Yeah. I think I've earned it a hundred times over by now.

"So what are we gonna do, Johnny? Huh?" Luther stopped his frantic darting around the back yard and sat to stare at his master.

Johnny closed the exterior panel on Margo's side and gave the hulking metal intelligence unit a solid thump of approval. "Finish all the things need finishin'."

"Right. Finish." His smaller hound leapt to all fours again and raced around the perimeter.

The bounty hunter turned and scowled at the rut Luther had managed to tear into the grass over the past few hours. "Git on outta the yard, huh? I'm gonna have a moat next time it rains if you keep this up."

Rex sniffed Johnny's toolbox where it rested against Margo's hull and uttered a low whine. "He won't stop."

"Have you tried racin' out into the swamp and letting him follow?"

"Yeah, Johnny. But then he comes back here to do…that."

The dwarf uttered a piercing whistle and Luther skidded to a stop halfway around his next loop. "Go chase somethin'."

"Yeah, yeah. Good idea, Johnny." The hound darted forward, paused, then raced toward the dock and stopped again. "We're going on a hunt, right? Gonna chase something big?"

"Not right now." He retrieved his toolbox and headed around Margo toward the shed. "The middle of February ain't the best time anyhow."

"Oh, come on, Johnny!" Luther barked and resumed his frenetic circuit around the yard.

Once he'd placed all his tools inside, he slid the shed door closed, rested his fists on his hips, and drew a deep breath of temperate Florida air.

You can't rightly call it winter and nothin' changes down here. Exactly the way I like it.

"Bro, cut it out!" Rex shouted.

"Can't, Rex! I gotta… I gotta…"

Rex snarled ferociously, followed by a yelp from his brother and a quick scrabble in the grass as the hounds tussled. When Johnny rounded Margo again to check the damage, the younger hound was on his back, pinned beneath Rex's forepaws with his brother's slightly larger jaws clamped lightly around his throat.

Luther whined before his tongue drooped out of his upside-down mouth. "Johnny! You're back!"

"All right, boys." He snapped his fingers and while Luther scrambled to get out from beneath his brother's hold, Rex didn't move.

"He won't stop, Johnny."

"Well, unless you aim to rip his throat out right here in the yard, let him up."

Luther's tail that had thumped on the grass even while pinned stopped immediately, and he licked his muzzle. "Wait, what?"

Rex snarled again but finally released the smaller hound and bounded away after his master. "We going for a ride, Johnny?"

"Oh, yeah!" Luther scrambled to his feet and almost tripped himself as he stumbled over the rut in the grass. "A ride! We could drive all day, Johnny. Nothing to do. No one else to talk to. Only the three of us with our heads out the window and our tongues hanging out."

Johnny snorted. "Don't put that on me."

He strode up the back porch stairs toward the door. "I have a few things I been fixin' to work on. Y'all go find somethin'."

"Like food, Johnny?"

"Oh, hey. If we find anything we think you might like, want us to bring it back?"

The back door closed with a bang behind their master, but the hounds raced up the stairs anyway.

Luther nudged past his brother to get there first. "Maybe he's talking about snacks."

A plastic scraping sound and sharp click came from the door. "Wait. Luther."

"He's playing hard to get, Rex. Hey, I'll take the trashcan. See if you can find any—" Luther's snout thumped against the dog door and he staggered back on the porch with a snort. "What?"

He pawed twice at the door, but it wouldn't budge.

"Johnny! Johnny, I think the door's broken!"

Rex lowered himself to his belly on the worn wooden planks and rested his head on his forepaws. "Thanks a lot, bro."

"You think he heard me? Hey, Johnny! *Johnny!*"

"Nothing is wrong with the door."

Luther's curdling howl stopped halfway through. "Except we can't get in."

"Because he locked us out."

The smaller hound cocked his head and nudged the dog door tentatively with his muzzle again. "Why would he do that?"

Rex stood, shook himself, and trotted down the stairs. "He probably doesn't want a moat in the house."

"Oh. Right. What's a moat?"

"You."

Luther sat and panted, and his tail thudded on the porch as he stared at the dog door. "Johnny! I promise I won't be a moat. We'll die out here! *Johnny!*"

The dwarf stood at the high, rough table in the center of his workshop. He pulled out the metal tackle box that held his smaller, finer tools meant for creating things instead of cleaning everyone else's destruction.

"Johnny, come on!" Luther shouted, his words interspersed with high whines that warbled in and out before they ended in urgent grunts. "What are you doing in there, huh? I can't see."

He sounds like a dyin' animal out there. I ain't fixin' to bring all that inside.

After he flipped the tackle box lid open, he left the table to walk down the long metal shelving unit that ran the length of the wall and turned the radio on. Static crackled through the speakers and he flipped through a few stations before he landed on a track by Tool. With a shrug, he let the tune play for a moment before Luther's urgent howl rose from the back door again.

"Johnny? Are you leaving us forever? Come on! We're your hounds. You need us!"

"Shut up!" Rex snapped.

"Johnny!"

The dwarf turned the volume up until he could feel the shredding guitar riff and the double bass exploded through his chest. The smaller tech pieces and devices beside the speakers rattled on the shelves but Luther's shouts had faded to a thin, incomprehensible buzz in his head.

This is why I don't have company. Too many folks hangin' around my place and the hounds go all soft on me.

He nodded his head slightly to the beat and returned his attention to the newest gadget he'd wanted to work on for the past month. The idea had brewed in his head for much longer and he finally had the time to put it all into action.

I ain't runnin' a cyborg ranch anymore. The kid's in school. Lisa's doin' her thing.

The dwarf froze and his hand hovered over the partially deconstructed remote detonator on the shelf.

This is the last time I'll be alone.

His brief and ineffective attempt to decide how he felt about that realization simply pissed him off, so he snatched the detonator up, selected the box of bolt tips encapsulating alchemized magic in various Boom Levels, and took it all to the table.

A moment later, his phone vibrated in his back pocket and he pulled it out to see a text from Lisa.

Just got my rental. Making a few stops before I head to the apartment. I'll call you then.

Nothing about her message implied that she wanted a response, so he shoved the phone back into his pocket and snorted. "I told her to call."

Shaking his head, he scratched in the tackle box for the small Phillips-head screwdriver and the tiny handheld welding gun. With the knowledge that he only had a few days left before Lisa officially moved in and Johnny Walker was no longer a bachelor dwarf with a shifter ward away at boarding school, he settled in and got to work.

His focus was interrupted at the end of the hour by the radio DJ saying he had a special treat for his listeners. "We're bringing on a new segment to the show, people. Heavy metal covers by acoustic string groups. Ever heard of rock violin? Trust me. This'll knock your socks off."

The second the violin started, Johnny's tools clattered onto the table.

"Goddammit! That ain't rock." He gritted his teeth, strode toward the radio, and punched the power button. The music stopped and he rolled his eyes. "You can't trust anyone to stick to the damn program."

Now, however, his concentration was gone.

The house was quiet and he was completely alone.

He clicked his tongue, cast another dubious glance at the gadget he'd been working on, then stormed out of the workshop and down the hall toward the front door.

It closed with a bang behind him. Before he'd even reached

the door of the screened-in porch, the hounds barked madly as they raced down the side yard toward the front.

"He's here! He didn't leave us!"

"We're coming, Johnny!"

Luther howled. "Whatever you want, we'll do it. Promise."

He marched down the porch steps and headed directly to Sheila. His hounds raced around him in excited circles while they yapped and cavorted until Luther stumbled into his brother. Rex ended the playfulness with a snarl and a sharp nip at the smaller hound's flank. "Cut it out."

Johnny snapped his fingers. "That goes for both of y'all. Come on."

"We're going somewhere?"

"Truly, Johnny?"

"Yes! Where are we going?"

As he opened Sheila's back gate, he nodded for the hounds to get in. "I'm gettin' an early lunch."

"All right!"

"You're the best, Johnny."

Both hounds scrabbled on the hard plastic floor in the back of the Jeep as Johnny closed the gate and headed to the driver's seat.

"Are we getting burgers, Johnny?"

"No way." Rex poked his head over the back seat to sniff the air like it smelled differently now that they stood in a Jeep without any windows. "Chicken."

Sheila's engine roared to life and Johnny slipped his black sunglasses on.

"Pickles!"

"Steak!"

Luther barked twice. "Oh! Oh! Squirrel!"

The dwarf glanced at them in the rearview mirror and snorted. "I ain't takin' y'all out for squirrel. You do that on your own time."

"But you are gonna get us snacks, right?"

"Yeah, Johnny. You'll share? You always share."

"If Darlene's feelin' generous today, sure." He shoved the gearshift into drive and accelerated away from his property with a jerk. Dirt and gravel sprayed in every direction behind the wheels.

CHAPTER SIX

The gravel parking lot in front of Darlene's held the usual trucks and beat-up clunkers owned by the locals in this part of the Everglades. Johnny's bright-red Jeep made it a total of six. He stepped out of Sheila with a glance at the other vehicles and shrugged. "It looks busy today."

The hounds practically pushed the back gate open on their own in their excitement to get out. "Food, food, food!"

"We get to go inside!"

"The hell you will." The dwarf snapped his fingers and pointed at the side of the raised trailer on stilts.

"Wait, what?"

Luther whined. "You said—"

"I said y'all might get somethin' if Darlene's feelin' good about it."

"So why do we have to wait outside?" Rex asked.

"Yeah. Again."

"That woman ain't lettin' two coonhounds inside until hell freezes over." He smirked. "And I reckon not even then. Go on. Wait out back."

"But Johnny—"

"If she don't bring you somethin', I'll take some to go. Git on."

The hounds slunk away toward the back of the trailer and sniffed the ground and the other vehicles as they passed.

"He can't mess with our emotions like that," Luther muttered.

"Especially hunger," Rex added as he stopped to lift a leg against the side of a local's ATV parked beyond the lot. "Hunger's the strongest emotion there is."

Johnny ignored them and headed up the stairs toward the narrow porch at the front of Darlene's. Only when he reached for the door handle did he realize how long it had been since he'd stepped foot in the place.

There's nothin' like Darlene's cookin' to set a fella's head straight when he needs it.

He opened the door and stepped into the dimly lit trailer-turned-diner. The door closed softly behind him and the low murmur of good-natured conversation from the locals died down for a second.

"Johnny!" Tripp grinned from his table in the center of the space. "We thought you died."

"Or got up and left to tag along behind that pretty partner of yours without tellin' us," Harry added from his booth along the far wall.

The other old-timers at their solo tables exploded in shared amusement.

"That would have been a hell of a blow, Johnny," Rick said through his chuckle. "Shuckin' out with no goodbye or what for."

He shook his head as he strode toward the bar along the back wall. "Do y'all think I'd tell you a damn thing anyhow?"

"That's the problem, ain't it?" Tripp wiped the collection of gravy from the corners of his mouth and laughed gruffly. "He never tells us a damn thing—could be dead or could be gone, or he could be hidin' a nuke in his part of the swamp and none of us will ever be any the wiser."

Bobby choked on his mouthful of green beans and bacon and

cleared his throat. "Is that what you got out there makin' all that noise, Johnny? Your personal warhead?"

Seated at the table beside the door, Arthur smirked into his glass of sweet tea and set it down with a clink. "Walkin', talkin' warheads, from what I've seen."

Johnny sat at the bar and thumped a fist on the old, stained wood. "I never pegged you for the gossipin' type, Arthur."

"What the hell d'ya mean, talkin' warheads?" Harry asked and turned in his booth to stare at Arthur.

"That's what it looked like." Johnny's closest friend in the Glades twisted one side of his white handlebar mustache between two fingers and studied the dwarf's back hunched over the bar. "But I reckon maybe they might be what he said. Assistants."

"Johnny, what in the hell is this old goat spittin'?" Rick asked.

The bounty hunter turned around to meet Arthur's gaze and shook his head, although a small smile emerged beneath his red mustache. "He's blowin' smoke, fellas."

"Oh, sure." At the single table on the far end of the long trailer, Dennis nodded sagely, pointed at Arthur with his fork, and dug into the rest of his early lunch. "If Johnny ain't hidin' warheads, Arthur's two lips short of a whistle. Either way, we done reached the end-days, fellas."

Arthur uttered a low whistle to make his point and the diner exploded with more laughter and thigh-slaps.

"It ain't the end yet," Johnny said with another glance at the door behind the bar that led to Darlene's kitchen. "I shipped those assistants out yesterday. Things are quiet again and y'all won't have to deal with the noise."

"Don't sound so disappointed, Johnny," Tripp replied with a chortle.

The dwarf cocked his head. "I can't speak for the state of Arthur's sanity, though."

The old-timers laughed and jeered at the white-haired man with the handlebar mustache.

"So it's that kinda day, huh?" His old friend chuckled. "Are you tryin' to start a fight?"

"With you, old-timer?" Johnny snorted. "I wouldn't dream of it."

"We're all gettin' old, Johnny." Harry stuck his thumb out toward Bobby at the table beside him. "Some of us more than others."

"You're one to talk, Harry. Janice told me she heard Mary Lee at the corner grocery talkin' 'bout those disposable drawers Beth Anne done wrapped up in two paper bags last week."

"Whoa, now, Bobby." Tripp shook his head at the fisherman in overalls. "No need to take it as far as that. A man's got his private business."

"Not accordin' to Mary Lee."

"Mary Lee's mouth is bigger than her head and you know it."

The other locals looked away and hid their expressions beneath lowered heads as they focused on their food and ignored the uncomfortable turn of conversation.

The dwarf swung toward the bar and stared at the door. *I didn't come down here fixin' to get everyone's personal details. Where the hell's Darlene?*

"Disposable drawers?" In his usual place at the end of the bar, Fred lifted his inebriated head from his arms and turned on the stool, weaving as he tried to focus on Harry. "Them's for babies 'n togs—tots…an' them little'uns pepperin' round…round floor."

"You hush up your pickled mouth, Fred." Harry pointed at the drunkard and glanced scathingly at Bobby. "And you go ahead 'n tell Janice she don't need to repeat everythin' she hears at the corner grocery."

Bobby cleared his throat and gave the embarrassed old-timer a stiff nod before he drained his mug of coffee.

"Mary Lee done already took that job anyhow," Dennis

muttered across the diner. The other locals sniggered and uttered wordless groans of agreement.

"Who the hell wants to spend the middle of the day yappin' 'bout old folks and loudmouths, huh?" Arthur slapped his table, stood, and headed toward the bar. He clapped a hand on Johnny's shoulder and gave the dwarf a little shake. "Johnny's got years on all of us. In both directions. Old man livin' a young fella's life, huh?"

The other patrons chuckled, their good humor restored by the change of subject.

"You sure got more ahead of you than the rest of us, I tell you what." Tripp scooped the rest of his mashed potatoes up, shoved them into his mouth, and dropped his utensil so he and everyone else could go back to pretending his hand didn't shake the whole time.

The bounty hunter nodded at the door. "Where's Darlene?"

"She had a delivery to sign for or somethin'." Arthur sat on the stool beside him. "She'll be back."

"Go on 'n tell us 'bout your young fella's life, Johnny," Rick called. "I been seein' a lotta Lisa's rental car rollin' through town the last month or so. Runnin' errands."

The old-timers whistled and laughed.

"Last time I checked, errands ain't a part of bounty-huntin' an' investigatin', right, Johnny?"

"It's been a long time since we seen you keep a woman 'round longer than…hell." Tripp removed his trucker hat to scratch his almost bald head. "Come to think of it, though, it ain't never happened."

"So when you gonna pop the question, Johnny?" Dennis asked. "Women like Lisa don't hang 'round for long otherwise."

"Christ." Johnny shot Arthur a scowl and his friend grinned. "I ain't talkin' about Lisa and my business with old guys who already put themselves out to pasture."

Harry laughed. "Yeah, ain't you fellas got more interestin' things to take your time up?"

Tripp cocked his head. "Are you kiddin'?"

The diner filled with laughter again and some of it turned into a croaked cough as Rick pounded on his chest and washed his food down with iced tea.

The bounty hunter waved them off. "Y'all can mind your own."

"You might as well give us somethin', Johnny boy." Bobby pointed at the trailer door. "We don't get any these days anyhow 'cept through hearin' a few good stories."

He turned on his stool to face the patrons and spread his arms. "When did this place become a gossip house, huh? Y'all are as bad as Mary Lee."

The old-timers howled with laughter. Dennis slapped his thigh with a hoot. "Sure. Maybe we'll go ask her 'bout Lisa!"

"Arthur."

"Johnny."

"Next time I step in here and you're sittin' at that table, remind me to hightail it right out again."

His friend chuckled. "All in good fun."

"Uh-huh." Johnny's stomach growled and he wished he at least had a drink to nurse while he waited. "Doesn't Darlene have someone to help her with the delivery?"

"Oh, sure. The delivery man helps her with plenty else besides," Harry called. The old men erupted with laughter again but it cut out immediately when the door behind the bar opened and Darlene finally entered her establishment. She looked flushed but still all business.

"What in the world's gotten into y'all?" The woman retied her apron swiftly behind her waist and frowned at the locals, who tried to hide their smiles. "I step out for five minutes—"

"More like twenty," Bobby muttered.

"You keep your nose in your own business, Bobby." She

turned to shoot the door a glance and briskly rearranged her hair piled high on her head. "And the whole shebang of you loiterers take twenty minutes simply to order. It's like I'm runnin' a— Johnny." She grinned at him when she finally noticed him seated at the end of the bar. "How long have you been sittin' there?"

"Twenty minutes."

"You hush, Tripp." She pointed at the man and swept a thick finger toward all the other patrons. "If y'all don't think I'll kick you out for getting on my nerves, you'd better think again. Sorry, Johnny. I didn't hear you drive up."

"You didn't see the hounds either, huh?"

She blinked, caught completely off guard, then laughed airily and rested hands on her wide hips. "You brought your hounds?"

"Honestly, I'm a little surprised they didn't sniff you out and interrupt your...uh, delivery."

The old-timers sniggered.

"Huh. Well, let me make it up to all three of you. I'll send you home with a little extra somethin' in a doggie bag. Literally."

"I appreciate you, Darlene."

"Ya'll hear that?" The woman turned to take a rocks glass from the bar that didn't display any liquor, pulled a bottle of Johnny Walker Black Label from beneath the counter, and poured the bounty hunter his drink. "Every man in here could stand to show a little more appreciation. Take a page outta Johnny's book. It looks like it's doin' him fairly well."

Johnny nodded when she slid his drink toward him.

"Speakin' of which...how are you and Lisa doin'?"

The trailer fell deathly silent for a moment before the patrons burst out laughing. Darlene started, stepped back, and scowled at the men who frequented her establishment almost every day.

"Well, I don't see what's so funny about it."

"He ain't gonna tell you, Darlene," Rick called. "The man's as shut-up as a bad oyster."

Arthur chuckled and shook his head.

The diner's owner looked at Johnny with a raised eyebrow. "Did I miss somethin'?"

He sipped his whiskey. "We're doin' fine, darlin'. I have no complaints."

"Oh, no complaints, huh?" She shared a pointed look with Arthur and tilted her head in approval. "That sounds good to me."

"You could say that, sure."

"Well, if things are so good, Johnny Walker, how come you didn't bring her in here with you for lunch?"

"She's outta town for a few days." He raised his voice without turning around. "And no, I ain't sayin' where she went or why, so y'all can drop it."

With a smirk, Darlene finished wiping a perpetual stain on the bar and slapped the rag down. "All right. Then what can I getcha?"

"Surprise me."

"Uh-huh." She studied him for a moment before she turned toward the kitchen and muttered, "Sounds good, he says. Ha."

Arthur lowered his head between his forearms folded over the bar and tried to hide his laughter. "It sounds like you got it bad is what it sounds like."

"And if I do, it still ain't none of your business." Johnny took another sip and couldn't help but smile over the rim of his glass.

Sure, I got it bad. There ain't nothin' wrong with it.

CHAPTER SEVEN

Halfway through Darlene's blackened catfish—which wasn't much of a surprise—Johnny's phone rang in his pocket. His fork clacked against the plate and Arthur popped a pickle chip in his mouth with a smirk.

"You're gettin' a little jumpy, ain'tcha?"

"It's easy to forget everythin' else when a fella has Darlene's cookin' in front of him." He nodded at the diner owner.

The woman put one hand on her hip and winked.

A glance at his screen confirmed that the call was from Lisa.

He answered it and lowered his voice, although he couldn't help a small smile. "Hey, darlin'. The folks at Darlene's were askin' about you—"

"Johnny, I don't know what to do." Her voice was hurried and urgent like she was on the verge of crying.

The bounty hunter's smile vanished instantly. "What happened?"

"It's Hamish."

"Your boy?"

"He's no longer a boy. But yes, my son. He's—" Lisa sucked in a trembling breath and couldn't finish.

Arthur gave him a curious frown, but Johnny dismissed him with a shake of his head and scowled at the half-eaten catfish in front of him. "Are you safe?"

"Physically? Yeah. Other than that… They were here, Johnny. Looking for him, apparently, and I have no idea why."

"All right. Take another breath and start from the beginning."

She sniffed and swallowed thickly. "Someone broke into my apartment. And yes, there are visible signs of forced entry on the front door so that part's covered. Whoever it was turned the place completely upside-down. It's trashed. I thought maybe someone noticed I hadn't been here for months and came to clear it out but nothing's stolen."

"Nothin'? Are you sure?"

"A hundred percent. I went through everything twice. And then I found…" Lisa panted a series of quick breaths—not quite hyperventilating but almost. "Hamish must have come by first. He left me several clues, Johnny. I had no idea he was back on Earth, but I think…I think whoever broke in was after him. He needs my help and I need yours."

"Yep. I'll call Felix and be there in a few hours."

"Thank you."

"You sit tight, darlin'. Stay there and keep your eyes open. We'll sort this out."

"Yeah. Yeah, okay."

She ended the call first but Johnny was already slipping his phone into his pocket as he stood from the barstool.

Darlene entered the bar from the kitchen with a white paper bag in hand. "I reckon we should start callin' these hound bags, huh?"

"Thanks, Darlene." He pulled two twenties from his wallet and slapped them on the bar before he took the bag from her. "I gotta run."

Her eyes widened. "Is something wrong with the catfish?"

"The catfish was perfect, darlin'." He wiped his mouth and

beard with a napkin and tossed it onto the plate. "I wish I had the time to finish it."

"Okay…" She slid the twenties closer to her. "I'll put the rest of this on your tab, then."

"That's fine."

"Who's Felix?" Arthur asked.

The dwarf frowned at his friend. "My pilot. Lisa…has a thing."

"Well, all right." Arthur and Darlene exchanged concerned glances as Johnny strode away from the bar toward the trailer door.

"Trouble in paradise, Johnny boy?" Harry called with a smirk.

"If that's what you wanna call a break-in, sure."

The diner fell silent as the bounty hunter jerked the door open and stormed outside.

I knew I should have gone with her.

"Johnny!" The hounds raced around the trailer and skittered across the gravel to meet their master at the Jeep. "Hey! You took forever."

"Yeah, we thought you'd moved in or something."

"Or maybe the lady two-legs killed you and decided to cook you up."

Rex sniggered. "I bet he tastes awful."

"Get up, boys. We gotta move fast." Johnny jerked the back gate open and Rex immediately leapt into Sheila.

Luther nudged his snout against the doggie bag in the dwarf's hand. "You did bring us something."

"I said up, Luther." With a grunt, he tossed the bag into the back with Rex.

The smaller hound yelped in dismay and bounded up beside his brother before the back gate slammed shut. "No fair, Johnny. You gotta give a little warning."

"Maybe you should do what he says the first time," Rex muttered as he rooted in the bag and instantly tore it halfway open. "Then you'd get what you want."

"But you're gonna share, right? Come on, bro, it's—yes! Thanks, Johnny."

"You're the best. Have we told you that?"

Sheila's engine roared to life and the bounty hunter wasted no time. The vehicle lurched away from Darlene's for a quick stop at the cabin.

The hounds stumbled and thumped against the back of the Jeep. "Whoa, watch it. We almost lost our lunch."

"Yeah, what's the hurry? Are we going hunting?"

"Yeah, we're goin' huntin', all right."

Luther gasped. "For real?"

"It ain't for game, boys. Bastards broke into Lisa's apartment."

"Whoa. Was it a fox?"

Rex lapped at the steak juice leaking all over the floor. "Foxes are the trickiest bastards ever. They get into everything."

"Or a squirrel?"

"Eat your steak," he muttered and glanced once into his rearview mirror before he tightened his fingers around the steering wheel. By the time they were halfway to his property, he'd made a mental inventory of everything he'd pack to take with them. Then, he called his pilot.

***

Johnny and the hounds arrived at Lisa's apartment five miles south of DC a little before 5:00 pm. Although the lock and knob on the front door had clearly been damaged, the door was closed.

"Hey. Johnny." Luther sniffed along the bottom of the hallway wall as they approached. "Smells like your lady two-legs over here. How'd she do that?"

Rex snorted and shook his head. "Even I remember what happened this morning."

"What happened this morning?"

Before he could tell the hounds to quit yammering, the front door creaked open and Lisa peered out at them with dry but red-rimmed eyes. "That was faster than I expected."

"Wow. You've got good hearing, lady."

Rex stared at his brother.

"Oh. Right. You can hear us."

"How you doin', darlin'?" Johnny tried to peer around her into her apartment before she stepped aside to let them all in.

"Better, I think. Or at least I've had a chance to calm and try to wrap my head around all this." She closed the door behind them despite how useless it was and ran a hand through her dark hair. "Thanks for coming, Johnny. I truly wanted to give you time to relax at home and—"

"Don't you say another word." He put a hand on her shoulder, nodded, and made sure to catch her gaze. "There ain't no relaxin' when I know you're out here with a break-in and who knows what else on your hands. I should have been with you in the first place."

"You couldn't have known this would happen. I didn't."

"Sure, but I had a gut feelin' anyhow. I'm glad you're all right."

"Yeah." She looked at him with glassy, exhausted eyes.

Damn, she's hurtin'. What the hell am I supposed to do?

"Come here." Johnny waved her forward.

Lisa stiffened and tried to hold her emotions back but was unable to stop her body from trembling.

"It's all right." He pulled her toward him and wrapped his arms around her. She didn't move and leaned against him like a statue. *Shit. I'm goin' about this all wrong.*

Before he could release her, she collapsed against him and finally hugged him with a tremendous sigh of relief. "I can't do this by myself, Johnny."

"Hell, that's why I'm here. We're…partners." He rubbed her back a little awkwardly and didn't even think about it before he added, "If you gotta cry or somethin', I reckon now would be the time."

Lisa sniffed and pushed him away. "I'm not crying."

"Naw. Sure. I'm only sayin'—"

"That I'm a woman and a mother so my emotions are sure to get the better of me?"

Johnny hesitated and scratched his head. "Well, now you're puttin' words in my mouth."

"I need your help, Johnny. Not your pity. So let's get to work."

"Yep." He cleared his throat as she turned away from him to walk through the complete mess the intruders had made of her apartment.

I can't win or lose in somethin' like this. It's best to let it go.

"Wow, lady." Luther stuck his snout into the huge rip along the cushions of Lisa's lime-green couch and snorted. "What were they looking for in your pillows?"

"The same thing I was looking for, probably." Lisa went to the bookshelf along the far wall of the living room. It had been completely cleared of books and knickknacks and these now lay on the floor. "And if I found it, it means they didn't."

The dwarf studied the destruction and frowned. "You stayed here for close to five hours in all this mess?"

She turned to shoot him a hardened frown. "I didn't want to touch anything else until you got here in case you find something I missed."

"Right. So what did you find?"

"This was the first." She bent to point at the wooden back beneath the center bookshelf. "I've had this since before Hamish was born and I certainly didn't put this here."

Johnny approached, ducked to take a glimpse beneath the shelf, then grabbed the shelf instead and ripped it free from its setting.

"Hey."

"We can put it back later." He tossed the board on the ground. "But I ain't hunkerin' down to crawl inside a damn bookshelf. What are we lookin' at?"

"This." Lisa brushed her finger against a number four etched into the wood.

He touched it and a dusting of fresh sawdust fell away. "It's fairly new."

"Yeah."

"Y'all got some kinda secret code with fours and bookshelves?"

She inclined her head and scowled at him. "No, Johnny. I'm very sure that would make your input unnecessary."

"All right."

"And over here." She led him across the living room again to the antique record player, which had been propped open with the bottom cabinet emptied. Fortunately, the player was still intact. "Look at the bottom left corner."

Johnny squinted and peered into the deep box of the record player. "Seven."

"Yeah."

"Do the numbers mean anythin'?"

"I have no idea what they mean."

"How do ya know it was your boy left these here and not some other nutjob breakin' in?"

Lisa closed her eyes and sighed heavily before she pointed toward the kitchen. "The note on the fridge."

"Well hell, darlin'. If he left you a note, that oughtta say everythin' we need to know."

"Read it."

The bounty hunter stalked into the kitchen and took a moment to assess the damage to the cabinets above and below the counters. Shattered dishware lay scattered across the otherwise clean floors. Both the oven and the microwave hung open, and every single drawer had been unceremoniously emptied as well.

There were only two things on the fridge. One was a square magnet that read, *If You Can't Beat 'Em, Make 'Em Bleed.*

He snorted. "It looks like somethin' that belongs on my fridge."

"Yeah, well, it's not mine."

Tacked to the fridge beneath the magnet was a torn sheet of scrap paper with a note written in large, blocky lettering.

Must have just missed you. Hope to see you soon. Give my love 2 Eddie.

Johnny frowned and leaned forward for a closer look. "And you're sure this was from him?"

"Yes, Johnny."

"Mother's intuition and all that?"

Lisa rolled her eyes. "Well, it is his handwriting. And—"

"Who's Eddie?"

"Our cat."

"Cat?" Luther yipped, spun wildly, and knocked over an already precarious pile of scattered junk with his tail. "I love cats!"

"Where is it, lady?" Rex added and resumed his active sniffing with renewed ferocity.

"Yeah, we'll rip its throat out."

She shook her head and tried to ignore them. "From when Hamish was little. He's the one who named the cat. It was more his than mine."

"Huh." Johnny clicked his tongue. "It's a little disappointin'."

"What?"

"I didn't peg you as a cat person, is all."

"Forget the cat, Johnny! My son was here, he left all these things in my apartment, and someone else broke in looking for something I don't think they found. Hamish might be in trouble, so let's focus on that part, okay?"

"Yeah. Sure." His gaze darted around the kitchen as he pressed his lips together, then finally looked at the seething Lisa with her fists clenched at her sides. "Sorry, darlin'."

"It's fine. I'm simply...I'm too close to this."

"You have every right to be upset. We'll get to the bottom of this. Did you find anythin' else?"

"No. That's it."

"As far as you know. All right." He headed across the kitchen and his boots crunched on shattered plates and mugs. Lisa didn't try to pull away when he caught her hand and led her into the living room. "So go ahead and tell me everythin' from the beginnin'. Walk me through it."

"Okay."

CHAPTER EIGHT

After the walkthrough of Lisa's destroyed apartment and her detailed account of every step she'd taken, Johnny didn't find anything new to add to the discoveries. "All right. So he left you three things."

She dropped onto the couch and sighed. "Yeah. Two numbers and a note."

"Three numbers."

"What?"

"He didn't spell out 'to,' He wrote the number two." He sat beside her and leaned against the armrest, which had also been shredded with what must have been a serrated knife. "A note about your cat. I'm guessin' Eddie wasn't some kinda magical feline with literally nine lives."

"He was a regular cat, Johnny. And yes, he died."

"All right. Then that was a personal connection so you'd know it was him."

"Right." She ran her hands up and down her thighs and stared at the loose pages ripped from some of the books that had been thrown haphazardly on the multi-colored area rug. "He left me a message without signing it or giving anything away about it being him. As far as anyone else is concerned, there's no proof to tie it back to him."

"And anyone chasin' someone connected to you named Eddie would find a dead trail." Johnny squinted at her. "Right?"

"The only Eddie I know is the one we saved from the swamp with the rest of the magicals from Philly."

"Yeah, he ain't gonna show up in lookin' through your personal life." Johnny looked at the hounds, who'd made makeshift beds for themselves out of the shredded curtains ripped from the rod above the windows. Luther snored lightly. "Does that magnet mean anythin' to you?"

"'If you can't beat them, make them bleed?' No, Johnny. Other than it sounds like something you'd say."

He snorted. "Your kid has taste."

All she had to do was cast him a sidelong glare before his crooked smile disappeared.

"Still, if we looked real hard into it, we might find it's a message on its own. He couldn't take down whoever's lookin' for him on his own. And I'd say someone is lookin' for him or he wouldn't try to hide the fact he was here to pay his mama a visit."

"But make them bleed? That doesn't make any sense."

"Sure it does. Did you ever get in a knife fight with someone three or four times your size and a helluva lot stronger?"

Lisa shook her head. "Johnny…"

"The aim right there is to be faster. That's it. Fast enough to not get hit yourself and to slice the fucker any which way you can."

Her eyes widened and she looked at him with sudden realization. "Make them bleed."

"Uh-huh. A hundred tiny cuts bleed as much as one big one if they're in the right places. So if your boy chose that magnet on purpose, it means he bit off more than he can chew."

"Oh, my God." She buried her face in her hands. "He came here asking for help and I was in the Everglades."

"It ain't your fault, darlin', so don't go beatin' yourself up. If he's anythin' like you, Hamish is smart. Everythin' he's doin' is for a reason."

"And I can't even see it." Tears shimmered in Lisa's eyes when she looked at the dwarf again. "I'm too close to this."

"Naw. You're right where you're supposed to be. Who can think like him better than his mama?"

"We should call this in—"

"The hell we should. We don't even know what it is. And I ain't handin' this off to someone else who doesn't give a shit 'cause it's only a job. So put that outta your mind. What about the numbers?"

"What about them?"

Johnny shrugged. "They gotta mean somethin' too. Four, seven, two. Or any other combination. Do they ring any bells?"

"No."

"All right." He rubbed his hands together and leaned forward to prop his elbows on his thighs as he studied the living room. "Eddie the cat. Bookshelf you've had since before Hamish was born. Is there any chance that record player goes back as far?"

Lisa blinked and straightened. "Yeah. My dad gave it to me for Christmas when Hamish was…one, I think."

"Should we give him a call?"

"My dad's been dead for…a long time, Johnny."

"Oh. Sorry."

"Don't be."

"So…numbers on everythin' your boy recognized. He didn't live with you here?"

She shook her head.

"Then he was lookin' for ties he knew you'd understand. What else do you have here from back in the child-rearin' days?"

"I don't know. A few pictures. We should look at those."

"Yep."

They both stood abruptly and headed to the hall and the

single bedroom. Rex twitched in his sleep, kicked out against Luther, and elicited a sharp whine from his brother before they both fell into contented snores again.

Johnny glanced at them before they stepped into the bedroom.

They'd best be on their toes after nappin' in the middle of a damn crime scene.

"Here." Lisa handed him a framed photo of her and a boy of nine or ten with dark hair and the same smile as his mom. "All our other pictures are packed in a storage unit. These are the only ones I kept with me."

He took the photo and his eyes widened. "Damn, darlin'. You don't look a day older than you do right here."

"That might be a compliment if magicals didn't age differently."

"Wait—you already have a storage unit?"

"Yeah." She cast him a fleeting glance. "When I took the job with the department, I put some of my things in storage from our last house as I downsized. Hamish went off to do his thing and I intended to get a bigger apartment. I guess I never found the time."

"Huh."

"That was part of the plan here too. I would move everything there into the other unit in Richmond when I clear this place out. You know, to cut down on bills."

"Well, I ain't makin' you pay rent in your own home."

Lisa smirked. "I appreciate that." She turned the second photo in her hands and studied the frame. "There has to be something else, right? Something I'm missing?"

"Check the picture." He opened the clasp on the back of his frame but there was nothing written there, tucked into the sides, or carved into any piece of it.

"Nothing."

"Yeah, me neither."

She set both frames on the dresser, which had been emptied like everything else. "I don't get it."

"Is that all he'd recognize? You kept two pieces of furniture and two pictures from life before the FBI?"

"It's called downsizing for a reason, Johnny. And it's not like Hamish knew the apartment inside and out. He'd only been here a couple of times before he left for Oriceran—wait."

"Yeah, follow that thought to the end."

Lisa ignored him and turned toward her closet. The door opened, the light clicked on, and she stood on her tiptoes to reach the shelf above her. Her hand slapped a few times on the dusty surface but she finally emerged again with a wooden figurine the size of a teacup.

"What the hell is that?" the dwarf muttered.

"A goodbye present." She gazed fondly at the figurine—a small tree with a twisted, gnarled trunk and incredible detail, even down to the leaves. "He made this for me before he left."

"Huh. And you hid it in your closet?"

"Yeah, I know that might seem a little weird. But it's…part of a thing we did with presents. You wouldn't under—"

The carving dropped from her hand and clattered onto the clothing-strewn floor.

"Lisa?"

"Okay." She bent quickly to pick it up again, then thrust the wooden tree toward Johnny. "I might be going crazy, so please look. On the bottom. Turn it over."

With a frown, he studied the intricate figure and flipped the tree upside-down. A number eight had been scratched into the dark-stained wood to show the lighter natural tone beneath. "Well, I'll be damned."

"It's a number, right?"

"Or a sideways infinity."

"What?"

"I'm kiddin'. That's an eight or my name might as well be Jack Daniel."

Lisa snorted and held her hand out for the figurine.

Johnny handed it over with wide eyes. "The kid must've passed shop class with flyin' colors, huh?"

"No, he was self-taught. And stop calling him a kid, okay? Hamish hasn't been a kid for a long time."

"Sure. But it's hard to imagine you bein' a mom to anyone over ten, and that's stretchin' it."

Seated on the bed, she rolled her eyes and fiddled with the wooden tree. "He was ten in that picture. Now, he's thirty-two."

A choking cough escaped the dwarf and he cleared his throat instantly to cover it. "That would put you in your mid-forties, yeah?"

Lisa's scathing glance only held a tinge of amusement. "I did not have a baby at fifteen."

"All right. Late forties, then."

"I'm not telling you how old I am, Johnny."

"Well, at least tell me if I hit the mark."

"No."

"Same decade?"

"Hey, let's focus on the numbers that matter." She scowled at him and wiggled the figurine. "Like the ones Hamish left me here in my apartment before the place was broken into by who knows how many assholes looking for him here. Or for me. I don't even know at this point."

"Naw, if they were lookin' for you, they would have stuck around." He sat beside her on the mattress, bounced a little, and raised an eyebrow. "Cushy."

She shrugged. "I like a soft mattress."

"How the hell do you sleep on this? It feels like you'd sink straight through the floor."

"Trust me, it holds up," she muttered, stared at the far wall, and mulled over all the possibilities of what these clues could mean.

"Huh." The dwarf pressed a fist into the mattress and watched the depression sink and then rise quickly into place again. "You never said a thing about sleepin' on my hard mattress."

"I don't mind it. But living alone means I get to choose my bed, and if I have to choose, I go with this every time— You know what? Let's table the couple's mattress conversation for after we find my son. How's that?"

"Sure. Sure. You're right." The bounty hunter exhaled slowed and gazed around the half-Light Elf's bedroom.

"Four, seven, two, eight. There's no other significance to where he left these numbers other than connection to him—"

"Yeah, we ain't takin' this mattress back to the swamp, though."

Lisa turned her head slowly to stare at him. "Are you serious right now?"

"I'm only sayin', darlin'. You don't gotta get rid of it. Put it in the Richmond storage unit. I ain't got space for another bed at home. Even if it's a damn cloud—"

"Wait! Storage unit." She ripped her phone out of her jacket pocket and opened her email to flip through the list of customized folders.

"Did you miss an appointment or somethin'?"

"No. But… Here we go. Receipts."

He ran a hand through his hair. "You lost me."

"Give me a sec." Her gaze darted up and down along the scrolling phone screen before she stopped to shove her phone under Johnny's nose. "That. Right there. Tell me that's not what this means."

"Darlin', I don't—"

"It's 2784. Right here on the receipt."

"Oh, shit. Capital Storage. Hamish know about the storage unit?"

"Yeah. He helped me move everything in there before I got this apartment." Lisa stood and slipped her phone into her pocket. "That was over ten years ago. I can't believe he remembered."

"Does he have a key?"

"No. He doesn't have a key to my apartment, either, but that didn't stop him."

"Well, when everythin' else is a dead end, I'd call that a helluva lead."

"Yeah, me too. Let's go." She didn't wait for him to say anything else before she raced out of the bedroom and headed to the front door.

Johnny strode out after her and whistled at the hounds. "Nap's over, boys. Let's go."

Luther snorted and leapt to his feet before he stumbled into his brother. "Where is it, Johnny? Say where, and I'll—"

"Get off." Rex snapped at the smaller hound, stood to stretch himself fully from snout to tail, and trotted through the piles of Lisa's broken belongings after his master.

"Yeah. Coming, Johnny. Wait up!"

CHAPTER NINE

Fortunately, the rush-hour traffic Johnny had somehow managed to navigate without killing anyone had decreased significantly by the time they headed out in his rental. At 7:34 pm, it was already dark when they pulled up at the twenty-four-hour Capital Storage premises, but the lot was well lit by bright street lamps. The rows of storage units were easy enough to navigate, also lit by the soft single floodlight mounted above each garage door.

Lisa got confused only once before they found her unit.

The dwarf stuck a thumb over his shoulder. "I think we were meant to turn right back there, darlin'."

"I know what I'm doing, Johnny." She spun quickly in the narrow avenue between the long, single-story unit buildings and continued to search the numbers. When they circled again to eventually end up in the row they would have reached if they had turned in the right place, he didn't say a word.

I gotta keep my mouth shut in this unless it's important. She's already on edge as it is.

"Here we go." She scowled at the number of her storage unit before she rummaged in her purse. "I haven't been here in years."

"It doesn't look like anyone else has been here either."

69

She paused to frown condescendingly at him. "Do you think Hamish broke into my apartment?"

"I dunno. Whoever else did it didn't leave any other sign there. Do you think there's a chance he trashed everything to cover his tracks?"

"Why would you ask that?"

He shrugged and gestured at the lock on the storage unit's handle. "There's no forced entry here."

"Break into my apartment and tear the place apart simply to leave a few personal clues? No. He wouldn't do that."

"Look, I know you have this image of your son, darlin', but he's been gone a long time. Maybe he's—"

"Stop. Please stop." Lisa whipped a huge keyring out of her purse and fumbled to choose the correct one under the bright floodlight above them. "I know my kid, Johnny. If anyone understands that, it's you."

"All right. Sure."

"No one else here, Johnny," Rex called from the other side of the building.

"Yeah, why'd you send us to go look around if there isn't anyone to take down and drag back to you?" Luther asked. "It's empty. Nothing but—ooh! Rex, check this out."

"What?"

"You smell what I smell?"

"Holy crap, Johnny. Someone's hoarding snacks in this one!"

Johnny snapped his fingers. "Good work, boys. Come on back. We're openin' the door."

Lisa finally found the right key and crouched beside the garage door handle to unlock it. After a quick tug, the door lifted with a loud rumble in the empty storage facility and she stepped inside to click the lights on.

The hounds trotted around the end of the building and stopped beside their master to take in the sight of Lisa Breyer's belongings from a different life.

"Whoa, lady." Rex stepped inside to sniff the plastic totes stacked close to the door, coated like everything else in a layer of dust. "I thought you had a ton of stuff in the last place, but this is intense."

The dwarf snapped his fingers. "Hush up."

"No, he's right." She walked slowly along the front row of her things with a nostalgic frown. "I do have a ton of stuff. I always meant to go through it but couldn't find the time."

"Ten years ain't enough?"

She glanced at him in exasperation. "I'd just gotten my job in the department, Johnny. I moved from Glen Allen to DC, Hamish moved out on his own, and then he went to Oriceran. Going through a storage unit full of everything from eighteen years of him living with me didn't exactly seem like a fun way to spend my extra time."

"Sure." He scratched the side of his face. "It's not like you could make a quick interplanetary phone call."

"Yeah. I dove into work instead." She stopped beside a long, low chest of drawers painted a dark blue-black with the solar system's planets and stars studded across the surface and smiled wanly. "This was his. I guess that's obvious."

"It's a decent paint job."

"Thanks."

Johnny raised an eyebrow. "You did that?"

"A single mom raising a kid at the start of magic's reveal on this planet? Yeah, Johnny. I gained all kinds of skills."

"How come I've never seen you paint?"

She shrugged. "You never asked."

"Hey, lady. You have a hound?"

"What?" She and Johnny asked it at the same time as they turned toward Rex, who sniffed furiously at the floor where a thick rope dangled over the side of an open box and trailed across the cement floor.

"Rex! You found a toy!" Luther padded toward him and tried to snatch the rope before his brother snarled in his face.

"I found it first."

"Oh, come on, bro. Sharing is caring—"

"Hold up." The dwarf snapped his fingers and both hounds sat. "Somethin' ain't right here."

"What do you mean?" Lisa looked dubiously behind her at the avenue between storage buildings and moved her hand toward her service pistol in the shoulder holster beneath her open jacket.

Luther panted and cocked his head. "I don't hear anyone, Johnny."

"That's 'cause they were already here and left."

"What?"

"No footprints." He stopped beside the hounds and glanced from the rope on the floor to the other side of the storage unit. A quick swipe of his finger against the top of the partially open box pulled up a thickly caked layer of dust. "You ain't been here in years."

"Right. Dust is a normal part of that."

"So why does all this open space on the floor look like it's been swept clean?"

Lisa stared at the cement beneath her feet. "He *was* here."

"Someone was." Johnny squatted beside the rope, which dangled from the open box but didn't carry any dirt at all. "What's in here?"

"Um...I don't know. Various garage items—tools, random junk, and rope, obviously."

"Do you have a flashlight?"

"Sure." She pulled her phone out to turn on the flashlight app. As she lowered it toward his outstretched hand while he inspected the box, she stopped halfway. "Johnny."

He looked at her and wrinkled his nose. "Since when do you have a problem lettin' me hold your phone?"

"Since you're looking in the wrong place." She nodded at the narrow row of space down the center of the storage unit with the two tall piles of her stacked belongings on either side. The walkway and back of the unit were completely dark at night, with the overhead light inside only bright enough to illuminate the front half of the unit. Her flashlight app, however, revealed everything they were looking for.

A thick layer of dust lined the floor to the back and a single line of large footprints cut through the dust.

"Well, look at that." The bounty hunter nodded and stood. "I assume you can't tell if those are your son's shoes, huh?"

"We're about to find out."

They moved slowly down the center of the unit and followed the tracks.

"These look new, Johnny."

"Uh-huh. And whoever made 'em either got too lazy to sweep the rest of the evidence or meant to leave 'em here exactly like this."

"There's only one set of prints." Lisa swept her flashlight across the floor and her frown deepened. "No one simply disappears like that."

"Is it more borgs, Johnny?" Luther asked as he sniffed along the edge of the plastic sheet covering a couch stacked with even more boxes. "That one guy could disappear."

Rex chuffed. "Yeah, before he tried to blow us up."

"He could have climbed back over this pile of stuff." Johnny scanned one side of the stacked belongings.

"No cyborgs in my storage unit. I can't handle that right—"

"Are you all right?"

The footprints ended at a low wooden chest in the far corner. It served as the base for a stack of much smaller boxes, although the front corner of the chest had lines of disturbed dust like something had been moved. The rest of its surface that peeked out from beneath the piled boxes was clean.

"Right here. Help me move these."

Johnny grasped a stack of three boxes, tried to lift them, but grunted and stepped away. "Who the hell puts bricks in tiny-ass boxes?"

Lisa propped her phone up against another stack of her things to give them light and took only one box in her arms. "They're books. Not bricks."

"You keep your books in storage?"

She dropped the heavy box on the floor with a sigh. "Again, this was supposed to be temporary."

With a disgruntled expression, he tried two boxes instead of three and barely managed to get them onto the floor without the cardboard slipping through his hands.

They worked quickly to uncover the rest of the chest before Lisa squatted in front of it and opened the lid slowly with a creak. He retrieved her phone and aimed the light inside.

"That's somethin'."

"Yeah." Despite how quickly she snatched up the single white envelope lying in the bottom of the chest, her hand still shook. It didn't stop when she tore the envelope open and unfolded the paper.

"Do you want me to hold that for ya, darlin'?"

"No. Only the light."

He aimed it at the paper and let her read the note in private.

She'll tell me what it says or she won't. It ain't none of my business what's in her stuff.

"Hey, lady." Rex pawed at a box slightly caved in one side. "This smells like the two-leg footprints."

"What?" Luther trotted toward his brother. "Lemme try. Ooh, yeah. Except it smells like…like…Rex, what's that stuff that makes two-legs grow bigger?"

"Food?"

"No. It's in them."

"Food?"

Luther grunted. "Same thing that's in Amanda. Come on, Johnny. You know what I'm talking about."

"The hell I do," the dwarf muttered.

"No, no. It's the thing that happens between pup and fully grown. Oh! Pheromones!"

Johnny frowned disapprovingly at his hound. "There ain't no pheromones shut up in a box."

"Hormones!" Rex added.

"Yeah, hormones." Luther sniffed the box again. "No hormones in the footprints."

The dwarf snapped his fingers. "Hush up."

Lisa sighed and lowered the note against her thighs where she knelt. After a moment, she turned to look at the box Luther still shoved his nose up against and shrugged. "It's probably a box of his old clothes."

"You saved his clothes?"

"Again, the plan was to go through all this later after the move and get rid of everything. You know, because this was—"

"Temporary. Yeah, darlin'. I get it." Johnny snapped at the hounds again. "Leave it."

"But it's the same guy, Johnny. This whole place smells like this two-legs without hormones and Lisa."

"Is that from him?" he asked Lisa.

She nodded slowly and handed the paper to him. "It sure is."

"What did he say?"

"Read it, Johnny. I need a minute."

He took the letter and leaned back against the stable stack of large boxes along the unit wall to read their next real clue. The handwriting wasn't nearly as blocky and bulky as the small note left on Lisa's fridge but it could have come from the same hand.

Hey, Mom. If you're reading this, it means I didn't find you at home. Sorry about not being able to call either, but I can't risk it right now. I'm in trouble.

I've been back on Earth for a week, trying to find a good time to reach out to you. But these guys are on me all the time. I can't tell you where I'm staying in case this falls into the wrong hands. It's not like any of these idiots are smart enough to work it out. Still, better safe than sorry.

It wasn't the plan to come back from Oriceran this early but I couldn't stay. It turns out the magicals I fell in with aren't the kind you'd want to write home to your mom about in the first place. They're worse. If I'd known what I was doing when I started, I wouldn't have kept going and now, it seems impossible to get out of it.

These guys are bad news. They are trafficking seriously dark magic like I've never seen before through the gates and trying to bring it all back to Earth. So much for taking a job as an "emissary." I can't tell you much more right now, but it's bad.

There's a bounty on my head. The last I heard, it was ridiculously huge, so calling you or meeting up with you out in the open isn't an option. And yeah, going to the FBI crossed my mind. But at this point, I'm basically a wanted criminal. I probably wouldn't even make it through the front door and I don't know anyone there but you. Which means if you can bring the information I have to your bosses, I might still have a chance.

I wish I didn't need your help but I'm running out of options.

I'll be at Tilted this Thursday at 9:00 pm. We can talk more then when I know we're both safe.

I love you. Sorry.

—H

Johnny frowned and scanned the letter again. "Damn."

"I know. What was he thinking? Working for smugglers and dark magicals? I thought—" Lisa pushed to her feet and took the letter from him. "I thought I'd taught him better than that."

"It doesn't sound like he did it on purpose."

"Well, maybe I should have taught him how to identify the wrong kind of magical from the start."

"That kinda thing comes with practice and experience, darlin'. It ain't your fault."

"No. It's his." She crumpled the letter and shoved it into her pocket. "I don't even know what to say."

"Let's focus on what to do, then."

"Do? I don't know that either." She lowered the lid of the chest with a bang and a puff of dust.

Rex sneezed. "Aw, jeez, lady. Easy on the dust clouds, huh?"

"Yeah, it's—" Luther sneezed and shook his head furiously. "It's not like—" He sneezed again. "Like we have—" The final sneeze was strong enough to stop him talking.

"We got what we came for." Johnny handed her the phone and headed down the center of the unit toward the open door. "And now we have to decide what comes next."

The hounds raced after their master and both continued to snort and sneeze. Luther bumped into a stack of boxes and skittered away even faster when the tower swayed at the contact.

Lisa brought up the rear and no one said a word until she'd turned the light off and pulled the garage door shut with enough force to slam it onto the cement. She locked the unit and thrust the giant keyring into her purse.

Johnny watched her staring at the closed door for a few minutes before he spoke. "You ain't gotta bottle it all up like that."

"Bottle what up? Hamish is back, I wasn't at my apartment to help him, and now I find out he's a wanted criminal on two planets who can't even reach out for help because no one but his mother will believe him. I…" She took a huge breath and brushed her dark hair away from her eyes. "I can't see where I went wrong here."

"You didn't." He placed a hand gently on her shoulder. "Look…normally, I ain't fixin' to step on anyone else's toes when it comes to bringin' down a few thugs or a dozen—"

She stepped away from him, her eyes wide with anger and pain and fear. "He's not a thug, Johnny."

She's tryin' so hard to not let it out. There must be a law about kids bein' a pain in the ass.

"I know he ain't, darlin'." The dwarf lowered his hand from where she'd stepped away from it and shrugged. "Which is why you're gonna meet him tomorrow and see what he has to say. If he's clean, we'll do what we can to help him."

"I won't go alone."

"Aw, come on. Don't tell me you're afraid of your own kid—"

"I'm afraid of my inability to look at this without bias, Johnny. This whole situation is one giant bias. I need you there with me."

"Me? Hell no. No."

"Johnny—"

"You ain't seen him in what? Ten years?"

"Nine. I think."

"I ain't crashin' a family reunion. He's your kid."

Lisa caught hold of both his shoulders and leaned toward him. "I'm serious. I can't do this alone. I wouldn't have even come this far without an extra pair of eyes. And there's no one else I trust enough at this point to bring with me. You read his letter. He has a dark-magical bounty on his head and who knows how many warrants for his arrest on Earth—if anyone here even knows he's back."

The bounty hunter's mustache bristled when he worked his jaw from side to side. "Seein' your son is a personal thing."

"I'm not asking you to meet the family, Johnny. I'm asking you to come with me as my partner—my business partner. On a case." She swallowed thickly and squeezed his shoulders. "Please."

He sighed. "Yeah, all right. I ain't goin' anywhere."

"Thank you." She finally released him and turned in a slow circle to scan the empty storage facility. "Can we maybe...get a hotel tonight?"

"I ain't sleepin' on that cloudy bed of yours if that's what you're asking."

She glanced at him and chuckled wryly. "Right. We wouldn't want Johnny Walker going soft on us, would we?"

"I ain't exactly sure what you mean by that, darlin', but I'm gonna let that slide." He pointed in the direction from which they'd come to direct them to the rental car, and they headed through the maze of storage buildings. "It ain't possible, anyhow."

"Of course not." She slipped her hand briefly into his and squeezed it.

Johnny looked at their interlaced fingers, opened his mouth in an attempt to find something reassuring to say, then stopped when she removed her hand and quickened her pace to get ahead of him.

All right. Give her time. I can't say she ain't given me any when I needed it.

CHAPTER TEN

They took a hotel room three miles away from her apartment complex and ate a quick dinner. Lisa barely touched hers at first but she managed to eat half of it. The meal was silent and strained until Johnny cleared his throat and asked, "Do you wanna drink?"

"No. I'm gonna go to bed." She pushed up from the small table in their suite, gave him a quick peck on the cheek, and headed to the bedroom.

The hounds followed her until she paused at the door to give them both a quick scratch behind the ears.

"You okay, lady?" Rex asked and leaned against her leg.

"Yeah, you look like you could use a good back scratch." Luther panted and his tail thumped against the old carpeting. "Or a snuggle. Sometimes that helps."

She looked questioningly at the bounty hunter.

"Don't look at me. If there's any snugglin', they're doin' it with each other."

Without a word, she stopped scratching Luther's head, frowned at her partner, then turned and walked briskly into the bedroom. "Goodnight, Johnny."

The door shut with a little more force and volume than necessary, although it wasn't exactly slammed closed.

Rex and Luther sat in front of the bedroom door and stared at it.

"I think she's pissed, Johnny."

"Keep it down, huh? If she's tryin' to sleep, the two of y'all yappin' on about her in the next room ain't gonna make it any easier." He finished the last piece of his burger, crumpled the to-go wrapper, and lowered his voice when he added, "Of course she's pissed. Her boy dug himself a hole and we have no idea how deep it is."

The larger hound stood, trotted toward his master, and glanced at the bedroom door. He sat at Johnny's feet and whispered, "I think she's pissed at you."

"What the hell did I do?"

"We gave you an in, Johnny." Luther padded toward the couch along the far wall, turned in two quick circles, then curled on the floor in front of the furniture. "Back-scratches or snuggles."

"Or whatever else two-legs do," Rex added.

"And you're still sitting there."

Shit. And that's why I don't do whole conversations based on heavy looks.

"You should fix it, Johnny."

"Yeah. Go make her feel better." Luther lifted his head from his forepaws long enough to prick his ears as he gazed at the bedroom door. Then, he whispered, "I think she's crying."

With a long sigh, Johnny stood from the table and headed toward the bedroom.

"Don't worry about us," Rex muttered and lifted his nose toward the table to sniff cautiously. "We'll take care of everything out here."

"Hey, Rex. Did they leave anything?"

"I'm checking."

Johnny opened the bedroom door slowly and stepped into the

darkness. The silhouette of Lisa's form under the thick comforter didn't move. He stepped out of his shoes, climbed into the bed beside her, and placed a hand on her shoulder. She was already asleep, however, so he lay down and kissed the back of her head as he muttered, "We'll work this out, darlin'. We always do."

The next morning, they bought bagel sandwiches and coffee for breakfast—with extra sides of eggs and bacon for the hounds—on the way to Lisa's apartment.

"This is gonna be rough," she said as she pushed the door open.

"Darlin', if you're worried about me bein' able to handle a little clean-up like this, you're forgettin' where I just came from."

She stopped to stare at him for a moment, then seemed to deflate. "Oh, jeez. I'm sorry, Johnny. You weren't finished cleaning the houseboat, were you?"

"Naw, I only had the top level left. Would it surprise you that the twins were the cleanest out of all four borgs? And even them sharin' a room. Or a floor."

"Not really..." With the toe of her sneaker, she nudged a book with the binding halfway ripped away from the hard-cover spine. "I need a plan."

"What you need is a distraction. Is there anythin' else you wanna go tackle today instead? I'll hang back. Maybe call in a few extra hands—"

"No, Johnny. This is my distraction."

He raised an eyebrow. "Cleanin' up your busted-into apartment and the mess made by a group of Oriceran asshats lookin' to put your kid in a bag? I ain't quite sure how that's gonna distract you from—I mean, it's the whole reason things are tense in the first place."

Lisa sighed and shook her head as she scanned the living

room. "We have all day to kill before we meet him at Tilted. I know DC inside and out. Unless you want some kind of tour—"

"Hell no." He cleared his throat. "Naw, darlin'. This city, district, or whatever the hell you wanna call it ain't my kinda place, and I know that without havin' to see everythin' in it. We could still go somewhere else."

"Like the hotel? No, I need something to keep me busy. And we might as well make ourselves useful here, right? Clean the mess and at least start the packing process."

"If that's what you want. Sure."

"Great. I think I have leftover boxes in the closet. We can at least get started with those." Lisa headed to the coat closet and called without turning, "There's a roll of packing tape in the kitchen. Bottom drawer left of the… Wait."

"Yeah, I don't think anythin's where you left it last."

"Well, I…okay, look through what's on the floor."

"Hey, hey, Johnny." Luther yipped, skittered around in the kitchen, and ran toward his master who paused to look at him with his hands on his hips. "This tape? That's what she wanted, right?"

The dwarf shook his head. "That's an oven mitt, Luther."

Lisa snorted as she pulled a stack of unassembled boxes from the back of a closet.

"Oh." Luther dropped it at his feet and shoved his nose inside to root around. "It's gotta be useful for something."

Rex pranced out of the kitchen, his head held high as he stepped proudly over piles of scattered utensils and shattered kitchenware. "You mean this roll?"

"What are you doin'?" Johnny pointed at the other side of the living room. "There are broken plates everywhere and I don't suppose the intruders stopped at the kitchen knives, either. One of y'all is bound to rip your paws or worse. Y'all need to stay out the damn kitchen."

With his prize clasped gingerly in his mouth, Rex walked slowly past his master.

The dwarf snapped his fingers. "Wait. Gimme that tape."

The roll dropped into his hand and the hound's tail wagged furiously. "It is what you wanted."

"Wait, how do you know what packing tape is?"

"I'm not an idiot, bro."

"Yeah, but—hey."

"All right, y'all make yourselves scarce. Go on."

"There's nowhere to go, Johnny."

"Try the corner. Wherever, but stay outta the way."

The hounds slunk off to sniff the ruins of the apartment.

"Here." Lisa took the roll of tape and handed him a trash bag. "Go into the bedroom and bundle all my clothes in here."

"Your clothes?" He took it and scowled at it. "Naw. I'll do somethin' else."

"Is something wrong with my clothes, Johnny?"

"Not for the most part, no. I like 'em." His gaze darted all over the living room. "But I ain't fixin' to go through 'em."

She chuckled wryly. "They're all clean, I promise. It's not a big deal."

"Sure, until it is. Here's how it goes, darlin'. It starts as an innocent favor, packin' your things. Then I find somethin' hidden in a sock drawer or shoved into a bag in your closet. You see me lookin' at it and freak the hell out 'cause it ain't somethin' I was supposed to see."

"Wow. You're seriously overthinking this."

"It's the same reason a fella would be damned if he went through a woman's purse. Personal stuff. It ain't..." He swallowed. "It ain't natural."

She laughed at his genuine discomfort and patted his shoulder before she pointed down the hall toward her bedroom. "Well, it's a good thing I don't use my closet and dresser as a giant purse. You have nothing to worry about and I have nothing to hide. So go shove the rest of my clothes into this trash bag for me, okay? I'm gonna put these boxes together, then I'll start going through the kitchen."

"Are you sure it ain't steppin' on your toes?"

"Get over it and help me, Johnny." With a nod, she sat on the floor beside the stack of flattened boxes and ripped off the first long piece of packing tape. "It'll take you twenty minutes tops."

With an incoherent grumble, the dwarf glowered at the trash bag as he half-shuffled reluctantly down the hall to do as his partner—domestic, business, or otherwise—instructed.

Rex and Luther turned out to be surprisingly helpful with cleaning and packing, fetching whatever Lisa asked for out of the few other rooms so she could focus on her task. The two coonhounds with their faces closer to the floor than either of the two-legs had a unique advantage when looking for random items beneath the piles of things turned upside-down.

Johnny finished with her clothes in the bedroom and relieved that it was over with, complied with her instruction to go through the apartment with the plastic trash can from the kitchen to pick up everything broken, bent, or torn that needed to be tossed out. "I think you're gonna need a bigger trash can, darlin'."

"The dumpster's downstairs behind the building. We'll make a few trips."

He crouched beside the smaller bookshelf in the corner and picked up a black shoebox that had been overturned on top of its contents. The lid lay two feet away, and when he lifted the box, a folded gameboard spilled off the top of the pile to reveal two bags of dice, multiple notebooks, and a small rulebook. "It looks like you forgot to pack this with the rest of Hamish's belongings, huh?"

Lisa peered around the corner of the kitchen. "Oh. No, that's mine."

"Yours." The bounty hunter peered into one of the drawstring bags of polyhedral dice. "I had no idea you were into nerdy board games."

"Dungeons & Dragons isn't a board game, Johnny. It's—"

"Hell, I don't need to you explain it to me." He thrust everything into the shoebox and closed the lid. "It's surprisin', is all."

"Why? Is it a deal-breaker for you?"

When he turned to frown at her, she smirked as she dropped a huge chunk of a shattered plate into the trash can. "Not as long as you ain't expectin' me to pick your hobbies up."

She laughed, unoffended by his statement. "Yeah, that goes both ways."

"'Cept for when you went into my stuff to build a cage for a borg bomb."

"That was different. That was by necessity. I like the game, but I'm sure D&D Action Surge won't get us out of a life-or-death situation."

"I ain't goin' to nerd meetings with ya, neither."

She rolled her eyes. "The fact you said that means you'll never make it to one anyway."

"Huh?"

"Put it in a box and move on, Johnny."

It took them the rest of the day to get all the trash and broken items out of her apartment and into the dumpster behind the building. Fortunately, the apartment itself hadn't sustained any real damage, so at least she wouldn't have all that money taken out of her security deposit—hopefully.

Half of her things had been packed in boxes, which amounted to three going into storage and only one of them labeled to go with them to the swamp cabin. It was only one-third full.

"All right. I think we should call it a day on this, darlin'." Johnny glanced at his watch. "We have about two hours before this meetin' with your kid. Do you wanna grab some—"

"Food?" Luther whipped his head up from where he'd rested it on his forepaws. "Like, actual food?"

"Come on, Johnny. It's perfect timing," Rex added. "I'm sick of eating crackers."

"You found crackers?" Lisa asked the larger hound, who looked away from her quickly and licked his muzzle.

"You can't prove anything."

Luther sniggered. "Because you ate the proof, bro. And you didn't even share. That's happening often lately. What's up with that?"

Lisa shook her head. "I don't want to eat until I see Hamish."

"It's not a good idea to go into anythin' on an empty stomach, darlin'."

"It's an even worse idea to stuff my face and puke all over someone at the wrong moment." She sighed and set the freshly emptied trashcan beside the fridge. "I only want to see him first, Johnny. Once I know it's him and that he's safe—or at least not seriously hurt—then maybe I can relax a little."

"All right. We might as well get goin' now. If we reach Tilted early, we can surveil it for a while and look out for any trouble before we're supposed to meet."

"Fine." She shuffled out of the kitchen after him, and the hounds bounded to their feet.

"Yes! We can at least get food first, right, Johnny?"

"Yeah, we've been so good. Cleaning's hard work, Johnny. Especially when you're doing it all with your mouth—"

The dwarf snapped his fingers. "Y'all are stayin' here."

"Wait, what?"

"Are you serious?"

"We're headin' into a bar, boys, to meet with someone who's tryin' but ain't exactly successful at stayin' under the radar. And I ain't fixin' to attract more attention to us or him by walkin' round with two coonhounds off-leash."

"You can put us on a leash, Johnny."

"Yeah, it's not like we don't know what they're for."

"Two coonhounds walkin' around in Virginia's kemana is

what's gonna draw all the attention. It's only for tonight, boys. Y'all can come next time. We won't be long."

"Aw, man…"

Johnny closed the door behind him as he followed Lisa into the hall.

"Hey, Rex. Did you eat all the crackers?"

"Duh. But I smelled a bag of beef jerky in the pantry. Help me with this handle, huh?"

"Damn hounds." Johnny turned to keep them out of Lisa's pantry, but she caught his hand and stopped him.

"They're fine, Johnny. Truly."

"Not when they think they can raid your kitchen."

She smiled coyly at him. "I ate the rest of the beef jerky three hours ago."

"Uh-huh."

"And normally, I'd say we should bring Rex and Luther with us. They've already proven how helpful they are in a pinch." She punched the call button for the third-floor elevator and folded her arms. "But it was the right call this time."

"Why is that? Hamish ain't fond of hounds?"

"Only until his face puffs up and the rash appears." The elevator doors opened. "He's allergic."

"Well, shit. I'll make sure to not hug him, then."

"Like that was something you would have done anyway."

CHAPTER ELEVEN

Lisa insisted she knew exactly how to get into the kemana outside DC and didn't need Johnny's help. He was happy to let her call the shots and choose their route from the hotel outside DC. As long as he was behind the wheel of the rental, he didn't mind.

"I ain't exactly a fan of this one," he muttered as they exited the dark, quiet, abandoned outskirts of the kemana—or mostly abandoned. Hundreds of eyes blinked at them from dark crevices and around shadowy corners. They glowed slightly beneath the dim light as the Willens who lived here watched the newcomers pass through their junk-built "suburb" at the edge of the larger city underground. "And we have hordes of spectators."

"What's the big deal?" she muttered. "You have other Willen friends."

"Yeah, but those I know. These are…closer to Washington."

"Oh, jeez."

None of the creatures came out of their dark homes to greet, address, or try to barter the magicals out of their shinier belongings. Fortunately, the two partners didn't have much on them that fit the description, and they proceeded quickly through the run-down parts of the kemana's outer ring before they reached the central part of the city. It was fairly busy, as kemanas tended to be, but Lisa stopped when she moved left and noticed Johnny had already turned right to head in the opposite direction.

"Hey."

"Huh?"

"Tilted's this way."

"Oh, sure." He sniffed, glanced at the other magical citizens going about their business without any human illusion disguises at all, and hooked his thumbs through his belt loops. "I'm followin' you, darlin'. All good."

She studied him for a moment with the ghost of a smirk. "You haven't been down here before, have you?"

"Naw. 'Course I have. Once."

"What happened?"

"Nothin'. But I ain't a fan."

"Yeah, you said that, but there aren't any Willens this close to the center."

He cleared his throat. "It's all too close to DC, darlin'—to the feds and to the center of this whole damn country. Give me the crowded New York kemana under the subway any day. Hell, I'd take the Detroit kemana over this."

She wrinkled her nose. "Detroit's...bad."

"It's better than this."

Shaking her head, she led him past the various shops and magical vendors who passed their Thursday evening by catering to other magicals instead of running around in the open above-ground. He squinted suspiciously at every dark corner between the buildings and every other magical who so much as glanced at him for more than half a second.

If Nelson found out we were here, he'd call us in to say hi. The safest place to be is right under the nose of the guy you don't want seein' ya. It still makes me as itchy as hell, though.

Lisa had no problem finding Tilted within the crowded

avenue of storefronts. It was a dimly lit, smokey dive bar for magicals at the far side of the kemana, separated from the majority of the underground city traffic. Johnny scowled at the sign dangling over the front door. "Have you spent a lotta time here, darlin'?"

"For the occasional drink after a particularly rough night, yeah. It's been a while, though." She opened the stained, slightly dented door, and the low beat of some alternative rock band he didn't recognize filled the air. "It's not like you were the first magical to introduce me to bars or drinks or blowing off a little steam."

"Nope. But it's hard to picture you rollin' round in DC bars by yourself."

"I guess you're getting the fast-track insider's look at my life before we met, huh?"

They stepped into the dark interior together and the wizard behind the bar gave them a glance of appraisal before he tended to the two other patrons seated in front of him.

She scanned the single row of booths and headed toward the back. "I need the restroom."

"All right." The dwarf watched her walk away.

It's only an excuse to check every single table for her son. There's no sign of him yet.

When she returned, her eyes were wide and her face was flushed. "He's not here."

He glanced at his watch. "We're half an hour early, darlin'. That was the point."

"Right. Okay."

"Did you see anyone else in those booths?"

"Only an old Wood Elf on his own reading the paper. Does that feel a little weird to you?"

"If we were in the Glades, darlin', sure. This city is a different kinda beast." He placed a hand gently on the small of her back and guided her toward the bar. "Let's take a seat and watch the door from a better angle. We can't spend half an hour standin' in the middle with our thumbs up our asses."

Lisa grimaced but didn't protest before they took their seats on the bar stools. "I guess."

The wizard approached them and wiped his hands on a rag. "What can I get for you?"

"Johnny Walker Black. Neat."

The bartender looked surprised but nodded. "And you?"

"Club soda with lime, please."

When he left to fulfill their ridiculously simple drink order, Johnny leaned toward her and muttered, "Club soda?"

"I'm not drinking before this meeting."

"Oh, come on. You're all nervous, darlin'. One ain't gonna hurt."

"Not everyone can drink like Johnny Walker and stay sharp on a case." She realized immediately how snappy that sounded and sighed. "Sorry. I merely don't want to take any chances."

"All right. That's fine."

The bartender brought their drinks and Johnny paid quickly before he downed the single two-finger pour of whiskey and they waited in silence.

Over the next forty-five minutes, only three more groups of magicals entered the dusky setting of Tilted—three shifters in business suits, a group of exhausted-looking Elves who'd brought their work with them in briefcases to attend to at one of the booths, and two witches. One of them looked terrified to be seated across from the table from her friend. The other smirked and leaned over the table and they held their conversation in low tones.

Naw, they ain't friends. It looks like everyone has their secret business down here.

But there was no sign of Hamish or anyone looking for Lisa Breyer to bring her a message.

By 9:30 pm, she had gone through three club sodas and taken

one more official trip to the bathroom. Johnny was on his third drink when she returned to the bar looking like she'd seen a ghost.

"What happened?"

"What happened?" Her gaze darted all over the bar. "He's not here, Johnny. He said nine o'clock. What if something is wrong?"

"Don't go lettin' that fear get the better of you. And stop lookin' everywhere like you're expectin' to get caught, huh? That's How Not To Draw Attention 101."

"He wouldn't make me wait this long. I know he wouldn't." She stared at her empty glass but didn't see it. "What if they got him? They were looking for him at my apartment. If they caught up to him before he had a chance to get here—"

"All right, slow down." Johnny rested his hand on top of hers on the bar, which made her look at him. "There's no use in worryin' yourself before we have any idea what's goin' on, right?"

"Johnny, I know that. But knowing it and feeling it are two completely different things."

"If anyone's watchin' us, darlin', we need to keep our cool."

"Right." She took a deep breath and nodded at the bartender.

"Another club soda?" the wizard asked.

"No. Gin and tonic. Hendrix."

"And another whiskey for me too," the dwarf added.

"Sure thing."

The mere act of ordering a drink settled her nerves enough to stop sweeping her gaze over the bar every ten seconds. "I don't like this."

"If you liked any part of this whole situation, I'd be more worried about you than him." He gave her his crooked smile. "It's gonna be all right."

"You don't know that."

"Well, we ain't got proof otherwise. We'll sit tight a while longer."

As soon as the wizard brought them their drinks, the music

playing through the sound system turned up a notch. The regular nightlife that flowed through Tilted at almost 10:00 pm surged through the front door like a switch had been flipped. The bar's patrons doubled, then tripled. Two huge Kilomeas in tight-fitting undershirts appeared to take their places as bouncers, one up front by the door and the other at the back at the entrance to the hallway that led to the bathrooms.

The conversations grew loud and chaotic around the bar as magicals jostled with one another to get their drinks and meet their friends for a Thursday evening of letting loose in a world below the one still predominantly made for humans.

Lisa drank half her gin and tonic in under a minute but forced herself to slow. "This will be impossible with so many magicals in here."

"Do you think you'd forget his face and miss him in a crowd?"

She frowned condescendingly at him. "Please tell me that was a rhetorical question."

"Sure." Johnny knocked his next drink back and turned casually on the barstool to study the growing crowd around them. He caught sight of the Kilomea bouncer outside the front door, who let the next wave of magicals inside and turned to watch them enter. His gaze flicked toward the two partners at the bar and he stared at the bounty hunter a little longer than necessary.

I ain't causin' a scene. He has no reason to single us out.

"We should go back to the storage unit," Lisa suggested. "He could have been hung up on something. Maybe he left something else there for us."

"Naw, we'll stick it out a while longer." He glanced casually at the other Kilomea bouncer in the back, who also watched him with way more interest than a quiet dwarf and his half-Light Elf partner warranted. "Somethin' else might be brewin'."

"What do you mean?"

"The bouncers are gettin' a little tense."

"It's packed in here, Johnny. Of course they're keeping their eyes open."

"But when they're makin' eyes at us? I don't think it's the crowd."

Lisa risked a quick look at the bouncer in the front, who immediately turned again to check the IDs of more magicals who waited to be let inside. "Okay. So what do we do?"

"We order another drink and wait for either Hamish or someone else to make a move." The dwarf raised a finger to catch the bartender's attention.

It took the wizard a minute but when he finished with the other laughing and drinking customers, he moved down the bar and shook his head. "Sorry, man. I can't serve you anything else."

Johnny snorted. "Funny. Another Johnny Walker—"

"I'm cutting you off. You've had four in the last hour and I don't need anyone to start trouble tonight."

"Are you kiddin' me? Those shifters over there have had six rounds in half the time."

"All right. I've had it with you." The wizard looked at the back of the bar and raised his hand. "Now you need to leave."

"This is ridiculous," Lisa said. "He's not even acting drunk."

"Oh, you want to give me that kinda lip too, huh?" The wizard folded his arms. "Both of you can get out."

"Now hold up a minute." The dwarf rested the side of his fist on the bar and leaned toward the bartender. "I ain't done nothin' to—"

"You need to come with me." A growling voice rose above the noisy conversation and the pumping music as a massive shadow fell across his back and the bar.

He turned on his stool to look up at an equally massive Crystal with a nightstick clenched in one meaty, frost-covered hand. "For real?"

"You can get off that stool and make it easy for yourself," the unexpected bouncer snapped and the nightstick in his hand released a zap of cold, blue-tinged electricity and a shower of sparks. Lisa jerked away from those that strayed toward her jeans. "Or you can make it easy for me and hard for you."

"Johnny…" Her eyes were wide as she stared at the electric nightstick.

The one time I didn't load up with weapons and I gotta face this asshole.

"Whoa, big guy." The bounty hunter raised both hands in surrender. "All right. I don't want any trouble."

"Then get moving." The Crystal jerked his head toward the back hallway.

Lisa slid off her stool and tugged on the sleeve of Johnny's black denim jacket. "Fine. We'll go—"

"Not that way." With a belligerent growl, their harasser caught her upper arm and hauled her down the bar toward the back.

"You get your goddamn hands off her," Johnny demanded. "What the fuck are they teachin' you in security trainin' these days, huh?"

She jerked her arm out of the Crystal's grasp a second before he shoved the nightstick into the dwarf's gut and launched a surge of crackling electricity.

"What are you doing?" she shouted.

Johnny staggered back, doubled over, and grunted as the breath that had been momentarily stolen from him returned in a rush.

"Do you want some of this too?" The Crystal brandished his weapon at her and she froze. "Then get moving."

"We're good, man. We're good." The bounty hunter shuffled past the bouncer and gritted his teeth against the pain in his abdominal muscles and the sting that faded slowly from his belly. Lisa still looked ready to protest so he caught her hand and tugged her with him toward the back hall as the Crystal followed, looming over them.

"They can't do this," she whispered.

"Roll with it."

"What about Hamish—"

"We'll think of another way."

"Pick it up." The Crystal shoved them both in the back and made them stumble forward, but he didn't take them to the back door of the establishment. Instead, they were herded toward a hidden door around the corner. He jerked the door open and more electric sparks surged from the nightstick in warning. "Time's up."

"This ain't the exit—" The bounty hunter grunted and staggered forward but managed to keep his footing when the magical gave him another almighty shove.

Lisa shouted in surprise and protest when she was pushed inside too and the Crystal pulled the door shut with a slam. The music in the bar cut out and made the sharp, metallic click of a lock being turned all the more audible.

They were left in silence and complete darkness.

CHAPTER TWELVE

"What the hell is this?" Johnny ran his hands along the door until he found the handle and tried to jiggle it open. It wouldn't budge.

"I don't like this, Johnny."

"Yeah, no shit. Hey, turn your phone light on."

Before Lisa could comply, bright overhead lights turned on with a sudden click to blind them momentarily.

Johnny squinted against the glare and returned his attention to the lock. "Do you have a hairpin on you or somethin'?"

"A hairpin? No. But there's another door." She moved across what looked like a storage room and he spun with a scowl.

"Well, why didn't you say so?"

"Because the lights weren't on—"

The door in question opened and a tall, thin Light Elf with short-cropped auburn hair stepped inside. Lisa froze.

"Someone had better start talkin'," the dwarf snapped. "And seein' as you're the only one in here, that someone is you. What the fuck is goin' on in this place—"

"Johnny, stop." The words escaped his partner in a gasp.

The magical standing before them frowned in concern before he hurried across the room toward her and wrapped his arms around her. A tearless sob left her lips when she hugged him in return and his man's face contorted in a grimace of pain and relief. "I'm so sorry it had to be like this."

"No, it's okay. You're okay." She pulled away to cup his cheeks and run a hand over his dark hair. "You said nine o'clock."

"I know. And there were eyes watching so I had to hold off a little longer. Thanks for waiting."

"Of course I'd wait for you. I'm only glad you're safe. Look at you…"

Johnny watched the reunion with a raised eyebrow before he finally cleared his throat. "Hamish, then."

The Light Elf stepped away from his mother as she turned and they both stared at Johnny. "Who's the dwarf?"

"Johnny Walker. You understand how much trouble you're causin', son?"

"Johnny—"

Hamish's lips twitched into a thin, tight smile. "I'm fairly aware of it, yeah. And I'm not your son."

"No, you're hers."

"Johnny's my partner," Lisa said hurriedly. "We work together. And yes, Johnny. This is Hamish."

"Well…" The bounty hunter studied him for a moment before he strode across the storage room to extend his hand. "I wish it were under better circumstances."

"Yeah, me too." The Light Elf stared at the outstretched hand, then turned toward his mom. "Did you go to the FBI with my letter?"

"What? No."

"No feds are involved." Johnny didn't lower his hand but stared at the man. "We went indie."

Hamish frowned. "What?"

"Independent," Lisa corrected. "Self-employed."

"Huh."

The bounty hunter inclined his head and raised an eyebrow. "It ain't right to leave a fella with his hand out."

"Sorry." The elf grasped his hand and they shook brusquely. "I merely wasn't expecting anyone else."

"Johnny's on our side. You can trust him."

Lisa's son ran a hand through his hair and sighed as he gazed around the room. "The only person or magical I know I can trust right now is you. And I'm already taking too many chances trusting a few others as much as I do."

"Your boys outside?" The dwarf jerked his thumb over his shoulder toward the locked door.

"Yeah. They're friends—for now. And they'll keep this a secret. But I can't ask them to deal with anything else." He grimaced at her. "It's bad, Mom."

"That was clear in your letter."

"But you found it. That's a good start."

"It was a nifty trick with the clues," Johnny muttered.

Mother and son looked at him with matching expressions of confusion and she inhaled sharply. "What's going on, Hamish?"

The Light Elf studied the dwarf for a moment and seemed to decide to take his mother's word that he could be trusted at least enough for this. "Have either of you heard of World Nexus?"

"No."

Johnny shook his head.

"Neither had I until about three years ago. They came to me on Oriceran and asked if I wanted to get involved in what they called 'worlds-changing improvements.'" Hamish scoffed. "The pay was unreal. The perks were…well, let's say it crossed my mind that it was too good to be true and I should've listened to my gut at the start."

"Your letter said something about being an emissary."

"Yeah. I was. I've met so many different magical families, big and small, known and unknown. Plus representatives from multiple corporations here on Earth. I thought they were normal trade deals, you know?" He shook his head. "Simple ones—too simple, honestly. My supervisor gave me enough information to know what I was talking about during the deal, and...Jesus. I thought I was making production deals, Mom. Imports and exports too. That kinda thing."

The dwarf hooked his thumbs through his belt loops. "I assume it ain't fancy rugs an' crystal dish sets."

"Far from it." Hamish grimaced and for a moment, his eyes looked haunted. "It turned out to be much worse. I got stuck in a negotiation about six months ago. I think the guy I was dealing with was newer at his job than I was. He kept asking questions about the details, and I had no idea what to tell him because it seemed like we were talking about two different things."

"What was he asking about?" Lisa prompted.

"Bodies."

"Bodies?"

"That's only one of the things World Nexus deals in. Human trafficking. Magical trafficking. I knew something was up immediately but I had to find out what was going on. No one would tell me shit other than to do my job and quit asking questions."

"But you didn't," Johnny added rhetorically.

"No. I followed my gut." Hamish clenched his eyes shut as if to ward off the memories of what he'd discovered. "It's way bigger than trafficking living beings. They have caches of dark magic ready to be bottled and sold to the highest bidder on this planet. Some kind of production plant on Oriceran does most of the work but I haven't seen it. I tried to find out where it is but the second I got close, World Nexus discovered that I was way in over my head and they came after me. Now, I'm out of a job, have been chased off a planet, and am locked in a storage room with the only person who can help me out of this."

Lisa bit her lip and stepped toward her son but didn't reach for him.

Yeah, he ain't a kid anymore. And she's gotta put away the mama hat if she's gonna get him through this.

"So what do ya need us to do?" the dwarf asked.

The elf's bright green gaze settled intently on him. "I have a list."

"That's a good start."

"It's the only thing I managed to get my hands on before I realized I couldn't stay on Oriceran any longer but it's big. World Nexus has connections to some of the largest crime syndicates on Earth. Organizations fronting any kind of illegal activity you could possibly imagine—mob bosses, crime lords, and all the high-ranking assholes who sent their mouthpieces to talk to me and make their deals."

Johnny almost winced at the sarcasm in his tone. "Damn."

"I know."

"So it's a list of names," Lisa muttered.

"Names. Addresses. Which organizations they're affiliated with. Some of them have notes on when they last dealt with World Nexus—with me. It's the whole roster, Mom. And I have to get it into the right hands to stop this."

"Not to mention callin' off the bounty on your head, right?"

Hamish scowled. "That's an added bonus, yeah. But I'm doing this because it's right. I can't even imagine the damage I've done by being so fucking naïve about the whole thing."

"Don't blame yourself." Lisa finally gave in and placed a hand on her son's shoulder. "This is the right thing. You didn't know before but now you do."

"And now you're draggin' us into it with you," the bounty hunter said bluntly.

She turned to look scathingly at him. "Don't."

"I'm only sayin' if he wanted to do the right thing, he'd go directly to the feds and the department without all this sneakin' around. There's somethin' else, ain't there?"

"Do you honestly think I'd be on this planet again risking my life every single second because I want to…what? Get something out of it?"

"That's a big incentive, yeah."

"Johnny, this isn't the time."

"We're finally chattin' in person. It seems like a perfect time to me."

Hamish pointed at the dwarf and frowned at his mother. "What's his problem?"

"He's like this with everyone." She frowned at her partner. "I merely thought he'd be able to put aside all the cynicism this once."

"It's part of the job."

"Well, sorry, Johnny, but I can't pay you for your work," the elf said with no lack of venom in his voice.

He snorted. "It wouldn't be my first pro bono case."

"Both of you need to stop right now." Lisa looked from one to the other and shook her head. "This isn't about money or deciding what part of this is true and what part isn't. Hamish is my son. I trust him and I'll do whatever I can to make sure he's safe. So if you're not on board with going down this road and believing what he has to tell us, Johnny, go ahead and say it right now."

The storage room fell silent.

Well, look at that. It only took a little squabble between the men in her life to get her into Agent Breyer mode.

He snorted. "I ain't backin' out, Lisa. You know that."

"Good. Hamish, I love you but if you can't trust Johnny, trust me. And if you can't do that, I won't be able to do anything for you. He's my partner. That's it."

"Got it." The Light Elf nodded stiffly at Johnny, who jerked his head in response with a grunt.

"Okay. So let's move on because I have a feeling this is a very time-sensitive situation." She folded her arms. "Who else knows about this list you have?"

"All the heads of World Nexus." He thought for a moment, his brow puckered. "And a few of their best head-hunters, I guess. The guys they trust to not try to sell something if they get their hands on it. But I had hoped you'd be able to take it to the FBI and have them sort the whole mess out. They have more resources than the two of you going… What did you call it?"

"Indie," the bounty hunter muttered.

"It's a PI firm, okay? Moving on." Lisa paused and tried to collect her thoughts. "I technically don't still work for the Bureau, Hamish."

"Yeah, I kinda picked that up with all this indie talk. When did that happen?"

"A few months ago. For…various reasons we don't need to get into right now."

"But you still have connections, right?"

Johnny clicked his tongue. "More like ball an' chain."

They both ignored him.

"Yeah, I think I can still pull a few strings."

"Okay." Hamish nodded and glanced over his shoulder at the door through which he'd entered. "But it has to stay anonymous, okay? Keep my name out of it. Say it came from one of your private cases or whatever comes to mind."

"You're in it that deep, aren't you?"

"Yeah, Mom. And I truly didn't want to drag you into it."

"You're not dragging me anywhere. Still, there will be questions when we hand this to the department. They have other resources for protection too, you know."

Her son jerked his head to the side with a pained grimace. "No offense, but WITSEC doesn't exactly cover the kind of protection I need from the guys World Nexus has on my tail. They're old-school Oriceran. Earth law doesn't exactly apply."

"It applies to everyone on Earth," Johnny interjected. "Whether or not they believe it."

"No WITSEC. And this has to be an anonymous tip. Please."

"Sure." Lisa pressed her lips together and nodded. "We'll find a way. What about you? Do you have anywhere to stay?"

"I have a few possible options that might serve."

"Hey, we have a few spare rooms in the houseboat," Johnny added.

The Light Elf frowned in confusion. "What?"

Lisa glared warningly at her partner. "Shut up."

He spread his arms placatingly and did as she said.

She wants him safe, sure, but not safe on the property she shares with a dwarf and calls home. Fine.

"We'll do what we can to get this moving, Hamish." She studied her son cautiously. "You brought the list with you, right?"

"Uh…no. Sorry."

"You didn't leave it with the taser-crazy asshole outside, right?"

"Adam? No, he doesn't know about any of this. Only the three of us do—and World Nexus. But the information's safe."

"Well, we can't do anything without that list, Hamish."

"I know. I have a number of moving parts to deal with but I can get it to you. Here." The Light Elf took a small slip of paper from his pocket and handed it to his mother.

She unfolded it quickly, read the note once, and slid it into her pocket. "What if I need to get hold of you?"

"I can't risk a phone right now, Mom. There are too many ways to track it."

"Smart move," Johnny muttered.

"But meet me there and I'll get you everything you need."

"Okay." Lisa's eyes glistened when her son pulled her in for a tight embrace that didn't last nearly long enough.

"I gotta go. Staying too long in one place makes it easier for them to—"

"No, I get it. We'll see you soon."

He nodded and turned toward the back door.

"Hamish?"

"Yeah."

"Please…be careful."

His smile wasn't anywhere close to reassuring. "It was nice to meet you, Johnny."

"Yeah, you too."

The Light Elf opened the door, peered into the passageway behind it, and stepped out before he closed it behind him with a soft click.

"Well." The dwarf folded his arms. "That was—" The lights turned off completely with another hollow click. "Aw, come on."

"He planned the whole thing," Lisa muttered.

"That don't mean we gotta stand here in the dark." He strode across the floor toward where he thought the other door was. It was easy enough to find and he pounded on it with a hard fist. "Time's up, fellas! The meetin's over. Open the hell up!"

"Why didn't he bring it with him?"

"'Cause he's bein' careful and smart. I woulda done the same. Hey!" He pounded again. "It ain't funny—"

The door opened with a rush of air and the overwhelming blare of loud music and even louder conversation. The Crystal—Adam, according to Hamish—stood on the other side with a smirk and the electric nightstick propped against one shoulder. "Have you had enough time to settle down?"

"Sure. Some fuckin' drunk tank y'all are runnin' back here." He brushed past the massive security guard, who chuckled briefly before he grinned at Lisa as she followed the bounty hunter closely.

The bar was even more crowded, and Johnny had no interest whatsoever in hanging around any longer now that their first meeting with Hamish was over.

And it ain't the last. The next place had better not be in a bar.

CHAPTER THIRTEEN

They left the rowdiness of Tilted for the quieter atmosphere of a coffee shop in the DC kemana. The sign over the door declared Magical Joe's to be *The only coffee shop in The District with magic in every cup.*

Johnny ordered them two black coffees to go with an added, "And I don't want any of that magic-whatever in here, understand?"

The half-witch barista smirked and nodded before she left him to fill their cups. He joined Lisa at a table in the back with the coffee in hand. Five of the other six tables were empty, which meant fewer prying ears could listen to their conversation. It also meant a greater likelihood that the barista and the one other patron would hear.

He sat across from her and handed her one of the cups. "How you doin'?"

She took it absently but didn't seem to hear him.

"Lisa?"

"Hmm?"

"Are you all right?"

"I...I don't know, Johnny." She put both hands around the to-go cup but didn't bother to sip the contents. "This is way worse than I thought."

"Yep. But it ain't worse than anythin' we've managed before."

"Except for the fact it's my son's life on the line if something goes wrong."

"Hey. How many times have we gone out on a case and screwed it up for the magical we went in to help? I mean seriously screwed it up?"

She raised an eyebrow. "It hasn't happened yet."

"And I ain't fixin' to start now." He sipped his coffee as he stared out the front window of the shop and almost choked. "See? This is exactly why I stay away from DC. The coffee tastes like dirt and politics."

"Now you're projecting."

"Go ahead and try it."

She took a tentative sip, swallowed thickly, and lowered the cup to the table. "Okay, I'll give you that one."

They sat in silence for a moment, and Johnny grimaced at the rush and deafening whir of the espresso machine as it pumped up to steam milk for the Kilomea who looked ridiculous in a business suit. He didn't let that stop him from getting his late-night energy shot, though. Johnny glared at the espresso machine until it stopped.

"Do you think he told us everythin'?"

Lisa shook her head. "I think he told us everything we needed to know in the moment. Which could go either way for us, honestly."

"Yeah, I thought the same." He lifted the coffee cup for another sip, frowned, and set it down again. "It makes sense to not put all his eggs in our basket. What still niggles at me is his happy little team inside the bar who got us into that room for him."

"What do you mean?"

"Think about it. If Hamish is tryin' to keep his head down,

tellin' four magicals in the same bar that he's here and in trouble and needs to use their storage room ain't exactly safe."

She shrugged. "He said he trusts them."

"Sure, but not all the way. Neither do I. There are now four fellas there who've seen his face and know at least this part of his plan—the part where you and I had to be smuggled outta the bar. Maybe it was a favor gettin' the bartender to cut me off. Tryin' to get a rise outta me so getting' kicked out by a Crystal didn't seem like somethin' outta the norm in a place like that."

"Right." A thin smile flashed across the half-Light Elf's lips. "It was well-orchestrated. I'll give him that."

"It has been from the beginnin', darlin'. Now I know he's a smart guy. And I assume he ain't lookin' too close to home 'cause he has big money and dark magic chasin' him for his head. I can't help but wonder if the guys in the bar are on some kinda payroll themselves."

She looked quickly at him in surprise. "You think the magicals who helped us meet with him should be on our suspect list?"

"There must be a helluva bounty on his head."

"No. No, if they planned to betray him, they would have done it already, knowing exactly where he'd be and when."

"Sure." The dwarf scratched his bearded cheek and watched the magical pedestrians milling around the kemana beyond Magical Joe's front windows. "Maybe they're waitin' for a chance to sweeten the deal a little and take him, his mama, and the dwarf bounty hunter all in one go."

"Which—again—they could have done half an hour ago with all three of us locked in that back room together." She leaned back in her chair and spun the full coffee cup in slow circles on the table.

"There might have been an update to the bounty too if word got out about what he's carryin' on him."

"You mean to grab Hamish and the list."

"Exactly."

"He didn't bring it with him to meet with us. How would anyone pursuing him know he doesn't have it on him?"

Johnny shrugged. "Okay, that's a fair point. It makes him even smarter in my book."

"And now we need to be extra careful. If World Nexus' hired hands expect him to have it on him at all times, he's a sitting duck."

"Uh-huh. It's a good thing duck season's over already."

She closed her eyes and took a deep breath to steady herself. "Is that supposed to mean something?"

"It means we're gonna get that list, keep your boy safe, and speed up what those assholes have comin' to 'em. Simple."

"There's nothing simple about this, Johnny."

"It only takes a little perspective, darlin'. That's all." He settled his hand over hers wrapped around the to-go cup and nodded. "We'll set this right. What was on that note he gave you?"

Lisa stared at him for what felt like a very long time but at least she no longer looked completely hopeless. "Saturday night at ten. An abandoned apartment complex in Richmond beyond the old train tracks."

"That's where we get this list."

"Yeah. The next two days are gonna be rough."

"Naw. We'll think of somethin' to pass the time."

She finally sipped the coffee again and grimaced. "This is seriously bad."

"See? DC coffee."

"Or magicals haven't yet learned how to master a cup of joe. I think I could go for a full drink right now instead."

"I can help with that."

They hurried to Lisa's apartment to pick up the hounds so they could all return to their hotel three miles away.

"What?" Luther whipped his head up from where he lay curled on the cushions. "Come on, Johnny. This couch is amazing."

"Yeah, we like it here, Johnny." Rex rolled on his back and wiggled on the thick multi-colored rug. His tail whipped wildly as he gave himself a good back scratch. "We can stay, right?"

"No." He snapped his fingers. "And y'all know you ain't supposed to be on the furniture. Get down."

"She doesn't mind."

"Yeah, lady. You don't mind, do you?"

"Y'all best mind me. Let's go." He snapped again and pointed at the door. The hounds slunk away from their comfy positions and their master turned toward Lisa with a grimace. "Unless you wanna stay. We replaced the locks."

"No, the hotel's a good idea, especially if anyone said anything about us meeting Hamish. There's still a chance someone else might come looking for him here and I'd rather not have to sleep with one eye open for the next two nights."

"Sure. All right, boys. We're headin' out. We're gonna make a liquor stop on the way."

"What about snacks, Johnny?"

"Yeah, we've been here on our own forever."

"Y'all done cleared out the pantry and don't even try to deny it. You're fine."

Lisa put away three shots of Johnny Walker Black at the hotel and didn't even seem to feel it before she decided to turn in around midnight. He wasn't too far behind her but again, she'd already fallen asleep by the time he crawled into the bed.

They took their time waking up the next morning, and Lisa was particularly silent over their breakfast from another bagel shop. The hounds picked up on her stress instantly and didn't even try to get the breakfast scraps. Instead, they curled at her feet and didn't say a word.

That's how most folks reckon their hounds should be.

When this silent tension continued past 10:00 am, Johnny couldn't take it any longer.

"All right. We gotta go do something."

"Like what, Johnny?"

"Like get you outta this hotel room to start."

"There's nothing to do but wait."

"Uh-huh. We can wait somewhere else." He took her hand and pulled her off the couch. "What happened to wantin' to stay distracted so you ain't sittin' around all day thinkin' about the worst-case scenario, huh?"

With a massive sigh, she looked around the small hotel room and shrugged. "Fine. But I think a walk's about all I can manage right now."

"Sure. We'll go for a long walk." He looked out the window at the gray sky and the light snow flurries that were supposed to have let up by now, according to the local weatherman. "A little cold never hurt anyone."

"That's not exactly true."

And it wasn't true for the bounty hunter, either. Five minutes in the mid-February chill in the nation's capital was enough to break his resistance. He relented to her suggestion to buy the first winter coat he'd owned in his life and that was the end of it.

For the first time since he'd arrived at her trashed apartment, her smile was completely genuine when he walked out of the outdoor apparel store wearing the puffy winter jacket that hung below his knees.

The hounds burst out laughing. "Woah, Johnny. Do they have an all-you-can-eat buffet in there too?"

Luther giggled and snorted as he pranced in front of Lisa. "It looks like you put on a few pounds."

"Y'all keep laughin'. I saw hound jackets in there too."

The laughter stopped abruptly.

"You look great," Lisa said.

"I look like a damn burned marshmallow." He lifted his arms

at his sides and looked at the bulky front of the garment. "It's for a walk, darlin'. Nothin' else. I ain't runnin' around DC in this when we're back on the job."

"You'll want it when we meet Hamish tomorrow night. It's cold in Richmond too."

"This is stupid."

She slipped her hand into his and nodded. "But now we can take a walk and you won't freeze. There's much to be said for a walk in the cold, you know."

"Yeah. Everyone who does it looks dumb and feels even dumber." His sidelong glance at her as they headed down the sidewalk was half-irritated and half-wary. "'Cept for you."

"Nice save."

Her good mood lasted only as long as it took them to walk the length of the outdoor shopping center and back again before her anxiety kicked in again. "This isn't helping."

"Sure it is. You know, I had my doubts about getting this damn jacket but I'm as toasty as hell."

She looked at the other pedestrians who had braved the elements to get their Friday shopping done. "What are we doing? Walking around the mall in the cold?"

"That's exactly what we're doin'."

"Hey, did you see those ladies three stores back?"

"The ones all wearin' the same maroon jackets and Ugg boots? Yeah, I saw 'em."

"They keep looking at us." Lisa stopped to face the dwarf and cast another wary glance at the women in question. "See? Like right now."

"Well maybe that's 'cause you keep lookin' at them." He tugged her hand so she continued to walk with him. "We ain't bein' tailed in a shoppin' mall, darlin'. There is nothin' interestin' about a couple enjoyin' some time outside."

Johnny grimaced at his words but she was too distracted by

her anxiety bordering on paranoia to realize what he'd called them.

Yeah, we're a couple. And the first time I say it, she didn't hear a word.

She stared after the laughing women as they left the sidewalk and headed to their parked cars in the lot. One of them glanced at her and flashed a grin, but that was all.

"See? You're kickin' yourself into high gear for nothin', darlin'."

"We should go back to the hotel."

"What?" Luther whipped his head up from the puddle he'd been sniffing. "No. Come on. You left us inside for hours yesterday. Or was that last week?"

"Look at this, though?" Rex sat and stared at the light snow still falling in defiance of all meteorological reports for the day. "What is it, Johnny?"

"It's bugs, bro. Everywhere."

"No, I think it's ash. What'd you blow up this time, Johnny?"

Their master snapped his fingers. "It's snow, boys."

"Rex, look at that big one! Get it!"

The hounds darted after the falling snowflakes and snapped their jaws at nothing. "They're fast!"

Lisa wouldn't stop peering into the alleys between buildings or through the front windows of the stores—not to window-shop but to identify any thugs hired by World Nexus and whoever else was looking for her son. "They could be anywhere."

"Do you hear yourself right now?" Johnny frowned. "I ain't sayin' you don't have a right to worry about your kid. But this is borderin'—"

"What?" She looked at him with wide eyes although her focus immediately strayed to other shoppers who stepped out of stores or left their parked cars to move toward them.

"Paranoid, darlin'."

"I'm not paranoid."

She was right. She's too close to this and now, we're dealin' with the aftermath.

"All right. It might be we need to get away from other folks, huh? Are you hungry?"

"Not even a little."

"I'm hungry, Johnny," Rex said and raced up behind them.

"Yeah, these white bugs are not filling."

Lisa gave the hounds a weak smile. "They've never seen snow before, have they?"

"Nope. I ain't a particular fan of it either."

"Okay. Let's go to the car. I know a place for lunch."

"Good idea."

CHAPTER FOURTEEN

The next day and a half of waiting for their next—and hopefully final—meeting to get the list of names from Hamish weren't any easier for either of them. Lisa was tight-lipped and jumpy around anyone. The hounds vacillated between cracking jokes to try to cheer her and whining pitifully as they rested their heads on her feet or thighs. Johnny, unfortunately, had to put up with all of it.

They did manage to put the rest of their free time to good use getting the last of Lisa's belongings out of her apartment. Three trips to the local Goodwill got rid of the furniture and anything else she didn't want to keep, and the rest of the boxes were loaded into the rental SUV to take into Richmond.

"We might as well make use of the drive, right?"

"Johnny, there's already a use for the drive."

"To meet your boy, sure. I know. I'm only sayin' it makes sense to get it all done in one trip. That's all."

With everything loaded, they and the hounds left at 2:00 pm to make the two-hour drive to Richmond and the second storage unit she had already reserved and paid for. It was much smaller than the other one but she didn't have as much to put in it. Even then, she was completely distracted as they unloaded the few boxes into the unit. On her second trip from the SUV, she turned to watch the only car they'd seen roll through the storage complex that day and stumbled over the last box she'd placed on the ground.

With a frustrated shout, she staggered to correct her balance and the carton she carried toppled from her arms and split open at the top. Silverware and random kitchen items spilled across the floor of the storage unit. "Dammit."

"Are you all right?"

"Yeah, I…uh, wasn't paying attention to where I was going." She knelt to collect the spilled items and flung them carelessly into the box. "Next time, don't put the boxes where people are trying to walk, okay?"

"Uh-huh. That's good advice." Johnny scratched his head as he knelt to help her. "Except I didn't put that box there, darlin'."

"What?" He raised his eyebrows, and she sighed regretfully. "I'm sorry, Johnny. This is… Okay, yeah, I'm having a hard time."

"I get it. Trust me. When your kid's life is on the line, things change more than you could ever imagine. I've been there."

Lisa dropped the last fork into the box and sat back on her heels. "Yeah. You have."

"And I tell you what. You're handlin' it better than I would have. You saw me when I had Dawn's case files."

She chuckled wryly. "You were a mess."

"Thanks. And you're keepin' it together the best you know how. You're maybe a little more distracted than normal, but at least you ain't in a one-track mindset focusin' on revenge and fueled by a whole bottle of whiskey in a few hours."

"Yeah, now that we're comparing ourselves parent-to-parent, I feel much better."

He snorted, stood, and offered her a hand up. "Well, you should. I ain't sayin' I was the best parent, either."

"Neither did I."

"Naw. Raisin' a kid ain't the kinda thing you can compare, is it? Or how we react when somethin' goes wrong." He slid the last box out of the SUV and brought it to the tiny unit before he closed the door, locked it, and handed her the key. "But you got somethin' I didn't, darlin'."

"Respect for the law?"

"Very funny." He tucked her hair behind her ear, a tender gesture that surprised them both before he cleared his throat. Still, he held her gaze until he was finished. "Your kid's still walkin' around, Lisa. He has a future—maybe one with fewer options now than he had in the beginnin', but that's the way life goes, ain't it?"

She swallowed thickly and studied his gaze as tears welled in her eyes. "Johnny, I'm not trying to be ungrateful—"

"Naw, stop talkin'. It ain't ungrateful to worry about helpin' a kid when there's still somethin' that can be done. He's a grown-ass man, sure, but he made the right choice comin' to you. You did a helluva lot more than I could have asked for when you helped me with Dawn's case, and I ain't fixin' to forget it. I'm not sayin' I'm returnin' the favor 'cause it ain't a quid pro quo situation. But we ain't stoppin' or givin' up until whatever Hamish got himself caught up in is done. Understand?"

The first two tears slipped down her cheeks and she sniffed and wiped them away with the back of a gloved hand. "Thank you."

"There's no need to thank me, darlin'. It ain't only about partnerin' on cases or in a business. Hell, we're standin' here outside a storage unit 'cause you're fixin' to make the Everglades your home too, and that's all right. But since we're doin' this whole thing, you and me, I ain't about to draw a line in the sand. I'm all in. And you ain't gotta do this on your own or shove everythin' down deep 'cause you think there ain't space for it. There's always space. Don't you go forgettin' that."

Her eyes and the tip of her nose were red now but she still didn't let herself cry. Instead, she flung herself at him, wrapped her arms around him, and kissed him fiercely. He barely felt her almost frozen lips on his—which he only now realized had started to go numb with the cold—but he kissed her in return.

Damn. This whole feelings thing kinda works.

"Holy shit." Luther sat in front of the closed storage unit and uttered a low whine. "Johnny? Are you feeling okay?"

He and Lisa pulled away from each other and turned to look at the hounds. "What's wrong?"

"Uh…you." Rex crouched close to the cold ground covered in a light dusting of snow and looked from master to the half-Light Elf with wide, glistening eyes. "What happened?"

"Y'all better say somethin' that makes sense."

"That was… You…" Luther snorted and shook his head vigorously. "You heard that too, right Rex?"

"Yeah. Johnny got mushy."

"Aw, hell." Lisa laughed when he pulled away from her to open the back door for the hounds. "Just 'cause y'all hear a thing two people say to each other don't mean you can't keep your opinions to yourself."

"Sure it does, Johnny."

"Yeah. Do you know how many hounds would do anything for their two-legs to hear their commentary?"

"It's what we live for."

"We can hear you, you can hear us, and it's way better than it was before."

He snapped his fingers and pointed at the back seat. "Git on up."

"Yeah, yeah, Johnny. See? It's a good thing." Rex leapt up first and his brother followed quickly.

Before the bounty hunter could close the door, Luther leaned forward out of the vehicle to sniff his beard. "Are you sure you're okay? Maybe you fell and hit your head or something, huh?"

With a snort, he nudged the hound in the chest so he could close the door.

"Hey, we're having a conversation here."

"Yeah, Johnny. You can open up to us too, you know."

"We've been around forever."

He ignored them and turned toward Lisa with a crooked smile. She was already at the passenger door. "I didn't hit my head."

"I didn't say anything."

They both slid into the SUV and he started the engine.

"You did get zapped in the gut by a Crystal's nightstick, though."

The dwarf buckled up and shifted into drive. "It takes much more than a few sparks to turn me upside-down, darlin'. I meant every word."

Without looking away from the windshield, she took his hand and squeezed it. "I know."

With a few more hours to kill until their meeting with Hamish, Lisa directed them toward a hole-in-the-wall pub in Jackson Ward called Happy's. "It's probably one of the best undiscovered gems here. Magicals only, too."

Johnny gazed across the street from the parking lot before he turned the engine off. "Did you spend much time here?"

"I did before I became an agent. I got a few extra jobs too by hanging around the place until something came up."

He narrowed his eyes. "Doin' what?"

"There was a temp secretary job. I worked at a dry cleaner's for a few months. Oh, one guy needed someone to test the Air BNBs he had on his list to choose the best ones. That was a great gig. Hamish and I spent the summer staying in some of the best places across the country, all expenses paid—on top of what he paid me."

"You tested…" Johnny shook his head. "I don't get it."

"He wanted full writeups so he could provide the best for his clients."

"Clients for what?"

"He didn't say, Johnny, and I didn't ask." She got out and closed the door swiftly behind her before she opened the back for the hounds.

The driver's door slammed shut a second later before Johnny rounded the front of the vehicle with a scowl. "Wait a minute. You mean to tell me you were paid to travel around and sleep in different beds for a fella wantin' you to tell him all about it?"

"It sounds creepy when you say it like that."

"It is creepy."

"No, it's not. It's like any kind of product-tester, okay? And I had my son with me. We were able to go places I would never have been able to afford on my own, and we made a summer vacation out of it. That's all it is."

"Uh-huh. And after that, you became a federal agent for the FBI's Division of Magicals and Monsters."

"Okay." She rolled her eyes and headed across the parking lot. "Believe whatever you want."

"So this Happy's place makes temporary hires while you get a burger and a drink, huh?"

"No, Johnny." Lisa waited for a car to pass and stepped off the sidewalk to cross the street. "It's a place for magicals to unwind without having to find a kemana and deal with all the craziness down there. Everyone does their own thing. You'll like it."

"Well, don't expect me to walk outta there as a brand-new bed-tester."

She laughed. "Not unless an Air BNB thinks a hard-as-rock mattress is a selling point."

"It smells funny here, Johnny." Luther peered over the edge of the sidewalk and sniffed the drainage grate at the curb, which was mostly covered with snow.

"That's the sewer, dummy." Rex nipped his brother's neck as he passed.

"Oh. Right."

Lisa led them down an alley that should have ended in

another street when the buildings on either side did. The end, however, was sectioned off with another brick wall and nothing else.

"What are we doing here, lady?" Luther sniffed along the bottom of the wall. "It kinda smells like a sewer here too."

She sighed and ran her hand along the bricks before she found the one she wanted and pressed it inward. The illusion charm vanished to reveal a door and she grasped the handle. "That might simply be the smell of desperation."

Johnny sniffed. "Desperate how?"

"To survive." Her smile was thin and tight again but carried a hint of nostalgia he couldn't understand. "But it's safe to kill a few hours here. I promise."

"Uh-huh."

With a shrug, she opened the door to reveal a long, darkly lit hallway.

"Hey, lady." Luther trotted after her and passed Johnny on the way in. "Are these two-legs okay with hounds?"

"We've been kicked out too many times," Rex added. "Oh. Yeah. You remember."

"As long as you guys don't start any trouble, you'll be fine."

"That's us. No trouble at all."

"Yeah, we're the best hounds ever. Right, Johnny?"

"Sure." The bounty hunter squinted into the darkness, glanced over his shoulder at the empty mouth of the alley, and stepped inside and let the door close behind him.

I'm supposed to be the one with contacts and all the back ways into secret places. She has more up her sleeve than I expected.

CHAPTER FIFTEEN

Before they reached the end of the dingy hallway, the slow beat and warbling acoustic guitar from some kind of country ballad echoed toward them from the pub beyond. Johnny wrinkled his nose in something close to disgust. "It sounds like desperation too."

"If anyone would appreciate Johnny Cash and Willie Nelson and Merle Haggard in their later years, Johnny, it would be you."

"Sure. Only that I share a name with one of 'em."

Shaking her head, she slowed at the end of the hall when the main room of Happy's came into view. It looked like any other hidden bar and pub known only to the locals but the magicals there were as comfortable in their natural forms without illusions as those in any kemana.

A dwarf who appeared to be twice Johnny's age—so was probably much older than that—manned the long bar at the back and glanced up occasionally from drying freshly washed glasses to check on his customers and smirk at the good-natured jests thrown at him.

Two old Kilomeas hunched over a chessboard in the far corner, their draft beers beside them on the next table. The barstools were mostly empty except for an elderly witch with a poorly executed hairstyle that was supposed to have dyed her thin, puffy hair a deep maroon but had only succeeded in creating a dull violet with red stains at the roots. She and the dwarf bartender looked up at the partners' approach and the lighting revealed the elderly witch's caked makeup and mascara smeared down her wrinkled cheeks.

Johnny cleared his throat. "Damn. You weren't kiddin' about the desperation part."

"Be nice." Lisa moved toward the bar and the old dwarf behind it broke into a wide, snaggled-toothed grin.

"Lisa. It's been a while."

"Hi, Murray."

"How are things?"

"The same as always, right?"

"Yeah." The bartender chuckled. "Me too. It's good to see you bringing a friend in."

"It's good to bring one. Johnny, this is Murray. He's been running Happy's for…jeez. As long as I can remember."

"As flattering as that might sound, it's not that hard a job." Murray nodded in the general direction of the patrons scattered around the establishment. "As you can tell. We don't get much action around here."

She grinned. "Exactly the way everyone likes it, right?"

"Ha. That's right. Nice to meet you, Johnny."

"Yeah, you too. Lemme ask you somethin'."

Lisa and Murray exchanged a worried glance before she said, "That's not how things work here."

"What? There ain't nothin' wrong with askin'. I'm only curious what kinda place—"

"Oh, my goodness!" The old witch at the bar squealed with delight and a light shower of dried and smeared makeup flakes fell from the creases of her face when she leaned down to extend her hand toward the hounds. "What cute little puppies!"

"Hey, lady." Luther sniffed her fingers and snorted immediately. "Whoa. You're more pickled than Johnny on his worst day."

Rex giggled. "You hear that, Johnny? We're cute little puppies."

"Oh, how sweet." The witch looked at Lisa, her eyes hazy and unfocused with intoxication. "Are they friendly?"

Johnny grunted. "Didn't she think to ask before she stuck a hand in their faces?"

Lisa elbowed him in the side. "They're friendly, yes."

"Of course we are," Rex added. "As long as you don't pull any weapons on us and come after our two-legs. Hey, old lady. You got any weapons on you?"

"Whew. Bro, the way she smells, she couldn't hold a weapon long enough to aim it, let alone point and shoot."

"Oh, can I pet them?"

Johnny shrugged. "If you want to."

The witch wobbled off her stool but managed to keep her footing before she lowered her multi-layered skirts to the floor in a surprisingly agile crouch to pet the hounds. "You two remind me of my Lucy and Hein. So sweet. Look at those eyes. Oh, if they were still around, you would all have such a good time."

"Oh, man." Luther snorted and backed away.

"Yeah, I'm done." Rex retreated to sit at his master's feet. "There's only so much stink a hound can take. Luther, put this on the list of bad stink."

"Times ten."

Oblivious to the hounds' distaste, the witch looked at Lisa with tears in her eyes. "I miss them so much."

"I know you do. It's hard to lose a pet." She looked expectantly at Johnny and nodded subtly toward the witch who seemed lost in her moment with his coonhounds.

The dwarf ran a hand through his hair and tried to smile. "They, uh…recently left ya, huh?"

"What?"

Murray shook his head in warning but it was completely lost

on Johnny.

"Your hounds, right? I know fresh grief when I see it."

"Oh, my Lucy and Hein." The witch stood, Rex and Luther forgotten, and fumbled to lift her half-empty drink from the bar. "It's been fifteen years without my babies. I don't think I can ever get over them."

He leaned toward Lisa and muttered, "Fifteen damn years? I know I ain't exempt from holdin' onto something for that long, but it sure as shit wasn't over a couple of hounds."

"Shh."

The witch swallowed the rest of her drink and thunked the glass on the counter. "Hit me again, Murray. It's been a hard day."

"Yep." The bartender looked scathingly at Johnny before he turned to pour another glass of grief on the rocks and shook his head.

The pub was almost perfectly silent until he handed the witch her fresh drink. "There you go, Beth. I put a little something special in there for you."

"Is it the absinthe? Please tell me it's the absinthe, Murray. I can't bear to…to…" She clambered onto the stool, almost fell off, sipped her drink, and fell silent again.

Murray watched her warily for a moment longer and walked down the bar to stand in front of Lisa and Johnny. "Okay. That's done. I assume you want something strong yourself or you wouldn't be here."

"Gin and tonic, please." She nodded and set her hands on the bar.

"And your friend?"

"Do you have Johnny Walker Black?"

The older dwarf chuckled. "Johnny Walker's a favorite around here."

"You don't say." He looked at his partner and wiggled his eyebrows. She scoffed and nudged him with her elbow again.

"Sure. I keep the whole rainbow of Johnny Walker labels here.

Hold on a second." Murray turned to search through the liquor bottles on the shelf behind the bar, then shook his head. "No regular Black. Sorry. But I got a Double Black Label Twelve-Year. If you're not too choosy about—"

"That'll do me fine, Murray. Neat. You know what, go ahead and make it double too."

"You got it."

The bounty hunter grinned and rapped his knuckles on the bar. "You should have brought me here sooner, darlin'."

"Oh, because of the sophisticated liquor selection?"

While the barkeep wheezed a laugh, he remained silent as he poured their drinks.

"Well, yeah. The place could use a little more fixin' up, though. Maybe some brighter lights and better music for sure."

"Hey." Murray pointed at him in mock insult. "Anyone who insults the Highwaymen has to go."

"The who?"

"No. They're different. I wouldn't play those guys in here if someone held a gun to my head."

"It's another band, Johnny."

"Hell, I know that." He folded his arms and scowled as the old dwarf finished their drinks.

Murray slid the glasses across the bar with a brisk nod. "That'll be—"

"I got it. Thanks." Lisa gave him her card and he laughed softly. "What's so funny?"

"I remember when you were in here cutting yourself off at two drinks of well liquor. Now you're buying twelve-year whiskey without even waiting to hear the prices." He returned her card. "Whatever you've been doing, Lisa, it looks like it's working. Keep it up."

"Yeah, thanks..." She signed the receipt quickly and took a long sip of her gin and tonic. "Hey, is anyone in the back room tonight?"

"Oh, yeah. Harold, Champ O'Finn, and a couple of the newer guys who come around often. Do you want a few tokens?"

"Yeah. Give me ten."

Murray winked and opened a drawer beneath the bar to pull out ten black plastic tokens. "Enjoy yourselves. Hey, and keep those dogs out of people's way, huh? We have a reputation for calm, quiet, and escapism."

"No problem. Thanks, Murray."

"Have fun."

Lisa nodded for Johnny to follow her into the back room at the opposite side of Happy's from where they'd entered. The hounds followed quickly but looked repeatedly at the old witch who seemed to have fallen asleep at the bar.

"Yeesh. You think someone should tell her fifteen years is a long time?"

"Forget that, bro." Rex stopped to sniff a stain beneath the bar before he caught up. "You think she even knows her hounds weren't actual hounds?"

"What?" She frowned at them as she opened the door to the back room.

"Definitely not hounds. Hey, Rex. She smelled like that kid who used to screw with Johnny's airboat when we were pups, right?"

"Oh, yeah." Rex sniggered. "I forgot about that."

The hounds walked through the open door and Lisa waited for Johnny to join her before she muttered, "Do you know who they're talking about?"

"Yep."

"So he didn't have dogs. What did he have?"

Even a forced cough couldn't quite cover Johnny's low chuckle. "Ferrets."

"I… Huh."

The back room of Happy's looked almost identical to the front except it lacked a bar. The lights were low and the music from the bar played there too. Johnny caught the words of Johnny Cash covering "Hurt," stopped, and inclined his head toward the closest speaker. "I stand by what I said. Change the music in here and you change everythin'."

"This is what magicals come here for, Johnny. It's a mood."

"Mood-y, sure."

She led them toward a table in the corner, where they had an unobstructed view of the five older magicals seated at a large round table and spinning some kind of contraption in the center. None of them paid any attention to the two newcomers and the coonhounds.

"A sad, depressin' place with sad, depressed folks and y'all have a roulette set up in the back?"

"Not quite. And it's not gambling if you don't put any money into it." Lisa dropped the black chips on the table and sipped her drink.

"What are those for, then?"

"The first person to double what they came in with gets a drink on the house."

"So it is gamblin'."

"No. It's a…game." She smiled and watched the old magicals huddled around the table, who muttered to each other and placed their chips in the center. "I think I came back here to play almost every time I stopped by. It's a nice way to forget your problems— or at least to shed a little light on how much worse things could be. It's…cathartic."

"All right. See." Johnny cleared his throat. "I'm havin' a hell of a time tryin' to understand what kinda place you took me to, darlin'. Correct me if I'm wrong but this looks like a bar where magicals at the end of the line come with all their lifelong regrets so both of 'em can die together. Or at least drown themselves in booze."

She chuckled. "It's not that bad."

"Seriously? 'Cause you and me are the only ones who don't

look like we're ridin' on the tail end of an old folks' home. Y'all got depressin' music in here, a bartender who ain't about to let folks ask questions, and a secret back room where those guys are playin' some morbid version of Spin the Bottle, or How Bad Could It Get. Whatever you wanna call it."

"Well, it doesn't have a name, okay?"

"Fine. It don't need a name to be as weird as hell, darlin'. Exactly how much of your free time did you spend here back in the day?"

Her smile faded and she licked her lips slowly in suppressed irritation. "A ton, Johnny. You know what it's like to be a single parent."

"Uh-huh, and I didn't need the Washed-Up Club to help me get through it."

With a sigh, she nodded toward the magicals around the circular table and lowered her voice. "It's surprising how many magicals here are living paycheck to paycheck exactly like the humans who…I don't know. Were dealt a hard hand. You'd think the reveal of magic would have changed things a little for us but it didn't."

"It did for you."

"Right. And I merely got lucky. But before that, I was struggling. I was all on my own with Hamish as a kid, working whatever odd job I could find to make ends meet. Most of the time, it was two or three at once. And this place…I don't know. It offered an escape." She laughed softly when he raised a dubious eyebrow. "I know. It seems counterintuitive. But seriously, everyone here is in some kind of bind. It takes a while to get used to, but Murray has only one rule in here. Don't get into other people's business and don't share your own."

"A pub for secrets, huh?"

"Something like that." She sipped her drink with a nostalgic smile. "And it seems weird now but I brought Hamish here on his tenth birthday. We played a round of the back-room game with…

oh, it must have been at least ten other magicals that day. He took the entire pot at the end and used it to buy a round for everyone else who was here. He couldn't drink but he didn't keep any for himself. Not even for a root beer float or anything."

"You brought your kid to a serious downer of a pub for his birthday?"

"Yeah, well… It was either that or mortify him with a trip to McDonald's. Hamish didn't have many friends when he was younger. I don't think he was all that interested in friends, honestly."

"I guess he cared more about makin' the other half of the team with his mama."

"I think you're right." She met his gaze and wrinkled her nose. "That was when I decided I had to do something else, you know? It took a while for me to finally change things. We moved often. I took any number of weird and crazy jobs. Not the kind I'd ever be ashamed to come home and tell my kid about but it was very heavy for a long time."

"Damn." Johnny took a long sip of whiskey and scowled at the table. "I didn't know about all that."

"Of course not. How could you?"

"All the same, I'm sorry that had to be your life for a while, darlin'."

"Don't be. It made me better in so many ways. After magic was revealed and I heard about the openings in a new FBI department for magical agents, I jumped at it."

"And they let you in just like that, huh?"

"I had my degree, Johnny. Three of them. And I was close to getting into the police academy when I found out I was pregnant and had to put most things on hold." She inhaled sharply and shook her head. "Luckily for me, the department wasn't all that selective about how much field experience their new magical agents had. At least, they cared far less back then than they do now. And they were willing to train me.

"Hamish had barely moved out at that point and I didn't have to worry so much about taking care of him as I did about where he was and what he was getting up to on his own. He said he was completely happy with the new job and the new apartment but honestly, it was a shitty place. Sometimes, he'd call me the next morning to tell me about the break-ins that happened or the fight that broke out in his neighbor's apartment. He wanted to laugh about it with someone, you know? I think it was his way of making it not so scary. When he said he was taking off to Oriceran to take a look at what a different planet had to offer, I was relieved."

"He was doin' well at that point?"

"Oh, yeah. He truly was. Of course, I should have guessed that bad situations and even worse magicals exist everywhere, no matter what planet you're on." She fell into another thoughtful silence and he glanced at the hounds seated at his feet.

Rex and Luther stared at the round table but didn't say a word. Their ears twitched continually as they zeroed in on whatever conversations were held over the Worst-Case Scenario game.

Finally, Lisa chuckled self-consciously. "So there you go. That's why I got into the FBI working as a special agent for the Department of Monsters and Magicals. I don't think I've ever told that story."

"I'm glad you did, though." Johnny raised his glass toward her in a toast. "There's nothin' wrong with goin' into somethin' tryin' to make life a little easier for you and yours."

"No, there isn't." She clinked her glass against his and they drank.

"But someone shoulda told you the money ain't in workin' for the FBI."

With a snort, she ducked to keep from spraying gin and tonic all over the table, forced herself to swallow, and coughed the rest of it out. "Well, you're the exception to that rule, aren't you?"

"Sure. I'm damn expensive. They gotta pay me and put up with me. Not that I ever asked for it."

"No, I know."

"It doesn't mean you ain't a damn fine federal agent—as far as federal agents go."

"What an incredibly thoughtful backhanded compliment, Johnny."

"Aw, come on."

Lisa smiled coyly and stirred the straw in her drink so the ice clinked against the glass. "I went into the department for a stable job, yes. But I also wanted to make sure I had more of a say in…I don't know. I guess how magical criminals were handled after the reveal. When that happened, I couldn't stop thinking about how a world full of humans adjusting to this mind-blowing existence of other races already established on Earth would react. How they'd deal with someone like my son who was starting in life and trying to navigate it all on his own. There had to be a different way to deal with magicals who found themselves in trouble, whether or not it was intentional."

"Well, there is now." The dwarf shrugged and twirled his glass on the table.

"Right. And until only a few months ago, I worked exclusively for the FBI and on the same team with everyone else who would handle Hamish's current problems very differently than we are right now."

"It's a good thing we met when we did, then."

"Yeah, I'll drink to that." They toasted again and she stared at him and wrinkled her nose. "That whole 'Everything happens for a reason' saying used to rub me the wrong way until about two minutes ago."

"Huh. I never much cared for that overly simplistic positivity shit either."

She rolled her eyes. "Of course not."

"But I think it might mean somethin' this time."

CHAPTER SIXTEEN

They finished their drinks and Lisa finally scooped up the black chips from the table before she stood. "We still have another hour. Come on."

"What? Naw, I ain't into confession."

"It's a game, Johnny. You won't be disappointed, I promise."

"Darlin', do I look like the kinda guy who likes playin' games?"

She stopped, darted a pointed look at the magicals seated at the round table, and raised an eyebrow. "Do they?"

"Aw, hell."

"Come on. Look, you don't even have to play if you don't want to. Just watch for a few rounds."

"Yeah, Johnny, go on." Luther stood and shook himself from head to tail. "If you say anything half as interesting as what's coming out of those two-legs' mouths, you'll win!"

"What's comin' outta their mouths?" the dwarf muttered.

"Some seriously messed-up shit."

"It's fun, Johnny," Rex added. "And you're good at lying."

Lisa laughed and caught his hand to draw him out of the chair before he had a chance to protest. "You picked up on it fast, boys.

If not for yourself, Johnny, then for me, okay? After the last four days, I could use this kind of distraction."

"I have no idea what the hell this even is." Still, he let her lead him to the table.

The washed-up magicals looked up at their approach. The Wood Elf with a completely shaved head and burn scars up his bare, sinewy forearms offered them a wan smile. The two gray-haired shifters studied the dwarf warily, and the old Kilomea with cataracts clicked his pile of black chips against the table. The only wizard at the table was missing all his teeth and only smiled briefly, and the Kilomea woman seated next to him stuck a sharpened claw between one bottom jutting eyetooth and the regular molar beside it.

This is one hell of a peppy bunch.

"Do you have room for two more?" Lisa asked.

"How many chips did Murray give you?" the Kilomea woman asked.

"Ten."

"Oh-ho!" The toothless wizard slapped his knee and cackled. "This young lady's coming in with an unhealthy amount of confidence."

She dumped her chips onto the table and grinned at the wizard. "Don't worry, Champ. I know it won't last."

"Hee-hee." Champ waved his shifter neighbor away from him. "Come on, now. Give the woman some space. She's one of the best. Unless, of course, you have your kid hiding somewhere and waiting for his moment to strike."

"I can't believe you remember that."

"I forget nothing, Lisa." He shook a crooked finger at her. "Better yet, keep your kid out of this. He's not a kid now and I bet he could clear the pot in half the time these days."

"Probably, yeah."

"Does your friend want a round too?" the shifter in a Washington Mystics baseball hat asked.

"Naw." Johnny folded his arms and shook his head as Lisa pulled a chair up beside Champ. "I think I'll watch. I ain't much of a game-player myself if you catch my meanin'."

"Huh?" The Kilomea man with cataracts must have been as hard of hearing as he was visually impaired. He leaned toward the bald Wood Elf with his mouth hanging open. "What did he say, Harold?"

The Wood Elf chuckled. "I honestly didn't catch it either."

"Wha?"

Harold raised his voice and enunciated each shouted word slowly. "I... Don't... Know."

"Well, why not?"

"His accent's a little thick—"

"Huh? I can't hear you!"

"Forget it, you tusked behemoth." The elf gave the blind Kilomea a reassuring pat on the shoulder, then nodded at Lisa. "What did he say?"

"He's gonna sit this one out."

"Oh, great. More for us." One of the shifters rubbed his hands together vigorously and stared at the spinning wheel in the center of the table that looked more like a roulette wheel than anything else. "Let's do it."

Johnny leaned forward to peer over Lisa's shoulder at the questions written on each compartment of the wheel instead of numbers.

Biggest fear? Deepest secret? Worst thing I've ever done? What the hell kinda game is this?

"My turn, isn't it?" the Kilomea woman asked.

Champ clicked his tongue. "Quit asking and play the darn round, Jenny!"

"Wow. Someone woke up on the wrong side of the hellhole this morning."

"Unless you've found a good side to wake up on," Harold muttered, "quit holding the game up."

After another quick pick between her teeth, she reached out to spin the wheel and it clicked and whirred as it moved around. She dropped a white ball into the slot and they all watched it move through the compartments with repeated clicks and a rumble as it turned.

Luther sniggered. "Hey, Rex."

"Yeah."

"Her name's Jenny."

The hounds giggled until Johnny snapped his fingers, then they sat perfectly still and tried to pay attention.

When the wheel finally came to a stop, a green light flashed at the top of the dome in the center of the contraption, followed by an elevator-type ding. The ball had stopped in a compartment with *I've thought of killing_____* written across it.

"Ha!" Champ rubbed his hands together again and smiled his toothless grin. "Murderous daydreams. I love this one."

Johnny leaned down to mutter in Lisa's ear, "Cathartic, my ass. Are you sittin' down with a huddle of washed-up killers—"

"Shh." She turned to smirk at him and raised her eyebrows. "Watch."

"You first, Jenny. Queen of the tusked-damned." Champ crowed in anticipation.

"Fine. It's you, you old codger. I've wanted to shut you up for years."

The old magicals broke into uproarious laughter, including Champ, who slapped his thigh madly and cackled through his open mouth and puckered lips around his toothless gums.

"Join the club!" the old wizard shouted. "And me? I've had my eye on this Bichon Frise who lives down the street from me. The little bitch has barked like someone died in that house for weeks!"

Luther whipped his head up and stood immediately. "Did he say bitch? Hey, old guy. I'll go check it out."

"Hush." Johnny snapped his fingers.

"Maybe someone did die," Harold quipped.

"All the better!"

As one, the group erupted into laughter again and Lisa chuckled almost silently.

The bounty hunter narrowed his eyes and glanced at all the worn, haggard faces of magicals on their last legs.

Ain't they all havin' a time? These folks have completely lost it.

"You…ha! Hoo. You next, Lisa." Champ nudged her in the shoulder. "Go on. Lay it out."

Her smile widened and she reached behind her to pat Johnny on the arm. "This guy."

"Wait, what?" Johnny did a double-take and stared at her with wide eyes.

"Killing a good friend, eh?" One of the shifters nodded. "It's always a good bet."

"Or a lover," Jenny added in her low, gruff voice. Johnny expected her to pull a pack of cigarettes out and light one up, but she didn't. "Maybe that's what he is, hmm?"

"What the hell?"

Lisa didn't bother to address the Kilomea woman's guess but gave his arm a little squeeze. "It's okay."

"You're up, Harold!"

As the Wood Elf went into staggering detail about exactly when, where, and how he'd kill the object of his murderous daydreams, the dwarf crouched near Lisa's ear again. "I can picture you wantin' to give me a good beatin' or two in the past. But kill me?"

"It's part of the game, Johnny. You'll see."

The other three magicals at the table all described who they wanted to kill. The blind Kilomea shouted his answer with slow annunciation. Finally, everyone raised a hand at the same time and gazed expectantly at the faces next to and across from them.

"One…two…three!"

Seven hands came down on the green-lit dome in the center

of the wheel and the magicals' faces were all contorted in grimaces of discomfort. The light on the dome turned bright orange, emitted an obnoxiously loud buzz like a question answered wrong on a game show, and a zap of electricity raced into Lisa's hand and up her arm.

"Ah!" She jerked her hand away and rocked back in her chair.

The old magicals laughed and pointed.

"All right, that's enough!" Johnny slammed a hand on the table. "Whatever ya'll are tryin' to pull, you took it too far."

"Johnny—"

"No. I ain't standin' here listenin' to all this morbid shit spray outta y'all's mouths. It's fine if you wanna play a game but hurtin' someone who ain't tryin' to hurt anyone else? That's—"

"Johnny," Lisa repeated more sternly and caught her breath after her round of silent laughter the dwarf had been too pissed off to notice. She shook her hand out and turned in her chair to look at him with a smile. "It's part of the game."

"Naw. That's torture."

"I knew it!" Jenny snatched one of her black chips and slid it across the table toward Lisa. "You are lovers."

"Oh, don't pester her, woman." Champ smacked Jenny's shoulder and waved his hand in front of her face. She leaned away from him with a snarl. "You know the rules. She won't tell you even if you asked."

"I was making an observation, thank you very much. And the rest of you need to pay up. The Light Elf won."

"Wait…" Johnny frowned at all the black chips that rolled and slid toward Lisa's pile. "That was your prize for winnin'?'

"Yeah." She stacked her chips—now almost two-thirds of the way to doubling her original buy-in—and grinned. "It's like a lie-detector test."

"Except they're all lies," Champ added and wiggled his thin eyebrows. "It's brilliant, right?"

"No, it's as dumb as hell."

"Psh." One shifter waved a dismissive hand toward the bounty hunter. "This dwarf's seriously uptight about everything. You need an outlet, pal."

"Pal?" Johnny stepped toward the table. "Listen, old-timer—"

"Johnny." Lisa stood and half-guided, half-shoved him away from the table. "I'll be right back, guys. Go ahead and spin without me."

"You're up, Bruno. Here. I have your hand and here's where you spin the wheel."

The dwarf glowered at Lisa as they moved away from the table. "You brought your kid here to play that? It ain't a game, Lisa."

"Trust me, it is." She put her hands on his shoulders as she tried and failed to force back her smile and another chuckle. "And I had no idea you'd react like that. I should have told you the rules beforehand. Sorry."

He glanced at the table while the blind Kilomea struggled to find the mechanism for spinning the wheel, even with Harold's help. "So explain. 'Cause I can think of ten ways to Sunday why that should be demolished."

A surprised laugh bubbled out of her and she covered it up immediately by clearing her throat. "Sorry. Okay, look. All the things written on that wheel are admittedly horrible."

"No shit."

"But the goal is to lie, Johnny. To make up the most outrageous thing you can think of for a horrible thing most of us spend the least amount of time as possible thinking about."

"And y'all wanna think about it here to get a free drink?"

"No, it's…" She turned to look at the table with a fond smile. "Like I said, Johnny. It's about realizing how much worse things could be, especially when everything else feels like it's going to hell."

"So why were you the only one who got that nasty zap in the arm, then?"

Her face broke into the most genuinely happy smile he'd seen in the last week and her eyes sparkled, even in the dim light. "That's a special device Murray made—or he had someone make it or bought it at some weird magical auction or something. But it responds to the biggest lie."

The bounty hunter stared dumbly at her.

"Johnny, I won because out of everything that was said around the table, my lie was the farthest from the truth."

Realization dawned on him and his eyes widened. "I knew you weren't fixin' to kill me."

"Ha! Well, it shouldn't have taken this game to convince you a hundred percent, but okay."

"Hey, Lisa's friend," Champ called. "Now you've seen it. You want in on the next round?"

"You bet your ass I do," he called without turning. He gave Lisa a quick kiss on the cheek and muttered, "We both know I'm a better liar on the fly."

She took his hand and led him to the table as one of the shifters pulled up another chair. "We're about to find out for real. A word of warning, though?"

"Yeah?"

"The shock stings like a bitch."

CHAPTER SEVENTEEN

When 9:00 pm arrived, Lisa excused herself and Johnny from the table.

"What? Are you kidding me?" Champ shrieked. "No one's won the pot yet."

"That's okay. Here. Share these however you want." She slid the massive pile of chips toward the center of the table. "We have to head out."

"All right, all right. We're walking away with something special tonight, aren't we?"

"And your friend's not bad at lying," Harold added.

"Not bad?" Johnny scoffed. "Try amazin'. I can lie my way outta almost anythin' you set in front of me. Ask Lisa. She'll tell you the same."

The bald Wood Elf chuckled. "I have no idea what you said but it was nice having you here."

"You see that kid of yours anytime soon, Lisa, you tell him I said hi," Champ called.

The much better mood that had filled her for the last hour dampened slightly and she swallowed. "I will. See ya."

The hounds followed them through the door of the back

room and looked over their shoulders as the old magicals spun the wheel again. "I don't get it, Rex. All that work and no one even gets a treat."

"They probably stopped eating a long time ago."

"Yeah. Smells like it."

The door closed behind them and the front room of Happy's held only five more patrons than when they'd arrived. Murray nodded at them from behind the bar before he leaned forward to hear his newest customer's drink order.

"Okay. Tell me you didn't have fun with that."

Johnny tilted his head from side to side. "I can't say that."

"Oh, come on."

"But I didn't not have fun." He smiled at her. "It's one hell of a way to make your troubles seem smaller in comparison."

"I told you. Thanks for stepping out of your comfort zone for a while. I had no idea how much I needed that."

"All right, well, we ain't makin' this a regular Saturday night pastime."

Her smile faded a little. "No. It's not a regular thing for us, huh? Hey, unless Murray knows where to get one of those wheels and the lie detector. We could—"

"Uh-uh. Nope. I aim to focus on the good I have instead of tryin' to pit shitty against shittier. I ain't bringin' one of those back home with us, darlin'. That's simply askin' for too much trouble— Hey. What's wrong?"

She had stopped and now stared at the entrance to Happy's at the end of the long hall from the alley. "I only…"

Johnny turned to see a woman's massive figure filling the entryway. She must have been at least six and a half feet tall and took up almost the entire doorway with both her height and girth. Her gray hair was pulled into a tight bun, and while she wore heavy, multi-layered skirts, thick snow boots, and an expensive-looking peacoat of pure gray wool against the February cold, something more than a little dangerous glinted behind her eyes. Her lower lip depressed slightly in two places where what looked like small upper fangs made divots in the skin. Those became craters when the giant woman's smile widened.

"Whoa. That there's a helluva woman."

That snapped Lisa out of her staring and she punched his arm a little harder than what could pass as playful. "Or hell in a woman's body."

"Say what now?"

Happy's front room quieted instantly and the other patrons cast wary glances at the giant woman who scrutinized everything like a starving predator closing in on its prey.

"All right, I'm missin' somethin'." Johnny cleared his throat. "Who's the—"

"Stop talking," Lisa whispered sharply.

The large woman's gaze fell on her and her predatory smile widened even further. "Well, look who the cat dragged in." She looked at the hounds, then the dwarf. "Or should I say dogs?"

"Oh, I see," he muttered.

"Murray, don't you think it's time to start raising the standards a little? You're letting simply anyone and their dirty animals walk in these days."

The old bartender rubbed furiously at a spot on the bar and shook his head at the woman. "That would completely defeat the purpose, Hannah. And you know it."

"Hmm." The floorboards shook when the giant whatever she was stepped slowly into the pub. Her dark eyes scanned Lisa intently. "Lisa. What a surprise to see you in here after all this time. I thought you were off doing work for the feds."

"And I thought you'd either be off-world by now or behind bars."

Johnny snorted and folded his arms when Hannah turned her attention to him.

"Yes, well, times change, don't they? Your choice in company, on the other hand…"

Rex and Luther crouched low on either side of Lisa with barely audible growls as they curled their lips in matching snarls.

"You say the word, lady."

"Yeah, we can take her down, no problem."

"Might take a while, though. Damn, she's big."

Johnny glanced at her with narrowed eyes. *If she says the word, I sure as hell won't stop 'em.*

Lisa responded with a completely humorless laugh. "Have a nice night."

"Oh, I plan to." Hannah turned slowly as the two magicals and two coonhounds gave her a wide berth on the way to the exit. "Oops. I almost forgot to ask. How's Hamish doing?"

The agent stiffened, stopped at the mouth of the dark hallway, and clenched her fists at her sides. Her head tilted slightly like she was trying to work out a sore muscle and she turned halfway to face the massive woman goading her. "You haven't seen me in…what? Twenty years? And that's the first thing you ask me?"

"I miss seeing his handsome face." Hannah clicked her tongue in mock pity. "But that's right. He's all grown up now so calling him handsome is probably a drastic understatement. Tell him I said hi, won't you?"

Lisa glanced at Murray, who grimaced so furiously that it looked like he was trying to pull a three-inch nail out of his foot. "Thanks, Murray."

She headed down the hall without another word and Hannah's booming laughter followed them to the exit door into the alley. It cut off the second she slammed the door behind them and she drew a deep, gasping breath of frigid night air.

"Do you feel like tellin' me what all that was about?" Johnny asked.

"No. Not really." She ran a hand through her hair and sighed heavily. Her breath misted in the alley lit by two exterior lights high on both walls. "Hannah Penton. She's a... Well, honestly, the only thing anyone needs to know is that she's a conniving bitch."

"Whoa." He scratched the side of his head and glanced at the door again. "I guess the two of y'all got into somethin' of a bad deal."

"Yeah, you could call it that." She focused on the asphalt beneath her feet and shook her head. "It's so weird how all the things you thought you left behind you flood back the second a bad memory pops up in your face."

"Uh-huh. And she knows Hamish."

"Yeah. She tried to...employ him. Several times. Can you believe that? A twelve-year-old boy as innocent as they come, and she did everything she could to get her claws into him."

"Doin' what?"

"Drug runs, probably. You know, I tried going after her during my first few years working with the department. It was impossible back then and it's still impossible now."

"Naw." The bounty hunter jerked his thumb toward the door. "You say the word, darlin', and I'll hightail it inside. I'll give the giantess a piece of my mind—"

"No." She caught his arm. "It's okay. If you don't ignore her, what should be five minutes with her turns into five hours before you know it."

"And how does that work, exactly?"

"Hannah has a way of making you forget everything else in your life except for how badly you want to smash her face in."

"Whoa, lady." Luther sat at Lisa's feet and stared at her with wide eyes. "You okay?"

"Yeah, when Johnny says that, we know he's joking. But serious," Rex added. "And you look...serious."

"I think I am. But we have a meeting to get to." She shook her hair out of her eyes. "So let's focus on that."

Johnny looked at his hounds and nodded after Lisa as she hurried down the alley. "You heard her, boys. It's time to move."

"Yeah, yeah, Johnny. We're on it."

"Hey, I'm wondering. What was that walking mountain of lady two-legs?"

"She's a Kilomea," Lisa called over her shoulder. "And I don't think anyone on either world has seen her with less of an illusion up than that."

Luther shuddered and flicked his tail before he padded after his master. "Ew. I don't even wanna picture it."

"Bro, imagine the thing we saw inside and picture it covered in hair with four giant teeth—"

"Aw… Now I'm picturing it…"

Rex giggled. "Gotcha."

When they reached the rental car, the dwarf turned the engine on, activated the heat, and paused before he drove away.

"What's wrong?"

He sniffed. "I don't like what happened there."

"Yeah, Johnny. Join the club."

"No, I mean, the way she was talkin' about Hamish. Like she knows he's back."

Lisa shook her head and strapped her seatbelt on. "She was only trying to be a pain in my ass. And she didn't have to try very hard, either. There's no way she knows."

"But if she did, it would mean someone's been flappin' their lips."

"She was bringing up a twenty-year-old issue. It's not out of the question to ask someone about their kid. People do it all the time."

His hands tightened on the steering wheel. "Sure. But did Hamish keep it a secret when he went to Oriceran?"

"No…" She rolled her eyes and slumped in the passenger seat. "Shit. She would have asked if I've seen him lately or had any word from him on Oriceran if she thought he was still there."

"Yeah, that's what I'm gettin' at. And she didn't word anythin' that way."

"Again, there's always a chance she was only trying to get under my skin."

"Sure. But we can't take any chances bettin' on that option. We gotta assume the giant-ass Kilomea woman knows somethin' most folks don't. And then we gotta work out who the hell else has that information and how it got to her 'cause it sounds a hell of a lot like the wrong magicals know about it now."

"Yeah, the wrong magicals being anyone Hamish didn't specifically tell. Minus those on World Nexus' payroll trying to hunt him. Jesus." Lisa rubbed her face with both hands.

"I reckon Hannah has somethin' more to do with this than most. You said she was a drug trafficker, right?"

"Right. Last I checked."

"Hamish has names and addresses of all the big-time crime lords on Earth, apparently. If we can trust what he's tellin' us."

"Johnny, we can trust him."

"I'm only playin' devil's advocate." The bounty hunter rubbed his mouth and frowned at the parking lot outside the SUV. "If that Kilomea's more involved in this than simply tryin' to unravel your yarn, she'll take note of the fact that you're hangin' around your old haunts like Happy's. It might be she's thinkin' you're findin' places you and Hamish used to go to together, maybe even to meet up with him. And that information's gonna get out too. Includin' the part about us leavin' at nine on a Saturday night."

"You know, now would be the part where you say something reassuring."

"Hell, darlin'. When I think of anythin' that fits the bill, I'll be sure to let you know."

She turned in her seat and scanned what little she could see of the parking lot around them. "We might be followed to this meeting."

"I'd say that's a very safe bet."

"Dammit. Couldn't he have carried a burner phone for a few

nights?" She pounded her fist on the door's armrest. "We can't even warn him."

"He's been on the alert for a long time, sounds like." Johnny leaned over to give her thigh a reassuring pat. "We can assume he's assumin' someone's always on his trail. He'll be ready."

"Okay. Fine." She took a deep breath, then nodded firmly. "We can deal with the rest of it later. Right now, we have about half an hour to get to the rendezvous point, and I'd still like to be there a little early."

"Uh-huh."

Lisa laughed humorlessly. "Listen to me. Rendezvous point. With my own son."

"Old habits die hard, darlin'." He shifted into drive and rolled them out of the parking lot in Jackson Ward to head to the mostly empty neighborhood on the other side of the train tracks in South Richmond. "Whatever happens, it's nothin' we ain't dealt with before."

"Except for having my son involved. No big deal."

"That's right. Now you're gettin' it."

CHAPTER EIGHTEEN

They pulled up on the opposite side of the street from the address Hamish had left her in the note. The clock on the dashboard read 9:53 pm and Lisa's knees bounced up and down in the passenger seat. "Do you see anything?"

"Nothing outta the ordinary. And we ain't gonna see anythin' but empty street and abandoned buildin's if we don't get out the car. Come on." He turned the engine off and exited to open the back door for the hounds.

"What are we looking for exactly, Johnny?"

"Yeah, give us a clue." Luther sniffed the sidewalk in a tight circle, his tail high in the hair until he found a leafless shrub beside the cement and lifted a leg against it. "We'll find it. You know we can, Johnny."

"All right, so we'll start with this." The dwarf waited for Lisa to join them, then nodded across the street at their intended location. "Y'all keep an eye out for anyone extra showin' up where they ain't wanted, understand?"

"Eyes open."

"Ears up."

"Noses in the wind. Got it, Johnny."

"And let us know quietly if you hear or see or smell anyone. The main word there bein' 'quiet' in case ya'll missed it the first time."

"Yep. Quiet."

"Hushed-up all the way, Johnny."

"We can do quiet."

"We're the kings of quiet. We're the—"

He snapped his fingers and both hounds whipped their heads up to look at him. "Startin' now, boys."

"Right."

"Yeah, yeah."

Johnny nodded at Lisa. "Ready?"

"No. Let's do it."

They crossed the street together, neither of them surprised by the lack of cars in this part of Richmond. The elevated train tracks on the other side of the buildings in front of them were easily recognizable in the light of the streetlamps. Moments later, they walked around the abandoned apartment complex with its front doors and windows on every level boarded shut.

"I shouldn't have to meet my kid in a place like this," she muttered.

"Quit thinkin' about it like that, darlin'. I know it's easier said than done but try to think about it as merely another case. Disconnect."

"Sure. Much easier."

"I don't smell anything over here, Johnny," Rex said from the row of untended bushes along the path.

"Yeah, me neither. Wait. It's him. The guy without hormones!" Two seconds after Luther whipped his head up to look at his master, a shadow stepped out from behind the gate that had once surrounded the complex's dumpster. "Oh, hey! There he is!"

"It's me," Hamish said before Lisa or Johnny could say anything else. "Do you think you could call your guard dogs back a little?"

"There ain't nothin' wrong with my hounds."

"Nope. Only me." The Light Elf stepped away from Luther and shook his head before he pulled an inhaler out and took two long puffs.

"Oh, shit." Johnny raised his eyebrows at Lisa. "You weren't kiddin'."

"Why would I joke about something like that? You know what? Never mind. Hamish, how are you doing?"

"Uh..." He replaced the inhaler in his jacket pocket and glanced around. "I've been better. Honestly, we probably shouldn't have even kept this meeting tonight. I...I think someone might have followed me."

"That's okay. It's okay." Lisa stepped toward him. "We'll make this fast and soon, this will all be over."

"Right." He studied his mom for a moment, then closed the distance between them and wrapped her in a tight hug. It lasted all of three seconds and caught her off guard but before she could react, he released her and stepped away again. "Listen, we don't have that much time so we need to hurry."

"Sure." Johnny nodded. "So where's the list?"

"Yeah. About that—"

"Johnny, someone's here." Rex said it at the same second that a small pile of discarded gravel on the other side of the parking lot's median toppled onto the asphalt with an unmistakable clatter.

"Lots of someone's, Johnny," Luther added. "Wait, how come we didn't smell them?"

The bounty hunter caught sight of someone's summoned red magic as it flared twenty feet away. He raced toward mother and son the second the conjured spell moved toward them. "Get down!"

He caught them both around the middle and took all three of them to the ground. Lisa grunted and gritted her teeth against the pain in her elbow and hip. Hamish hissed in surprise. In the next moment, the air filled with the crackle and buzz of more magicals casting many more spells than anyone had anticipated.

The whole damn place is an ambush.

"Boys!"

"We got it, Johnny!"

"Oh, hell yeah! It's on!"

He pushed to his feet and snatched an exploding disk from his utility belt—for this particular meeting with Lisa's son, he'd planned ahead just in case. Without hesitation, he punched the button on top of the disk and hurled it in the direction from which the first magical attack had come. The disk exploded while still airborne and threw metal shrapnel in all directions to elicit cries of surprise, anger, and pain from the magicals who had begun to close in on them.

The air in the parking lot wavered in the darkness and the illusion used by at least three dozen magicals pursuing Hamish Breyer eroded.

At least I can now see who the hell I'm fightin'.

"They're hidden," Johnny shouted. "Hold 'em off."

"Christ, Johnny." Lisa drew her service pistol and swung it to face the oncoming attackers as more illusions failed and multi-colored spells streaked toward them. "There has to be at least forty—"

"Don't count, darlin'. Just shoot." He activated two more exploding disks and hurled them toward the incoming assault.

"FBI!" Lisa shouted. "Don't—"

A bolt of frigid, ice-encrusted magic hurtled toward them from the hands of a Crystal who strode across the parking lot. Hamish yanked his mother aside barely in time for her to avoid a spear through the back before the parking lot filled with bitingly cold air and a haze of blizzard magic that obscured everything.

"Johnny!" Luther called and snarled as he jerked the leg of a wizard caught between his jaws from side to side. His captive screamed. "Why is it so cold?"

"Hey, I can't see anything!" Rex shouted. "Where's the—"

He stopped in mid-snarl to pounce on a Kilomea who lumbered through the instant blizzard. The enemy roared in pain but couldn't see who he was fighting.

Johnny activated and hurled disk after disk from his belt. The explosions created a violent, drawn-out barrage until the latest one caught the Crystal who'd been casting the storm. The snow, frigid wind, and cutting shards of ice died down with a howl and the full extent of what they were up against was clearly visible.

Holy shit. They sent a whole damn army to assassinate one Light Elf.

"Johnny," Lisa called as she launched fireballs into the fray. She'd returned her service pistol to its shoulder holster now that there were too many attackers and not nearly enough bullets. "We have to get him out of here."

"Yep." He threw another exploding disk and saw it hit this time. The wizard who limped away from where Luther had taken a chunk out of his leg screamed and catapulted across the abandoned parking lot while blood sprayed from his severed hand.

We gotta get ourselves outta this mess.

"All right, on my mark." He nodded at Hamish, who was less skilled than his mom at fireball attacks but wielded light-energy attacks with terrifying precision. "The hounds will cut us a path back—"

A whistle pierced the noise of battle and grew louder and lower in pitch. Johnny had enough time to see the tip of some kind of altered RPG ripping across the darkness overhead before it struck the apartment building and erupted. He, Lisa, and Hamish were all thrown forward and down by the explosion. His chest hit the asphalt first, then the side of his face. The deafening explosion cleared everything in his range of hearing except for the damn ringing that threatened to split his skull.

The shock of being hurled flat on his face seemed to last

forever. The sound slowly returned and Johnny tried to force himself to stand.

Rex and Luther barked madly from somewhere very far away and it took a moment longer for their voices to return to Johnny's mind with any clarity at all.

"…getting away!"

"…on it, Johnny…too many…won't make it…"

He tried to blink away the dizziness and the shitty feeling when all bodily sensations returned at once. Finally, the bounty hunter managed to get one foot on the ground and supported himself on the opposite knee.

"Hamish!" Lisa's cry came through loud and clear.

The darkness carried an extra layer from the ruptured apartment building—a billowing dust cloud of plaster, exploded brick, drywall, and whatever else the damn RPG had destroyed. Strips of shredded, moth-eaten curtain fluttered in front of his face, most of them still flaming as they fell.

"Johnny, help him!"

He turned to Lisa who was propped up on one elbow and pointed with the other outstretched arm at her son twenty feet away. Hamish lay face-down on the asphalt, his eyes closed and blood smeared across his forehead and cheek. More of it trickled in a thick, heavy stream from a cut somewhere beneath his thick dark hair.

She struggled to rise but her leg was pinned beneath a pile of rubble.

"Shit." The dwarf grunted and finally struggled to his feet and staggered toward her. The whole world tilted sideways.

"No!" she shouted, her eyes wide with terror. "Not me. Get Hamish!"

The rest happened too quickly to think about. He turned toward Hamish as a massive shifter with a red, swollen nose grasped the Light Elf under the arms and hauled him away. Rex and Luther howled madly and launched themselves at the closest attackers, who still flung magical attacks but missed due to such poor visibility. The dwarf ducked beneath a blast of crackling blue light and staggered after Lisa's unconscious son who was half-carried, half-dragged away from the fight.

"Johnny!" she shrieked and fought desperately to free herself.

He drew his utility knife, flicked it open, and focused his blurred vision on the huge shifter and the tops of Hamish's shoes as they scraped across the asphalt. With a burst of speed and determination, he pushed into a jog but his boot came down on a smaller pile of crumbled bricks and his ankle twisted and gave out beneath him. He landed hard on one knee, growled at the sharp pain that seared up and down his leg, and threw the knife.

It struck the shifter squarely in the back beneath the shoulder blades. The guy fell and dragged Hamish with him and for a moment, the bounty hunter thought he had enough time to reach the Light Elf. He struggled to stand again but the pain in his injured ankle made him hesitate for a split-second.

Even without that tiny delay, he would never have had the time to reach Hamish and get him away. Two gnomes and another wizard rushed toward the captive, ignored the shifter with the knife in his back, and picked their target up between them.

"Hamish!" Lisa flailed wildly under the debris pinning her down.

The kidnappers disappeared through the thick cloud of dust, smoke, and destruction. The sound of multiple car doors opening and closing competed with the crackle and roar of more magical shots fired. Those were only meant to keep the two partners from following them. That was the most obvious explanation because as soon as the multiple vehicles raced away from the abandoned and now half-destroyed apartment building and faded into the darkness, the attacks dwindled and stopped entirely.

Rex and Luther raced after the getaway cars. Their frenzied

howls and baying followed their progress down the street as they did what he might have asked them to do if he could have.

Time seemed to stretch as Johnny stared at the fallen shifter and the wreckage.

Just like that. I let 'em get away just like that.

Lisa's agonized cry made him turn and he limped toward her as he scanned the clearing dust cloud. Taillights winked through the thick dust and smoke and a moment later, it was only the two of them.

"I can't… It's on my leg." She was panting now, her face pale as tears streamed down her cheeks. "Johnny, help me!"

He dropped to his knees with a grunt of paint and placed a hand on her shoulder. "Do you think it's broken?"

"No. I don't think so." She gritted her teeth and met his gaze. "Get it off me."

"Yep." He fumbled in his pocket and retrieved a handful of detonating black beads. After he'd crushed them between his fingers, he pressed them against various points on the largest chunk of concrete and bent over Lisa to shield her from the small, popping blasts.

Chunks of concrete and brick peppered his back when the beads exploded. She cried out again but this time, it didn't sound like pain. Not the physical kind, at least.

He helped her clear the largest chunks so she could finally pull her leg out of the rubble. "It don't look broken to me."

"I'm fine." The tremble in her voice said otherwise. "Johnny, they took him."

"I know." He studied her leg with a scowl. "We'll find him, darlin'."

"How? Those assholes came out of thin air! How are we supposed to find him when they fooled us both with those illusions? We'll never—"

"Don't start that now, darlin'." With a grimace, the bounty

hunter stood and helped her to her feet. "Don't even think about it. We'll find him. It's only a matter of lookin' in the right place."

Lisa's lower lip trembled as she set more weight experimentally on her leg. She closed her eyes and took a deep breath. "I knew someone would be here."

"Yeah, so did he. We all knew the risks, darlin'." *We merely didn't expect them to be as high as this.*

It took visible effort but she managed to pull her emotions together and turned to scan the destroyed property. "Where are Rex and Luther?"

"They ran after the cars." Johnny tried to scratch an itch on his face but instantly jerked his hand away with a hiss. "Damn."

"What?"

"It's nothin'. Listen, if the boys find anythin', they'll let us—"

"Johnny?" Luther called. "Hey, Johnny?"

"Where are you?"

The dwarf whistled shrilly and both hounds trotted around the side of the building, panting heavily.

"We lost 'em, Johnny."

Luther lowered his head and let out a low whine. "Cars are too fast."

"We followed them about a mile before they got away. Sorry, Johnny."

"Sorry, lady. We tried."

Lisa closed her eyes and remained silent.

"Naw, y'all did all right. Come on. We'll regroup, check our injuries, and decide on our next steps." He moved toward the street but paused in front of Lisa to place a hand on her arm. "We gotta move—"

She jerked away from him and stormed toward the rental, although it was more an impression than fact as real storming was out of the question for both of them. Hers was more of a hobble that favored her almost crushed leg, while he limped after her with sharp pain shooting up his ankle. The hounds followed dutifully and sniffed at the wreckage.

"Don't blame yourself, Johnny."

"Yeah, you're not the one who blew a building up this time."

"Blame the idiots who—wait." Rex ran in the opposite direction and his claws skittered across the asphalt in the darkness. There was a metal clink, a wet, slicing sound, and the larger hound raced to catch up with Luther and Johnny.

"Whoa, dude!" The smaller hound bounded aside. "Watch where you're swinging that."

"You want this Johnny?" Rex looked at his master with wide eyes, his tail wagging.

The dwarf glanced down and would have laughed if circumstances were different. Instead, he took his utility knife from between Rex's jaws, shut it before he strapped it onto his belt, then sniffed and crossed the street. "Good boy."

"Ha-ha! You hear that, bro?" The hound stuck his snout in the air and pranced across the street.

Luther stopped on the sidewalk, looked up and down the street, then brought up the rear of their partially wounded procession and muttered, "You look stupid."

CHAPTER NINETEEN

"Ah. Shit." Johnny hissed and pulled the rag drenched in rubbing alcohol away from his face. It was stippled with blood, most of which had spread through his beard. He could still feel some of it trickle between the wiry hairs and trace a line along his jaw toward his chin.

Lisa paced constantly across their hotel room. "We were so close."

He watched her for a moment, then slapped the rag to his face again with a grunt. "It ain't gonna get any closer walking a path into the floor like that."

"Well, right now, Johnny, the alternative is to start breaking things. If you're cool with an outrageous damages bill for this hotel room—"

"Naw, that's all right." He cleared his throat and checked the rag again. The blood was darker now and more of it seeped through the cloth, and his face felt like someone had tried to scale him like a carp.

"We need help." She spun away from him and continued to pace across the room while she scowled at the outdated pattern of the carpet. "This is too big—way too big for the two of us. What were we thinking?"

Rex stopped licking the underside of his forepaw to look at her. "Um…you forgot two hounds, lady."

The dwarf snapped his fingers. "Hush."

"It wasn't supposed to be this bad," Lisa continued. "How could we let this happen? I don't…I don't even know if he's still—"

"All right, that's enough." He dropped the soaked rag on the table and stood to move toward her. "We're thinkin' about our next steps, darlin'. That's the plan. Anythin' beyond that is a waste of energy."

She stopped to shoot him a completely crushed look, then staggered toward the couch and practically fell into it. "My son—"

"I know." Johnny limped to the couch and sat beside her. It didn't seem nearly as strange now for him to rub her back in reassurance. "We'll find him."

"And now World Nexus and whoever's been looking for him has that list."

"To hell with the damn list. Your kid's more important by a long shot, and I know you ain't gonna try arguin' against it. There's more than one way to skin a catfish, darlin'."

"Skin a cat."

"Huh?"

"The saying is 'More than one way to skin a cat.'"

He snorted. "Not in my neck of the woods." He removed his hand slowly from her back and studied her profile before she lowered her head into her hands. "What do you wanna do?"

Lisa whipped her head up and glared at him with blazing eyes. "I want my son back."

"'Course you do. I'm only sayin'—"

"I need my phone." She searched one back pocket, then the other. "Shit, it's in my jacket. Where did I put it?"

"Right there." He nodded at the hook beside the front door of the hotel room.

"Right."

"Naw, darlin'. You stay sittin'. You ain't spent enough time off that leg."

She scoffed as he stood. "Johnny, your ankle's the size of a grapefruit."

The dwarf lifted the leg of his black jeans to peer at his injured ankle. He'd iced it for a good ten minutes but it had still turned nasty shades of blue and purple. "Naw. More like one of them little, tiny oranges that are real easy to peel."

"Cuties."

He glanced at her and winked. "You ain't so bad yourself."

Lisa sank into the couch and closed her eyes as he hobbled on his swollen ankle toward the front door and the coat hook.

"Who you gonna call?"

"Ghostbusters!" Luther shouted. When his brother and the two-legs frowned at him in exasperation, he whined and slumped with his head on his forepaws. "Fine."

"We need to call Nelson," she said.

"What? The hell we do."

"Johnny, this is completely out of our hands. We can't do this on our own and we were stupid to try in the first place."

"We merely didn't see the full extent of it. Now we have." He hauled her winter jacket off the hook and rifled through the first pocket. "What the hell is Nelson gonna do, huh? Call in his best bounty hunter and the guy's partner to go in and get the job done? Oh, right. We're already on it."

"I'm too close to this and the department has resources we don't."

The first pocket was empty so he flipped the jacket and patted it impatiently to find the other one. "We have resources."

"Well, I won't fly to the Everglades so you can run a search through Margo. Do you know how much time we'll lose?"

"Margo could do it. 'Course, it'd be a helluva lot easier if Hamish stepped outta the Iron Ages and got himself a damn phone."

"Wow. You choose now to advocate for modern technology?"

"Darlin', I've had a phone on me since cell phones became a thing. Remember those big ol' bricks folks used to carry around in the—" With a frown, he removed his hand from her jacket pocket and stared at the item in his hand which certainly wasn't a cell phone. "What's this?"

"What's what?"

"It was in your pocket, darlin'." He hung the jacket absently on the hook again and hobbled toward the couch. The two-inch vial of sludgy, viscous liquid glowed bright orange and held both their attention until he stopped in front of her. "Does any part of this ring a bell?"

"No. I've never seen that before."

"And you didn't put it there?"

"Without seeing it? Not likely."

"Uh-huh." The bounty hunter squinted at the vial and turned it to study the quarter-inch-thick silver base. "Damn. He's good."

"I have no idea what you're talking about."

"We have one thing goin' for us, darlin'. Hamish got taken by the bastards he's been tryin' to stay ahead of, but we got the list."

"What?" Lisa leapt to her feet and grimaced when she put too much weight on her bad leg too soon.

"I'd bet the whole damn houseboat that's what this is."

"He didn't give us anything, Johnny."

"Not that we knew of. We had…what? All of two minutes with him? He was jittery and nervous. He knew someone was tailin' him. Maybe he even knew exactly who it was and how much time we didn't have." He went to the dresser across from the bed, snatched the remote up, and pried the back off to dump the batteries onto the floor. Then, he pulled the dresser away from the wall and studied the back of the TV.

"What are you doing?"

"I'm improvisin'."

"With the hotel TV?"

He set the remote down to draw his utility knife and flicked it open. "If you're more concerned about keepin' somethin' outta the wrong hands than you are about your well-bein', what would you do with that somethin'?"

"I don't know… Make sure it's safe."

"Uh-huh. And stickin' it in a place isn't exactly the safest bet. So how about givin' to someone you know would keep it safe?"

"That doesn't work, Johnny. There is no one he truly trusts."

"Except for his mama—ow!" The exposed wires at the back of the TV sparked when he cut through the ones he wanted. He shook his hand out, dumped the wires on the dresser, and got to work taking apart another section of the TV.

"Right." Lisa heaved a sigh. "And I completely let him down."

"Nope. Do these World Nexus assholes know who Hamish Breyer's mama is? Most likely. They went through your apartment and didn't find what they were lookin' for 'cause there was nothin' to find. For them, anyhow." The TV creaked in protest before he finally pulled another panel off the back and dug even deeper. The panel thumped on the floor. "But even when the bad guys know who you are, your boy still trusts you."

"It didn't do any of us any good."

The dwarf froze, sniffed, and abandoned his work to step around the dresser and meet her gaze. "You gonna stop with all the pessimism anytime soon? 'Cause that ain't helpin' either."

"Johnny, I don't—"

"It's safe to hand something to someone you trust. Sure. But even a person you know would never turn you in runs a risk of havin' the knowledge forced out of 'em. Yeah, I know, darlin'. You'd do fine in an interrogation. We've both been there. I ain't sayin' you couldn't hold your own."

Lisa closed her mouth and frowned as he disappeared behind the dresser and the disassembled TV again.

"You know what's more secure than handin' that special somethin' to someone you trust?"

She rolled her eyes. "If you're trying to make a point, Johnny, make it already. It's almost midnight and I was almost crushed by an exploding apartment building, so—"

"Givin' it to a person without tellin' 'em what's what. You can't torture information outta someone who don't even know they have it."

"What?"

When he was satisfied with all the TV components he'd unceremoniously ripped away, Johnny strapped his knife on again and took the handful of wires and components—plus the battery-less remote—with him to the small table near the door. "Your boy knew what was comin'. You wouldn't think it weird 'cause you're his mama. But that hug he gave you took precious time, didn't it? And he knew."

"I have no idea what you're saying—"

"This, Lisa." He held the orange vial up so she could see it clearly. "This is the list."

She squinted. "It looks like one of your bolt tips."

"On steroids, maybe." He set everything down again and went to the alarm clock on the nightstand to take what he needed from that too. "And full of information."

"Do you have to take everything apart in here?"

"Come on. We ain't got a TV in the Glades, darlin'. Or an alarm clock. You ain't gonna miss not havin' one now."

Lisa leaned forward and propped her forearms on her thighs. "So much for avoiding that hotel room damage bill."

"Naw. This is a piece of junk." The clock clattered onto the nightstand, rolled off, and thumped onto the carpet. "The TV might run a little high, though."

"Johnny, are you sure that's the list?"

He paused beside the table and raised an eyebrow. "As sure as you are that Hamish ain't done nothin' but put himself in the wrong place at the wrong time. And maybe take a little too long to grow out of his gullibility."

"Fine." From her place on the couch, she watched him work with the various pieces he'd stolen from their hotel room using his utility knife as the only tool to fit it all together.

Half an hour later, he set the knife down and turned toward her again. "Do you have your laptop on you?"

"The real one or the fancy one?"

"Huh?"

"Yes, Johnny. I brought my laptop."

"Good. Go ahead and get it, will ya? I need it for this."

She stared blankly at him. "Are you serious?"

"As a heart attack, darlin'."

"I won't let you tear my laptop apart."

The bounty hunter gestured toward his newly built contraption on the table. "We have the list and I built us a magical flash drive reader. Do you wanna be able to power the damn thing and read what your son gave you or not?"

"Fine." She stood and walked toward her overnight bag beside the bed. For a moment, she stared at the weird machine with wires poking out of it before she forced herself to look away to find her laptop.

When she returned with it clutched tightly to her chest, he laughed. "Come on, darlin'. I ain't gonna destroy it."

"I need some kind of reassurance."

He sighed. "How about a promise?"

"Fine." She handed it to him, then tried to sit in one of the two chairs at the table before she noticed the blood-stained rag he'd tossed aside. "Johnny."

"Yeah."

"Where are you bleeding?"

"Huh? Oh, only my face."

"What? Let me see?"

The dwarf jerked his head away from her and pointed at her laptop. "We have better things to look closely at right now. They are a helluva lot less boring than a little scrape."

"I wouldn't call that a little scrape."

"All right, fine. But it would have been far worse without the beard."

Lisa wrinkled her nose and stared at his blood-flecked beard.

"Extra cushionin' and all that. Hey, open the damn screen, will ya?"

"It's already open."

"I need to get in."

"Oh. It's asking for the password."

He sighed with exaggerated patience. "Which is?"

"Yeah, I'm not giving that to you. Move over."

CHAPTER TWENTY

With everything finally connected—and Lisa gritting her teeth in silent anxiety over the way her laptop was being used—Johnny placed the orange vial where an AA battery would have gone in the remote. Now that the remote had been completely repurposed, it was propped up at an angle to give him full access should anything go wrong.

"All right. Here goes nothin'."

"Wait, what?"

He attached the final two wires to the second set of open battery terminals in the remote. Sparks spat from the connection. The orange liquid inside the mounted vial glowed with an internal light. The light behind the laptop screen grew brighter and brighter until Lisa thought it would explode.

"Johnny—"

"Hold on!" Smoke rose from where the wires made contact with the battery terminals before the impromptu device emitted a sharp crack and another spray of sparks.

She cried out in surprise and shielded her eyes. The laptop screen went completely black.

"Huh." With a scowl, Johnny pulled the wires away and leaned back to look at the screen.

"Great. You promised."

"That was supposed to work. I guess there's an extra—"

"Johnny, don't!"

He pressed the wires against the terminals again but nothing happened. "Shit."

"Wait. Don't move."

"What?"

Lisa stepped around him to peer at the laptop screen and the rows of information in white text that scrolled from top to bottom. "Holy shit. It's working."

"Damn straight it is." He grinned at the hounds. "You hear that, boys? Another success in the bank."

"Smells good." Luther licked his muzzle and rolled onto his back, his hind legs splayed and his forepaws dangling in the air. A deep snore escaped him, and his upper jowls peeled slowly away from his teeth in the deepness of canine sleep.

I can't even count on a coonhound for support.

Rolling his eyes, he returned his attention to the wires to hold them in place. "What's on there, darlin'?"

"Names. Exactly like he said." Lisa laughed weakly in disbelief and scanned the information. "A few addresses—wait. There's information here too that doesn't make sense. This whole section."

He glanced at the screen. "All right. I don't claim to know a helluva lot about code or nothin'—"

"You don't say."

"But I think that part there is either a bug there ain't no workin' around, or it's still encrypted."

"But not the rest of it. Do you think there's a higher level of security on more important information?"

"Sure. Either that or whoever put this together wanted to be sure the only folks who got everythin' on this list were the right ones with the right tools to get everythin' in one place." With a growing crick in his neck, Johnny pulled away from the screen to focus on the wires again. "Is Hamish into all this codin' stuff?"

"Yeah, he is."

"So he's the one who put it together, then. He's a smart kid."

"He's not—"

"Smart man." He raised his eyebrows at her when she turned to study his expression. A small, knowing smile grew on both their faces. "Let me know when it's done."

"Yeah, okay."

The information from the alchemized data list took another forty minutes to download completely. Lisa had pulled a chair up behind Johnny so he could sit and the dwarf now hunched over the table with his chin resting on one forearm while he stared at the wires attached to the battery terminals. His fingers had grown stiff and even though his right arm had fallen asleep, he still didn't lift his head.

"Okay." Lisa nodded. "I think that's the rest of it."

"Are you sure? 'Cause if it ain't, we might lose whatever else is there."

"No that's it. The screen's blank again."

With a sigh, he straightened and removed the wires slowly. The remote spat another spray of sparks but that was all. He stretched his cramped hands, leaned back in the chair, and frowned at the vial in the battery dock. The liquid was still there but now it only held a stain of orange, barely visible even under the hotel room's bright light.

"All right. It looks like we got our list."

"Or most of it." Lisa sat in the other chair and turned the laptop toward her before she typed in a few commands. "Here we go. It definitely downloaded."

"It sure as shit better have."

"Wow." She scanned the information pulled up on her screen and her eyes widened more by the second. "This is incredible."

"Are there many names?"

"Yeah, and many I recognize. Take a look." She spun the laptop toward him and he squinted at the screen.

"It's a little hard to make out, ain't it?"

"Only the encrypted part."

"Naw, I mean the whole thing." He leaned forward. "Who the hell makes shit this small?"

"Uh-oh."

"What?"

Lisa folded her arms and smirked. "It sounds like Johnny Walker needs reading glasses."

He snorted and returned immediately to the list of names and addresses. "It ain't happenin'. My eyesight's never been better."

"Not if I can read all that."

"Darlin', you've seen me shoot. I can hit a rabbit forty yards away. What the hell would I need glasses for?"

"Reading glasses. For up close." She chuckled. "Which won't be a problem for hunting unless you plan to shoot rabbits point-blank."

With a grunt of irritation, the dwarf ignored her to look at the list of names until his vision doubled and formed the tight knot of a budding headache between his eyes. He leaned back and pinched the bridge of his nose. "Yeah, I recognize some of these too. Garreth Browel. Malek Ordus. Clyde Ambros."

"Yeah. They were all at the Monsters Ball in New York last year."

"Damn. He's in deep."

"We already knew that." She stood and closed the laptop before she squeezed his shoulder. "We'll find the best place to start in the morning. Right now, we need to get some sleep."

"Yeah." Johnny stood, then shook his head. "I'm gonna see tiny-ass letters every time I close my eyes for the next week."

"It's better than dreaming about them."

"Now why would you go and put a thought like that in a guy's head?"

She smiled and climbed into bed.

CHAPTER TWENTY-ONE

The most promising lead from what had already been decrypted
off Hamish's list pointed to Leonard Osterman in Manchester.
They stopped for breakfast on the way, made sure to get the
hounds the canine-friendly versions, and finally stopped outside
a large building in a factory district on the south of town.

Three other vehicles were parked in the lot, which made the
location look fairly empty on a Sunday morning.

*Lack of cars don't mean shit. We found that out the hard way last
night.*

"It was very convenient to leave the address for us," Johnny
muttered as he shoved the rental keys into his back pocket.

"That's the point of the list, isn't it?"

"Uh-huh. Have you ever heard of this Osterman asshole
before now?"

"No. But he was the closest to Richmond so it's a decent start."

The hounds padded after them and sniffed the cold morning
air beneath a clear blue sky.

"There's a ton of stuff going on here, Johnny."

"Yeah. A ton of magicals, too."

"What kind?"

"Um…all of them?" Rex snorted. "And shifters. Lots of the big kind too."

"And that about covers every magical race on Earth."

"It makes sense," Lisa said and glanced briefly at the security camera mounted on the building's exterior wall. The front door, though, was unmanned. "Leonard Osterman does have a record."

"Uh-huh. Illegal gamblin's the most of it."

"That's what his rap sheet said."

"All right. So maybe we can get him to bet on his own life versus some other asshole's. We only gotta get inside his head a little." Johnny opened the front door and they stepped into a small reception room with low lighting and only one piece of furniture. That was the stool set outside another door on the opposite side of the room, and on it sat a massive Azrakan wearing a dull gray vest and jeans.

The bounty hunter stifled a shudder at the sight of the magical's curved horns like a crown of antlers.

One shriveled Azrakan hell-bent on global mind control was more than enough. Now I gotta look at this one smirkin' at me?

The guard didn't move until they approached. Slowly, he raised a clawed hand and studied Lisa. "What do you need?"

She raised her chin and gave him her most apathetic stare. "We're here for the party."

The bouncer grunted and looked at the hounds. "No dogs allowed."

"The hounds stay with me," Johnny said.

With a growl, the Azrakan met his gaze. "Who sent you?"

"Garreth Browel," Lisa replied.

The bouncer's eyes widened.

"We met him last year at the Monsters Ball. He dropped a few names and we decided we'd finally come to see for ourselves."

The Azrakan ran a tongue over his teeth while he frowned in thought but finally stood and opened the door behind his stool.

He held it for them and nodded. "Those dogs make any kind of trouble down there, you know what'll happen to them."

"It ain't a problem," Johnny muttered as he followed Lisa through the doorway.

The hounds brought up the rear and sniffed the doorway and the stairs leading under the building. "Another talking moose, Rex."

"I know, right? They pop up out of nowhere."

The door slammed closed behind them but the stairwell was lit well enough. Shouts and cheers echoed toward them from the room below and drowned out the background beat of heavy metal music. Johnny didn't recognize the song or the band but he already approved of the soundtrack, at least. They reached the base of the stairs and stopped to scan their surroundings.

The single massive room below the factory had most likely been used for machine storage. Now, a large pit surrounded by a three-foot cement wall took up the center of the room. Snarls and the sharp crack of snapping jaws rose from the pit, and even from where he stood, Johnny could see the top halves of two wolves fighting.

Shifter fights. It's the lowest of the low down here, ain't it?

"Smart thinkin' droppin' Garreth's name like that, darlin'."

"Thanks. I thought it couldn't hurt if they're all on the same list together."

"Uh-huh. We might have to drop it again when we find Osterman."

"No problem." She glanced at him with a coy smile. "I'm good at improvising too. But with words instead of bombs."

"Don't we make a fine pair?" Johnny snapped his fingers. "Y'all stay close, understand?"

"No problem, Johnny."

"Yeah, they're fighting shifters in there. I don't even wanna think about what they'd do to us."

Magicals crowded around the cement wall of the pit to shout

and roar encouragement to whichever shifter they'd placed their bets on. A spray of sand arced out of the ring and showered the spectators, who jeered and bellowed even louder as the fight got dirty.

A bar had been set up along the far side of the room, and two gnomes poured drinks for the magical underground scum in this part of the state.

Some of 'em probably came from farther around too to get their rocks off in private.

Pockets of other magicals stood around the crowd focused on the shifter fight. No one bothered to lower their voices as they conversed, laughed, and sipped their drinks and occasionally exchanged money to bet on the next fight. No one paid the newcomers any attention either.

"I guess we oughtta head to the bar."

"It's not even eleven in the morning, Johnny."

"That ain't stoppin' the rest of these folks, now is it?" He didn't give her a chance to protest before he moved forward.

Lisa frowned at him as Rex turned to look at her, his tail sticking straight out behind him.

"Stay close, lady."

"Yeah, no telling what's gonna happen down here. These two-legs smell like sweat and rage."

With a sigh, she headed after Johnny and muttered, "I'm coming."

The gnome bartender at the closest end of the bar widened his eyes when he saw Lisa coming toward him. He opened his mouth to say something but Johnny cut in with, "Gimme a Johnny Walker Black and…what d'ya want, darlin'?"

"Soda with lime."

The gnome looked particularly disappointed to see Lisa was with Johnny instead of on her own but he turned to pour their drinks anyway.

"Look at that." The dwarf smirked and rapped his knuckles on the bar. "The one redeeming thing here. They have my drink."

"I wouldn't call that redeeming, Johnny."

"Sure, but pair that with the mood music?" He pointed at the ceiling and raised an eyebrow. "It ain't all that bad."

She leaned toward him and muttered through the side of her mouth. "I think you're forgetting about the giant pit in the ground where they're betting on which shifter can tear the other's throat out first."

Luther sidled closer to Johnny's leg and gulped.

"Naw, I ain't forgettin' that. I'm tryin' to ignore it and stay focused." *Or I might rip someone else's throat out.*

"Here," the gnome said brusquely and shoved their drinks toward them.

"How much do I owe ya?"

With a sharp, unamused laugh, the bartender looked from one to the other of his latest customers and grimaced. "You don't have to rub it in."

He left them standing there to fiddle with the inventory.

"Look at that. It's an open bar and we didn't even have to pay to get in." The bounty hunter picked his drink up and took a small sip. "Sure. I think this could be my kinda place."

"Except for the—"

"Yeah, I know, darlin'. I'm tryin' to stay positive."

Lisa paused with her drink raised halfway to her lips and stared at him. "Well, that's a first."

They took their time to surveil the room and the various groups of magicals holding their private conversations. None of these looked particularly promising. They were there to get in on the action and the particularly noisy crowd gathered around the fighting ring could be dismissed completely.

They don't care about anythin' but which wolf walks away and which one bleeds.

"Maybe we could've thought this through a little better," Johnny muttered. "I have no damn clue what he looks like."

"We don't have to." Lisa nodded across the room at the overweight wizard who stood in front of another door. He was flanked by two burly Kilomea who, for some reason, had decided to shave from the backs of their hands to beneath the cut of their rolled-up shirtsleeves. The effect made their arms look almost human if it weren't for the pinkness of their flesh.

The dwarf snorted. "Those arms look like shaved puppies."

"I don't even want to know what purpose that serves." She shook her head. "Forget about their arms. My guess is that's Osterman between them."

"He ain't the only asshole in this place with giant bastards on both sides of 'em."

"True. But he hasn't left that position in the last twenty minutes."

"Have you been watchin' him the whole time?" He lowered his head in approval. "I ain't even noticed."

"Yeah, that's the whole point of an undercover stakeout." She gave him a half-playful frown. "I might not officially work for the Bureau now but I still know how to do my job."

"I never said you don't."

"The bookie's errand boy keeps circling. He stops at Mr. Large-and-In-Charge over there after every circuit."

He snorted. "I thought I was the one who made names up."

"No, you're the one who has to say them all out loud."

Johnny raised his hand to scratch the side of his face but pulled quickly away from the raw sting beneath his beard. *Good. She's back in Agent Breyer mode and the mama hat is back at the hotel.*

"Is there anythin' else I should know before we call this one Osterman and move in?"

"Maybe. Three different magicals have stopped to talk to him since we've been here. The chats only last about fifteen seconds and he directs them to someone else in a different part of the room. I think he has at least thirty guys here on his payroll. And yes, that's including the bartenders."

"Well, all right, then. That must be our guy."

"We have to get him alone, though. Asking about World Nexus and whatever he knows about who's holding Hamish won't exactly go over well in a crowd this size."

"Uh-huh." The dwarf swallowed the last of his drink with a grimace. A gnome dressed like the bartenders came through pushing a silver serving cart with an ice bucket and a bottle of champagne nestled on top. Johnny placed the glass on the tray as it passed and ignored the gnome's disgusted glare. "You wanna take point on this or should I?"

"Wow, Johnny." Lisa fixed him with a teasing look and pursed her lips in an attempt to hide a smile. "You're making a plan."

"I think we need one, is all. It's on a case-by-case basis."

"Yeah, okay. I'll take it. You can be my bodyguard."

"What about us, lady?" Rex asked, gazed at her, and panted.

"Yeah, we can have jobs too. We're real good at jobs. Tell her, Johnny."

She nodded toward their master. "You can be his bodyguards."

"All right!"

"We've never been bodyguards before."

"Hey, Luther. What's a bodyguard?"

"Lean, mean, killing machines."

"Okay, cool."

Johnny snapped his fingers. "Y'all hold it together until I tell y'all otherwise, understand?"

"Yep. No problem, Johnny."

"You say otherwise, and we'll say die."

The undercover private investigators and their two coonhounds wove through the groups of laughing, drinking, and betting magicals and took time to act interested in the various activities offered for the underground room's more nefarious patrons. At least four tables had been set up to take bets for more than the shifter fights in the ring.

Lisa glanced at one of them and forced herself to not scowl as she leaned toward Johnny. "They're betting on the gnomes."

"Huh?"

"The bartenders."

"About what?"

"I don't know, but I have a feeling they won't get the bonus catering tip they were expecting."

He sniffed and wrinkled his nose. "Never mind what I said, darlin'. This ain't my kinda place."

"I never believed you before."

The snarls and sharp barks from the pit grew in intensity and urgency. The spectators roared at the fighters, pumped their fists in the air, and leaned forward over the cement wall like crazed animals. An earsplitting yelp echoed through the room, followed by a nauseating crunch that ended in a wet snap and gurgle. The crowd around the pit became utterly frenzied—both the winners and the losers of this particular fight.

The uproar stopped the two partners and they turned to study the ring.

"My God…" she murmured.

"At least they ain't takin' the poor bastard home to patch him up."

"No, because he's dead."

The dwarf shrugged. "Better than havin' to endure the wounds simply to do it all over again."

"That's…morbidly optimistic."

A man straightened from the sandy floor of the pit amidst the howls of victory as the spectators prepared to collect their bets and place new ones. He stood completely naked and was covered in huge gashes with a layer of sand stuck to what looked like rivers of blood. Even when the announcer for this screwed-up fight joined the victor in the ring and grasped his wrist to hoist his arm high, the shifter stared at the far wall of the room while his chest heaved.

"Titus takes the fight!" the announcer cried. "If any of you chumps have a shifter you think can beat him in the pit, by all means, bring your wolf! We're here all day and the roster somehow keeps shrinking."

The crowd erupted with laughter. Only a handful of magicals paid any attention to the shifter who'd lost his life for their entertainment. As soon as two gnomes hopped into the ring to remove the body, the scum of Virginia's magical society turned away to find enjoyment elsewhere.

"There's no way he can handle another fight in the same day," Lisa muttered.

"It might even be in the same hour." The dwarf's nostrils flared as he turned toward Osterman and his shaved Kilomeas. Lisa didn't budge. "Come on, darlin'."

"This isn't right, Johnny."

"Most things ain't. Trust me, I don't like it any more than you do, but we gotta stay focused."

"Yeah." When Rex pressed his side against her leg, she reached down absently to run her fingers through his short hair.

Johnny didn't think either one of them was aware of their attempt to find reassurance.

Shit. We'll put the shifter fights on the list of things to blow up after we rescue Hamish.

He nudged her in the shoulder and broke her staring contest with the blood-splattered interior of the pit's cement wall. She met his gaze and her jaw worked visibly around the tight set of her lips.

"I'm focused, Johnny. Let's go."

CHAPTER TWENTY-TWO

Osterman was laughing with his massive goons as they watched the gnomes struggle to remove the dead shifter's naked human form from the ring. He didn't notice the two investigators approaching with the hounds until one of his bodyguards stepped forward to block the newcomers from getting any closer.

"Back up." The Kilomea grunted and folded his comically hairless arms.

Lisa raised both hands in a conciliatory gesture. "We only want a minute of Mr. Osterman's time. If it's all the same to him."

"Mister." The beast snorted and turned toward his equally shorn twin. "You hear that?"

"Do you have an appointment, sweetcheeks?"

She forced herself to smile even wider. "No. But I'd love to sit down with the mastermind behind this place."

"Go get yourself a few drinks. Mr. Osterman's not interested in any new—"

"Don't put words in my mouth, Ernest." His boss set a meaty hand covered with expensive rings on the Kilomea's shoulder and the bodyguard stepped back with a scowl. "And that's no way to speak to a woman. Feel free to take notes."

The guards glanced at each other and Ernest's counterpart rolled his eyes.

"Forgive their poor manners." Osterman extended his hand toward Lisa and leaned toward her, his eyes wide as he studied her from head to toe. "The folks we see here on a regular basis are rather rough around the edges and it's been a long time since I've seen such a beautiful woman brave the chaos. And to speak to me, no less."

She set her fingers in the wizard's open palm and he bent even lower to brush his lips against the back of her hand.

Johnny snorted. *If he leans over any more, he's fixin' to fall on her.*

"You can call me Lenny."

Lisa withdrew her hand and held the wizard's gaze. "Emily."

"Hmm. You wanted to speak to me?"

"In private, yes."

"Right this way, then." Osterman gestured toward the door he'd stood in front of since they had arrived and gave her another quick appraisal before he flashed a grin.

Johnny snapped his fingers and the hounds fell into step beside him as they followed Manchester's master of underground betting.

"Not so fast, bud." The second Kilomea thumped a hand against Johnny's chest and held him at bay. "You heard him. Private party."

The dwarf glanced at the hand on his chest, then looked slowly at the leering bodyguard. "Touch me again and you'll lose more than a little hair off that arm."

Lisa turned to see the altercation and acted quickly. "Oh, I'm sorry. Osterman."

He froze when she placed a hand on his arm and turned with a slightly perturbed frown. "Yes?"

"If you don't mind, I'd like my associate to join us."

The wizard chuckled. "I do mind. You wanted a private meeting."

"Yes, but it's not for me." She glanced at Johnny, who was now caught in a staring contest with one Kilomea, matched only by the hounds' staring contest with the second guard. She crooked her finger at Osterman so he had no choice but to lean toward her. "What he lacks in social skills, he more than makes up for with the work he does for Garreth."

The wizard's eyes widened. "Garreth? Did he send you?"

"No one sends me anywhere, Lenny." Lisa batted her eyelashes. "But I do have a few fingers in some of his...less-savory pies. He wants his dwarf to deliver information personally before he and I can complete our side arrangement. Which, I hate to say, we won't be able to do if your men keep the dwarf outside."

"Ah. I see." The wizard stroked his hairless, double-jowled chin. "I think I can make an exception for Garreth. And you, of course. I do have to ask about the dogs, though."

She nodded and cast Johnny a sympathetic frown. "Support animals."

"Seriously?"

"He's very attached to them."

"Hmm." Osterman straightened and turned away from her to gesture at the Kilomeas. "Let them through."

"You wanna shut yourself in the back with the dogs?" Ernest snarled his disapproval. "All three of them?"

His boss' accommodating smile disappeared instantly and a crackling shard of bright green magic flared in his meaty palm. "Don't forget yourself, Ernest."

The Kilomeas backed away and stared at the magic in the wizard's hand.

"Do I need to repeat myself?"

"No, boss."

"We heard you."

Osterman snuffed the conjured magic out, plastered his

welcoming smile on again, and nodded at Lisa. "Again, you'll have to forgive their manners."

"Those seem to be outrageously lacking these days, don't they?"

He chuckled and opened the back door. "I think you and I will get along fine, Emily."

Ernest glared at Johnny and his lips curled around his huge exposed upper fangs. "Get lost, dog. Before he changes his mind."

The bounty hunter snapped his fingers and the hounds were at his side in an instant. He leaned toward the admonished Kilomea and jerked his chin up. "Woof."

Rex sniggered. "He barked at the naked walruses."

With a high-pitched giggle, Luther shook his head as he padded at his master's side. "And it's funny 'cause he's not a two-legs."

Johnny let himself smirk but couldn't reply to the hounds only he and Lisa could hear.

They know what we're watchin' for. I can't say there ain't still a little fun to be had while we're doin' it.

Osterman led them into the back room of his establishment, which had been convincingly decorated to look like a large private study in a massive Victorian-style home in New England. An iniviting fire crackled in the center of the left-hand wall. A leather sofa of deep chocolate-brown and matching armchairs took up the center of the room around a glass-topped coffee table, the base of which had been intricately carved from what looked like petrified wood. In the back stood a mahogany desk fit for a magical of his immense size lit by the dim light from an expensive-looking lampshade made of stained glass. A long row of shelves lined the righthand wall, filled to capacity with iden-tical copies of the same hardback book in black cloth covering, none of which boasted a title or author or any identifying infor-mation on the spine.

No way in hell are those real books.

Their host gestured toward the sitting area. "Please. Have a seat. It's not quite noon but we've been quite busy this morning. And if you're here with word from Garreth, I imagine your schedule has been particularly full lately."

"That's one way to put it," Lisa said as she lowered herself into one of the armchairs and gazed around the study. The chaotic noises from the main room behind the door didn't send so much as an echo into the study.

"Brandy, then." The man chuckled. "You strike me as a brandy girl."

"How could you tell?"

The partners exchanged a glance and she shook her head slowly in warning.

Yeah, yeah, I know. You can take care of yourself, darlin'.

He sniffed and took the other armchair.

"I have a certain sense for these things," Osterman continued as he poured two glasses and moved across the room. "I promise you'll enjoy this. It's a HINE two-fifty."

"Very nice." She took the crystal glass from him and made a show of swirling the drink before she took a delicate sniff.

The bounty hunter forced himself to not smack the drink out of her hand and get them right the hell down to business.

The sofa groaned under the wizard's weight when he sat. At the sound, Rex and Luther stopped their curious sniffing and skittered to Johnny's armchair.

"He's gonna bring the whole place down on us, Johnny."

"He needs a bigger couch."

"Ah… Now." Osterman sipped his drink, leaned forward over the coffee table, and grinned at Lisa. "Should we get this other business of Garreth's out of the way first or is that better left as an afterthought?"

"Let's talk about what I want from you first, hmm?" Lisa set her glass down on the table and stood.

Johnny scowled at her as she stepped slowly around the table to approach the sofa. *What the hell does she think she's doin'? This ain't a 007 flick.*

The man watched her with greedy eyes and settled more comfortably into the couch. "Hmm. I'm already intrigued."

Lisa uttered a deep, throaty chuckle through her nose that the dwarf hadn't heard from her before. "And I haven't even said anything yet."

"But do keep talking."

"Uh…Johnny?" Luther stared at Lisa's odd display and lowered his head. "What's wrong with her?"

"Yeah, that's not right. Is it?"

The armrests creaked when Johnny's hands tightened around them. *Careful, Lisa.*

"Tell me what I can do for you, Emily." Osterman leered at her as she stepped around one of his huge legs.

She unzipped her jacket, shrugged out of it, and rested it casually over the arm of the sofa. "It's very personal."

Christ. She put the gun in her goddamn waistband?

"Oh. Even better." The wizard placed a hand on her waist and a sheen of sweat formed along his hairline.

Lisa paused and rested her small hand on his overlarge one to stop him from getting too handsy. "I only have one question first."

"Of course."

Her hand moved much faster than Johnny expected. In two seconds, she'd drawn her pistol from the waistband of her jeans and shoved the barrel under the wizard's trembling jowls. "What do you know about World Nexus?"

And…there it is.

Osterman's eyes almost doubled in size when they widened, then he laughed. "It's that kind of foreplay, is it? Put your little peashooter away, girl."

He tried to pull the gun away from the underside of his chin but she wrested her wrist free of his grasp and delivered a dizzying backhanded slap across his face with her left hand. The wizard grunted and would have fallen sideways on the couch if the expanse of his girth hadn't rooted him in place.

"Oh, yes!" He touched his cheek and frowned when he looked at his fingers. "Although things won't start heating up until we draw blood."

Lisa stepped away from him and leveled her pistol with both hands at his chest. "You're sick."

"Naturally. And do tell your associate he's welcome to watch. I also enjoy an audience."

"That's it." Johnny leapt out of the armchair, hiked his long winter jacket up, and drew his knife.

"Ooh. The messenger has a temper." The sofa creaked and snapped when the wizard's laughter bounced him on the cushions. "Feel free to join us."

The bounty hunter's blade flicked at his side. "You didn't answer her question."

"Why talk about World Nexus? That's so boring and the fun's only getting started."

This asshole needs a serious dose of reality.

"Boys?"

The hounds stood abruptly. "Is that the signal, Johnny?"

"Yeah, there are so many, it's hard to keep track."

Johnny inclined his head as Osterman continued to laugh. "Damn straight."

The wizard drew a sharp breath. "What was that—"

With matching snarls, Rex and Luther vaulted onto the sofa and landed one on either side of the crime lord. He shrieked and tried to bat the hounds away as they snapped at his arms and flailing hands.

"Get these—ah! Animals off my—"

The sofa had endured enough. One of the support planks

beneath the opulent cushions snapped, followed by another. It rocked the man in his seat and he flailed again before the entire piece of furniture, the hounds, and the wizard toppled back. The floor trembled on impact, although Rex and Luther were agile enough to leap to safety before the giant magical had a chance to grab or crush them.

"Huh." The bounty hunter grinned. "Handy sofa."

Lisa glanced at him in exasperation, then hurried around one side of the fallen criminal with her weapon in both hands. Johnny strode to the other side and rested his boot on Osterman's neck.

The wizard uttered a strangled grunt but didn't struggle to right himself.

"Here's the deal. We know you have ties to World Nexus and have seen your name there with some of our favorites. And now, we need you to answer the goddamn questions."

"Garreth didn't send you at all, did he?"

"Clearly not." Lisa smirked at him. "But I have met him."

"Whatever you're trying to get, you'll never—" The words ended in a croak as the bounty hunter pressed down with his boot.

"This isn't the time for you to talk, pal. Only listen. A Light Elf was taken during a bigass fight yesterday in Richmond. It took forty of you assholes to bring him in alive. We're lookin' for him."

"Ha! You and every other piece of trash on this side of the country." Despite his face turning an alarming shade of red, the wizard was remarkably calm. "Twenty million is a hell of a sum to put on one magical's head."

Johnny bent over with his boot still pressed into the guy's neck and tickled Osterman's ear with his blade tip. "I didn't ask for your opinions. Where did they take him?"

"Oh, you truly are desperate." The wizard choked a laugh. "I'm not in the habit of giving information away for free, dwarf."

"Sure. In return, I won't skewer your brains on my knife. Before I crush your trachea."

"Johnny."

He was already in too deep. A little warning from Lisa wouldn't stop him now. "Or how about I promise to not pay Tabitha a little visit of my own, huh?"

Osterman stopped smiling but said nothing. Johnny smirked, thankful that he'd taken the time to do a little research deeper into the list.

"That's right. She has a cute little house on the west end of town. Did you set her up in that? I bet she feels real safe there in that big house with the kids. Corey and Paige. How about I tell 'em their Uncle Lenny says hi?"

"They'd…" Osterman grunted. "They'd love to hear from me, I'm sure."

"Johnny, this isn't working."

The bounty hunter lifted his boot off the wizard's neck and replaced it with the tip of his knife as he shouted, "Where did they take the Light Elf?"

The wizard chuckled again and his eyes rolled back to focus on Rex and Luther who snarled at him from behind his head. "You should put both those dogs in the ring. It's most likely a faster way to make the kind of money you're after." A deviously unconcerned grin spread across his reddening face. "If you think they can last one-on-one with a shifter."

Johnny growled his frustration but finally pulled back and stepped away from the quivering mound of upside-down wizard. A trickle of blood ran from the center of Osterman's throat and around the back of his neck toward the floor.

"This ain't workin'."

"That's what I said."

"Fine. We'll try another way. Come on." Johnny stormed through the door out of the study.

With her pistol in one hand and aimed at Osterman's head, Lisa stooped to snatch her jacket up.

"You come back any time, Emily." The wizard ran his tongue

over his top teeth. "I'll get rid of the couch and install a few mattresses."

"Fuck off."

His laughter followed them as they exited. She tugged her jacket on and shoved her pistol into her waistband.

CHAPTER TWENTY-THREE

The Kilomea bodyguards were put at ease by their boss' laughter, even when it cut off as the door closed. It didn't stop them from glaring at the dwarf and the half-Light Elf followed closely by two coonhounds.

"See?" Johnny spread his arms and walked backward as he leered at the guards. "A few minutes never hurt no one."

They rolled their eyes and returned to scanning the main room for troublemakers.

"That didn't go anything like I planned," Lisa muttered.

"No shit. Are you seriously walkin' around with a loaded gun down your pants, darlin'?"

She glanced scathingly at him. "The safety's on."

"Oh, sure. That's what they all say before someone blows their own ass off."

"Stop." She zipped her jacket and scowled at the magicals enjoying themselves at the start of another fight. "This was a dead end."

"It's a good thing we have a list with at least another hundred names. More if we can get the others decoded."

"Fine. Let's start again with the next closest name on the list."

"It oughtta be somewhere close—"

The spectators around the fighting pit exploded in another uproar of cheers and whistles and bellowed shouts of encouragement. Johnny spun toward the ring and stopped when he saw the shifters who'd entered. One of them was a massive white wolf bigger than the shifter Aldo he'd defeated with his bare hands at the Everglades' local pack den. The other was a small gray wolf—much smaller—who snarled far more fiercely against all odds.

"Johnny?" Lisa backtracked to join him. "What's going on?"

"These sonsabitches."

"What—" She sucked in a sharp breath when she noticed the small gray wolf in the ring. "That's not her."

"I know it ain't her, Lisa!" His shout startled her but it was lost beneath the cheers of bloodthirsty magicals who had chosen the wrong day to come to Lenny Osterman's underground room. "It don't mean I gotta stand here and stomach it. Come on."

He stormed around the thickest group of spectators lining the concrete wall and she hurried after him with a glance at the Kilomeas. It seemed they hadn't noticed that anything was wrong.

Rex and Luther skittered after them and panted as they wove through the jostling magicals trying to get their bets in. "Uh-oh. He's seriously pissed now."

"You think? They put a pup in the ring, bro."

Luther whipped his head up to catch a glance at the shifters pitted against each other, but the crowd had already thickened and blocked the view. "Not our pup?"

"Nope. It could have been, though."

"Shit."

At the top of the stairs, the Azrakan bouncer hardly gave them a second glance as Johnny shoved the door open and stormed across the small reception area. Lisa had to double-check that the bouncer wouldn't come after them, but he sat as stoically on his stool as when they'd first arrived.

"Hey." She jogged across the parking lot to catch up with the dwarf. "Tell me what's going on."

"Nothin', darlin'." He jerked the back of the SUV open and slid his duffel bag toward him.

"That's not gonna fly, Johnny. I know that look."

"What look?"

"The look that means someone's about to get punched or stabbed or blown to pieces. Come on, talk to me."

"I ain't fixin' to do any of those things." He slammed the hatch of the SUV shut and opened the back door calmly for the hounds. "Up."

Luther leapt immediately into the back seat. "He's using one-word commands, Rex."

"Yeah, not good." Rex shoved his brother across the seat so they could both sit and stare at their master. "Someone's going down. You sure you don't want us in there with you, Johnny?"

"Yeah, we took the giant wizard down by jumping on a couch! We can—" The bounty hunter shut the door but it didn't do a thing to cut the hounds' voices in his head. "Wow. Rude."

"Jeez. The least he could do is give us an 'oh, thanks.'"

"Right?"

"Okay, see?" Lisa pointed at the back door. "Even your dogs know something's wrong."

The bounty hunter opened the passenger door and gestured for her to climb inside.

She folded her arms. "This feels like something you should explain."

"I gotta take care of somethin'. Y'all can wait a few minutes. This won't take long."

With a sigh, she climbed into the passenger seat and caught his arm before he could shut the door. "No explosions and death?"

"That's a promise, darlin'. I only need a minute or two."

They stared at each other until she finally released his arm. "Fine. But hey, don't slam the—"

The door slammed shut and she slumped in her seat. "Shit."

With painfully clenched fists, he stormed to the front door of the old factory building and flung it open. The Azrakan on the stool cocked his head in surprise.

"I forgot somethin'."

"Magicals don't usually come back in once they leave."

"Yeah, well, if I'm down there longer than five minutes, feel free to come drag me out again." Johnny threw the door to the descending staircase open and left the guard yet again with no reason to get off his stool.

He gritted his teeth so hard he felt the rugged places in his molars where they'd chipped tiny pieces off their neighbors. *Goddamn fighting rings. Usin' shifters as punchin' bags. Take whatever they damn well please. I've had more than enough of this shit.*

No one noticed the furious dwarf in the puffy black winter coat seething at the fighting pit. Nor did they notice him reach into his jacket pocket and draw an incredibly small silver pistol that wasn't a real weapon. When he pulled the trigger and both wolves in the ring howled in pain before they toppled into the sand, however, that sure as shit got their attention.

The spectators screamed with rage and pushed each other closer to the concrete wall.

"What the fuck are you doing?"

"Get up! This is a fight!"

"Who messed around with the shifters?"

More snarls and shouts of pain erupted from other shifters around the room—those who were recovering from the day's fights or preparing to risk their lives in the next few hours. They clapped their hands over their ears and doubled over in pain, their faces contorted in surprise and agony.

"Whoa, whoa. Hey! What's going on?"

Magicals stepped away from the tortured shifters all over the room and gave them a wide circle of space as they looked every-where to find the meaning behind the sudden and invisible attack.

"It's him! With the gun!" A witch with way too much eye makeup screamed and pointed—but not at Johnny. It seemed someone else had decided to spice things up a little at the same time and provided him with a perfect cover in the process.

Magicals roared in anger and shoved against each other as they all but ran over their neighbors to reach the stairs. The wolves fighting for their lives were left abandoned in the pit and no one bothered to stop to help the other shifters in their human forms who writhed in agony on the floor.

Half the room cleared in thirty seconds and angry shouts and snarls rose up the staircase as those who'd stayed looked around in confusion.

The back door across the room opened and Osterman emerged, red-faced and furious. "What the hell is going on out here?"

His Kilomea guards jumped to attention and took their places in front of the wizard to shield him, but their boss shoved them away.

"Someone better have a good explanation for why this place cleared out like someone cried 'bomb!'"

"It was only some dipshit with a gun," Ernest said. "We think."

"Well, did he shoot all the shifters? Jesus, I can't leave for ten minutes without the whole place falling apart. Find out what their problem is. Now!"

The Kilomeas raced away from him and skirted the remaining magicals who seemed too stunned to do much in the bedlam.

The bounty hunter had a perfect view of Osterman from where he stood. He made no effort to pocket the high-frequency blaster that had disabled every shifter present with a five-second squeeze of the trigger as he stormed toward the perverted crime lord of this underground domain.

The wizard didn't notice him until they were three feet apart. "Huh. Did you come back for another round, dwarf?"

Johnny raised the pistol—which his opponent couldn't possibly know didn't contain actual bullets—and grinned. "If it were me, I'd reassess your business, Osterman. Anyone could come in here and tear the place apart."

The man's eyes widened but he didn't raise his hands in surrender or even try to run. "What do you want?"

"I already told you. When you change your mind, I think you can find out how to find me." He left the gun trained on the man a little longer before he spun on his heel and stormed toward the stairwell.

Outside in the rental, Lisa pressed herself down in the passenger seat and tried to not draw any attention from the dozens of angry magicals who spewed through the front door of the building. "Johnny…what did you do?"

"He flushed the quarry out, lady."

Luther sniggered. "Hey, yeah. That means it's your turn to aim and shoot."

"Be quiet for a second, huh?" She scanned the parking lot and the front of the building, then straightened fully in her seat when the front door burst open again and Johnny stormed out.

"Hey, there he is!" Luther pressed his nose against the back window and his tail wagged furiously and thumped against his brother's face.

"Dude. Cut it out."

"Johnny! You made it!" The smaller hound barked, and Lisa turned to shush him harshly.

"Not in the car, Luther."

"Oh. Okay," he whispered. "He made it."

The dwarf opened the driver's door and slumped behind the wheel. He slammed the door and a moment later, the high-frequency pistol clattered into the cup holder at the base of the dashboard.

"Jesus." Lisa hissed her disapproval and leaned against the window. "Now who needs a refresher course on gun safety?"

"It ain't that kinda gun." He cranked the engine and checked the building's front door. No one seemed inclined to follow them.

"Is that the…shifter gun?"

"Uh-huh. And I tell you what. Osterman may be a disgustin' four hundred pounds of slimeball criminal but he sure don't scare easily. I'll give him that." With a quick jerk of the shift stick into drive, the vehicle lurched forward across the parking lot and accelerated onto the side street.

The shifter gun toppled to the floor at her feet.

"Hey, hey!" Rex yapped once. "Careful with that, huh?"

"Yeah, it took me a week to see straight after she pulled the trigger in the swamp!"

Lisa picked the tiny repurposed pistol up and held it safely in her lap. "So let me get this straight. You went in there, pissed off because they're fighting shifters in that pit instead of…I don't know. Roosters or Pitbulls. And your way of taking care of it was to torture them all with a high-frequency blast no one else can hear?"

"Yep. It might be it gave 'em extra time to get the hell outta there and start over."

"Johnny, please don't tell me you risked our very thin cover here simply because you wanted to free some shifters."

"What? It sounds like the kinda thing you'd be pressin' me to do under different circumstances."

She rolled her eyes. "These aren't normal circumstances at all and you know it."

"Yeah, all right. I wanted to give those shifters a chance so I broke up the whole damn schedule and got most of those scumbags outta there." He sniffed and glanced defiantly at her as his hands tightened around the steering wheel. "It coulda been Amanda down there in that pit if we hadn't gotten to her when we did."

"I know." She sighed heavily. "It's awful."

"But that ain't why I went back."

"Then why did you?"

He cleared his throat. "The motherfucker didn't even offer me a drink."

CHAPTER TWENTY-FOUR

They pulled over at the closest trucking rest stop and refuel station, both to buy a quick lunch neither of them was particularly excited about and to plug Lisa's laptop into a working outlet so they could review what they had of Hamish's list.

She sipped her Diet Coke in the giant plastic to-go cup, then pulled the straw away from her lips. "Okay, I have to ask."

"Go for it."

"What did you do to him?"

"Osterman? I gave him a warnin'." He shrugged and took the last mouthful of his soggy sub sandwich before he tossed the empty heel of bread onto the wrapper. "And put a serious dent in his business, which should take a helluva lotta time and money for him to build up again. It might be enough time to get him to change his mind about talkin'."

"Assuming he's the only one on the list we can get to who knows anything about World Nexus and Hamish."

"I ain't assumin' nothin', darlin'. Merely coverin' our bases. Has that charged enough yet?"

"Yeah, it's on."

"Let's take a look."

She slid toward him along the booth with her laptop, glanced around to make sure no one was watching, and pulled up the downloaded and still partially encrypted list. "So we're looking for the second-closest address to Richmond."

"Bonus points if the name attached to it happen to stands out in any way."

"Well, that's a real shot in the dark."

They leaned forward to scan the names and addresses as she scrolled slowly through the information.

Fifteen minutes later, Johnny slumped against the back of the booth and growled in frustration. "Christ. How long does it take to find a goddamn address? Can't you do the Google or somethin'?"

Lisa snorted. "I'm very sure that if I could simply Google 'magical criminal associated with World Nexus in the Richmond area,' we wouldn't be in this mess in the first place."

"Right. No reason for a list and no reason to go after the guy who smuggled it from Oriceran."

She leaned away from the laptop and glared condescendingly at him. "Seriously?"

"What?"

"Hamish isn't a boy, a thug, or a smuggler. And you can't blame him for any of this."

"I ain't blamin' no one, darlin'." He swallowed thickly. "I'm speakin' my mind, is all."

"Well, maybe keep your mouth shut and your mind where it belongs." She returned her attention to the screen with an angry shake of her head.

Johnny stared at the table in front of them, then glanced at the hounds, both of whom were busy licking the nonexistent remains of cold-cut meats and cheese off the paper plates on the floor. *Fine. Agent Breyer in a room full of bloodthirsty assholes. Lisa the mom when we're sittin' down for lunch at a damn truck stop.*

"Wait. Look at this."

"Can I open my mouth now?"

"Shut up. Here." Lisa shoved the laptop toward him again and pointed at the screen.

"Holy shit. Ameyna Frossard."

"The heiress. I guess we missed her name with all the others from the Monsters Ball. And look at the address."

"She has four."

"Yeah, the third one."

"Well, I'll be damned. Atlantean queen of crime spendin' her golden years in a damn beach house. What d'ya know?"

"We'll go see her next." She pulled her phone out and opened a GPS search. "Norfolk is only about an hour and a half from here. Two hours tops. Of course, that's assuming she's spending her time at the beach in the middle of February. It can't hurt to look, right?"

"Why the hell are you pullin' your phone out for that? You have a computer right there."

"And expose everything on it to anyone searching the Internet for us, Hamish, or this list? I don't think so."

"Wait, folks can do that?"

Lisa frowned teasingly at him before she turned her attention to typing in Ameyna's address. "Yeah, Johnny. It takes a high skill level—way above anything I can do on my own. But if someone wanted to, they could hack into any device connected to the Wi-Fi here and do some serious damage."

"So it's okay with your phone?"

"My phone doesn't have—" She glanced around the rest area again and lowered her voice. "Doesn't have sensitive information worth twenty million dollars to the asshole who turns it in."

"Huh."

"Okay, yeah. Ameyna's close enough for us to reach this address before dark. Are you up for it?"

Johnny raised an eyebrow. "Are you?"

"I'm not tired if that's what you're asking. And we already

spent way more time than I like waiting until the next meeting with Hamish. Only now, he's locked up who knows where and the clock is really ticking this time. I want to move on this."

"Well, you know I ain't gonna stop ya."

"Good." Lisa closed the laptop, unplugged the cord, and headed to the exit. "Oh, do you mind tossing my trash?"

"Nope."

"Thanks. I'll be in the car."

With a sigh, the dwarf bent to retrieve the hounds' paper plates before he dumped the rest of their lunch trash on top of them.

"Hey, Johnny, hold on!" Luther snorted and tried to lick the plate as Johnny stood to throw it out. "I wasn't finished."

"There ain't nothin' left but paper. And I ain't goin' through another round of your stomach issues when you can't lay off what ain't meant to be eaten."

"Aw, man. Rex, you got any—"

"It's all gone, bro. All gone."

He opened the door for them, and the hounds shuffled outside with their tails between their legs.

Aw, hell. Like I'm the guy who ruins all the fun.

Two hours later, the bounty hunter drove them down a long, immaculately paved driveway in Norfolk with high cliffs on one side and the white-sand beach beside the Atlantic Ocean stretching out forever on the other.

"Wow." Lisa peered out the window at the waves that crashed into the surf, then squinted through the front windshield. "We've been driving down this same road for…what? A mile? I don't even want to know what kind of money it takes to maintain something like this."

"The dirty kind."

She snorted. "Okay. Well, that goes without saying."

Johnny nodded. "It looks like that's the house up ahead."

"For all we know, it could be the groundskeeper's cottage. Or the mother-in-law suite."

"Aw, hell. That's a thing?"

"Yeah."

"Who in their right mind wants to put their mother-in-law in a suite at home? Shit, a guest room ain't enough? What's so funny?"

"That's what it's called, Johnny. It's like a separate living space for guests. You know, with its own kitchen, living area, and private entrance. Most of the time, at least."

"What does that have to do with a mother-in-law?"

"Nothing. You know what? Never mind." She tried to cover her smile as she looked out the window again. "You must have issues with in-laws."

"I never had 'em and I ain't fixin' to deal with that kinda headache anytime soon."

"Oh, okay. Well, it's a good thing I don't come with in-law baggage."

He glanced at her, then did a double-take. "Did I say somethin' wrong?"

"Nope."

"Shit, darlin'. Is it 'cause of the fact in-laws come with the whole m—" He cleared his throat and tightened his grasp on the steering wheel. "The M-word thing."

"Ha. The M-word thing."

"'Cause I didn't mean anythin' about you and me. I'm not sayin' that's ever somethin' comin' down the line, but it ain't not somethin'. Unless that little freak-out you had when I gave you the collar injection—"

"You're spinning yourself in circles right now, you know that?"

"Yep. I'm painfully aware."

"All discussions about the M-word thing aside, my parents aren't around anymore."

"Oh." The dwarf drew a deep breath and shook his head. *Why the hell didn't I jump to that answer first? Get your damn head back in the game, Johnny.* "You too, huh? I'm sorry to hear it."

"That's the way things go, right? Yeah, we live longer than humans, but there's no guarantee."

"Don't I know it. Well, hell, darlin'. If you wanted to build a mother-in-law suite, I guess it ain't the worst thing you could—"

"Stop."

He chuckled. "Come on. I'm only tryin' to have an open mind."

"No, Johnny, I mean stop!" Lisa pointed out the window at the metal bars of the automated property gate that the SUV raced toward.

"Shit." The dwarf braked hard and the vehicle skidded across the immaculate driveway with a squeal of burning rubber and a puff of dark smoke rose behind them.

Rex and Luther yelped and thumped against the backs of the front seats. "Whoa, Johnny. What gives?"

"Yeah, who taught you to drive?"

He turned to look at them. "Are you boys all right?"

"You almost made houndcakes out of us."

"Not the kind we'd wanna eat, either."

Johnny shook his head and shifted into park. "But I didn't. No blood or broken bones so y'all are fine."

"Oh, sure. Ignore all the festering wounds no one can see."

Rex sniggered. "What, you mean like you?"

"Hey."

"There's the camera," Lisa pointed out. "And a keypad for the code, I imagine."

"Too bad Hamish didn't think to put that on the list."

"Honestly?"

"Sorry."

They got out of the car to inspect the gate. The bounty hunter tugged on it a few times but the mechanism was too well-maintained to be forced without a warrant or an excuse to argue against forced entry. Lisa stepped toward the security camera mounted on the left-hand gatepost and peered into it. "Hello? We're here to see Ameyna Frossard."

"Do you think it picks up audio?"

"It might."

"Not with all the crashin' waves out here. It wouldn't be able to pick out a single word."

"Well, there might still be someone watching." She waved her hand in front of the camera twice, then stepped back. No beep and crackling voice came over the intercom and the gate didn't budge. "Great. Another dead end."

"You think?"

Lisa turned toward the ocean and folded her arms with a sigh. "Well, at least we had a great view while we wasted two more hours. I'd love to have a place like this on the water."

"You already have a place on the water."

"You can't honestly say the Atlantic Ocean and the Everglades swamp are comparable." She turned with a frown of mock disappointment, but Johnny was gone. "Where— Hey. What are you doing?"

The bounty hunter was on the other side of the gate and walked casually down the long drive toward the main house that peeked out around the bend ahead. He turned and spread his arms. "I'm takin' a closer look."

"Yeah, and trespassing."

"Do you see a No Trespassin' sign?"

"No." She frowned at Rex and Luther who scurried around the beach-side gatepost after their master. "But there's a gate. That says enough all on its own."

"The gate stops the vehicles, darlin'. If she didn't want folks walkin' up to her door on foot, she shoulda fenced it off."

"Oh, sure. With an electrical fence too, right?"

"It might be the only thing keeps me out. And even then, not for long." He disappeared around the bend of the cliffs that blocked the beach house from view.

"Hey, keep up, lady," Rex called.

"Yeah, he's not stopping now."

Lisa glanced at their rental, rolled her eyes, and finally walked around the beach-side of the gate before she jogged to catch up with them. "This isn't the best plan to go with."

"Sure it is. It's the only plan we have right now."

"If she's here, breaking onto her property won't make Ameyna any more willing to talk to us. Especially if she recognizes us."

"Naw, are you kiddin'? It's comin' up on a year since the Monsters Ball. No way is she gonna see our faces at her front door and know who we are."

"Johnny, she had the chance to kill us both in that penthouse and didn't." She hung back and folded her arms as the dwarf strode up the three wide stone steps toward the front door. "Which means she had a good reason to not do so. And if the queen of crime in the US grew a momentary conscience that worked in our favor, it's not something she'll forget."

"Or you might be makin' a mountain outta nothin'."

"Oh, sure. Okay. Remind me to say I told you so."

Johnny knocked briskly on the front door and they waited in silence. A low hiss rose from the other side before it faded and slow, light footsteps moved toward them. He turned to wiggle his eyebrows at Lisa. "Well, look at that. Someone is home."

With her lips pressed together, she shook her head and waited for Ameyna—or whoever was inside the house—to open the door. Hopefully without the added excitement of trying to kill them for trespassing.

CHAPTER TWENTY-FIVE

The door opened and Ameyna's bright green eyes peered out at the couple on her doorstep. The Atlantean woman's hair-snakes lifted from their roots in her scalp and hissed as one, followed quickly by the queen of crime's mirrored hiss. "You."

"Huh." Johnny regarded her calmly. "I didn't think you'd remember."

"What are you doing here?" The crime boss subjected them to her glowering scrutiny then snarled at the hounds who sniffed around her open door. "Out!"

"Whoa!" Luther skittered away from her and tripped once down the stairs before he righted himself and moved to stand beside Lisa. "Jeez! Is that how you treat guests?"

Rex backed away until his forepaws rested on the second-to-last step and his hind legs supported him on the drive. "You gonna teach her a lesson, Johnny or should we?"

The bounty hunter cleared his throat. "We ain't here for you, Ameyna. It's about—"

"I don't care why you think you can simply walk up onto private property for a personal chat, dwarf. The problem is that

217

you did." The Atlantean turned her gaze to Lisa again and her eyes narrowed. "And you don't look remotely surprised."

"I'm not. Come on, Johnny—"

"Now hold on a minute. We ain't gotten to the questionin' part."

"You said you weren't here for me." The two snakes at the center of her forehead undulated like long bangs in a light breeze and hissed in warning. "And I have nothing to say to you."

"We know you've been workin' with World Nexus," he said and spread his arms placatingly. "We have a whole lotta information that ain't gotta get made public. If you can tell us—"

Ameyna's lilting laughter echoed around the stone and cement courtyard built along the rising cliffs. "You truly are thick, aren't you? I could have wiped you off the face of this planet in New York, Bulldog. Not that I believed for a second that's your name."

"Johnny, actually."

"Of course it is. Only an idiot would come sniffing around the beach house of a vacationing businesswoman who spared his life for no reason other than because she felt like it."

He snorted. "That's what you're callin' yourself these days, huh?"

"Johnny, let's go." Lisa turned away from the front door.

"We're lookin' for the Light Elf World Nexus has been sendin' every Oriceran head-hunter and their sister after. Do you know anythin' about it?"

The Atlantean's nostrils flared again and she raised her chin to stare down the sharp line of her nose at him. "If I did, I certainly wouldn't tell you. I'll give you two minutes to remove yourself from my property. After that, I can't guarantee—"

She froze, whirled, and stretched her hand toward the single black snake that slithered urgently toward her from the other side of the house. When she stooped to reach it on the well-polished wooden floor, it wound itself around her hand and slithered up her arm and neck until it hissed in her ear.

With an aggravated sigh, the Atlantean pointed at the courtyard's exit. "Out! Now!"

"Is somethin' else happenin' back there?" Johnny tried to peer around her for a better view of her home. "Do you have company or what?"

"No, you stunted buffoon!"

"Hey, now—"

"It's a—"

The high-pitched whine reached them a second before an explosion wracked the rear of the beach house. The ground trembled beneath them and huge chunks of the stone wall toppled from the other side of the house and down the slope toward the sea. Ameyna staggered forward with the force of the blast, caught herself on the outer wall beside the door, and whirled to storm into her house.

"Ingrates!" she shrieked.

Johnny pointed after her and gave Lisa a knowing look. "Open door."

"No."

"It might as well be an invitation."

"Johnny—"

Another heavy explosion came from the far side of the house, this one much bigger and with twice as much force. The Atlantean's furious snarl filled the air and in the next moment, the gunfire started.

"Yeah, I'd call that probable cause." Lisa darted up the stairs and hurried through the beach house with Johnny and the hounds on her heels.

Bullets blasted through the walls and the glass of the sliding back door across the massive living room. A vase on the marble end table shattered a second before she passed it. She shielded her face but pushed through the chaos. Pieces of wall and glass and puffs of feathers from bullet-peppered upholstery filled the air.

In the next moment, everyone was outside again in the ocean breeze. Another high whine pierced the air before a third explosion wracked the dwelling. Two speedboats had skidded onto the sand at the water's edge. In one of them, a shifter knelt beside a massive rocket launcher and prepared to reload. In front of that speedboat, a Crystal wielding a fully automatic rifle sprayed the house and the back yard with gunfire. The second boat was empty because the three magicals who'd previously manned it now marched up the beach toward the residence and fired as they moved.

What the fuck do they think this is? Normandy Beach?

The bounty hunter snatched an explosive disk from his belt and punched the top button.

Lisa already had her service pistol drawn and shouted, "FBI! Lower your weapons!"

Of course, no one heard her over the rapid gunfire and the still crumbling side of the house. Johnny barely heard her before he tossed the explosive disk at the magicals who approached. It detonated a foot in front of the invaders and all three of them catapulted into the surf in a spray of sand, saltwater, screams, and more than a little blood.

His partner scowled at him in disapproval and he retrieved another disk.

Ameyna stood on the back stone patio beside the shattered sliding doors, her arms outstretched and her head completely devoid of snakes. Her hair had slithered down the mild slope toward the water's edge, almost invisible in the grass although they left trailing lines through the sand before they converged on the magicals who'd left the boats.

The Crystal thrust another magazine into the rifle and swung it toward the Atlantean woman.

"Take 'em down!" Johnny shouted as he hurled a second disk

and lunged toward Ameyna at the same time.

The hounds had already used his first explosion as cover to gain ground on the attackers. Luther leapt into the speedboat with the shifter who manned the rocket launcher. He struck the enemy in the shoulder and the weapon clunked against the side rail of the craft before the launcher toppled into the water.

At the same moment, the Crystal opened fire again, this time at Ameyna. The bounty hunter hurled himself into the Atlantean a split-second before the bullets ripped through the air where they'd stood. The two made impact with the stone floor of the patio and the freshly scabbed burn on the dwarf's left cheek broke open again on contact. She snarled and disentangled herself despite the bullets that whined over their heads.

The automatic weapons' fire lasted all of two seconds before Rex leapt at the Crystal and clamped his jaws around his forearm. The magical roared as his arm was dragged down by almost sixty pounds of coonhound, but he wasn't smart enough to release the trigger. The bullets sprayed in a wide arc across the northern corner of the house, missed Johnny and Ameyna by mere inches, and drilled into the sand to draw a line across the beach and toward the magicals recovering from his explosive disk.

"Whoa, whoa—ah!"

The Crystal eliminated two of his fellow attackers before he finally dropped the rifle in the sand to deal with Rex, who'd made himself an extra growth on the guy's forearm.

The shifter leapt from the other speedboat and landed on all fours as a shaggy gray wolf. Luther raced after him and snarled and snapped at the wolf's heels.

The single magical who'd escaped being gunned down by friendly fire trained his pistol on Rex instead and tried to get a clear shot as the Crystal swung his arm frantically and drove his other fist into the hound's flank.

Lisa ran down the beach. She fired two shots at the wizard with his gun trained on Rex, then shot one at the Crystal. Her bullet ricocheted off the giant magical's back, which made her pause with a confused frown before she shook herself out of it and summoned a fury of fireballs instead. Those drew her adversary's attention and he turned toward her with a bellow and summoned a flurry of icy shards in the hand not dragged down by Rex, who tried to jerk him along the beach.

With all weapons discarded, buried in sand, or washed out by the surf, Johnny drew his knife and raced toward the water. Luther and the gray wolf struggled on the sand and the wolf uttered a blood-curdling howl. It ended abruptly in a yelp and a snort, and the hound immediately disengaged when he saw the horde of black hair-snakes whipping around the shifter's paws and ankles.

"What the—" The hound backed away swiftly along the sand, his tail tucked between his legs as Ameyna's hair-snakes swarmed up the gray wolf's legs and covered him in what looked like a writhing mass of shimmering black scales.

Johnny reached the Crystal as the bellowing magical dropped to one knee and pounded his hound-held arm into the sand. Rex yelped at the impact and released his hold before he rolled away. The bounty hunter bulldozed into the Crystal before the guy could stand and he thumped onto his back in the sand. A larger wave crashed onto the beach and sprayed behind the magical's head, blinding him before the dwarf sat on his chest with the blade of his utility knife pressed against his throat.

"Don't move, asshole!" he warned.

The Crystal snarled. "Do it! We'll simply keep coming."

"Naw. You're still a little useful—until I decide you're not. I got a lotta questions and you're gonna answer every single—"

Ameyna shrieked in rage as she raced down the gentle hill toward them and seemed to float across the ground. Her hair-snakes disengaged from the shifter to rush toward their mistress and left the magical in his humanoid form on the sand. He gasped raw, ragged breaths, his eyes wide as he struggled to breathe while blood from hundreds of puncture wounds trickled across his body.

By the time the Atlantean woman reached Johnny seated on the Crystal's chest, her hair-snakes had swarmed up her body and attached themselves to her head. "Leave him!"

He scowled at her. "For what?"

"For me to deal with as I see fit, dwarf! He's a trespasser on my property."

"Oh, only for the tresspassin' then, huh? All right." He swung a leg over the Crystal as he removed the blade tip, then socked the guy in the jaw for good measure. "Do you think you can get a confession outta the bastard?"

Ameyna hissed and approached the invader. In one swift move, she dropped to one knee in the sand and thrust her palm on his chest. He grunted and all the woman's hair-snakes jerked toward his face to echo a furious hiss. "How long have you been watching me?"

The Crystal stared at the dozens of snakeheads. "Long enough to know you've gone soft."

"That's not an answer!"

The guy chuckled in an effort to keep his composure while the Atlantean pressed down on him with surprising force. "Devon's disappointed in you. He says it's time to—"

With another shriek of rage, Ameyna swiped her hand across his throat and blood sprayed across the sand. He choked, raised one hand halfway to his throat, then thumped back onto the sand and bled out in seconds.

"Aw, hell." Johnny's shoulders slumped. "There goes our interrogation."

Ameyna stood and watched the Crystal's blood stain the sand.

"Johnny." Lisa waved him toward her and the hounds, who stood around the naked shifter lying on the beach while his face turned an alarming shade of purplish-blue. His chest jerked and bucked but only a few strangled gasps reached his lungs.

"Damn." The dwarf pointed at Luther. "I guess that ain't from you."

"What? No!" Luther crouched low on the sand and studied the suffering shifter with wide eyes. "But it doesn't look good."

"He's finished," Ameyna said as she walked slowly toward them. "There's no saving him so don't even try."

"What happened?" Lisa asked.

"He got what he deserved." The Atlantean brushed one of her snakes away from her face and it wound itself lovingly around her finger.

Johnny frowned as he studied the shifter. "Your snakes did this?"

"I thought they were only for…you know." Lisa shrugged. "Reconnaissance?"

A small, unamused smile lifted the corner of Ameyna's mouth. "Not mine."

"Damn."

"Hey, Johnny." Luther uttered a low whine and stepped away from the dying shifter. "Where's Rex?"

The two partners turned to see the larger hound limp across the beach toward them, covered in sand and seafoam.

"I'm good, Johnny. All—" Rex yelped when he put his right forepaw down at the wrong angle and lifted it again quickly. "All good."

"It don't look like it." Johnny knelt at the hound's side to inspect the favored paw.

Ameyna frowned. "Doesn't look like what?"

Rex gazed at his master with huge, glistening eyes. "She can't hear us."

"It don't look like it's broken," the bounty hunter replied and nodded at the hound before he gave Rex's head a gruffly loving scratch. "He'll be all right."

"Then I suggest you come inside." The Atlantean looked from

Johnny to Lisa and back again. "It turns out we have something to discuss after all."

Without another word, she stormed up the beach and the hill toward the half-demolished back of her beach house. Her flowing, cream-colored pants and matching blouse whipped around her limbs in the rising ocean breeze as the sky darkened.

Johnny raised an eyebrow at Lisa. "Somethin' to discuss, huh? It only took a siege to make her open to the idea."

She shook her head and glanced at the shifter before she turned toward the house. He'd stopped moving.

CHAPTER TWENTY-SIX

"I don't take betrayal lightly," Ameyna said where she sat on her expensive, dark-purple divan like a queen on her throne. The fact that the furniture was riddled with bullet holes and leaked its stuffing on one side somehow didn't diminish the effect in the least.

"Yep." The two investigators sat on the sofa opposite their previously unwilling host. "You made that very damn clear with the whole…" He drew a finger across his throat and made a choking sound.

Ameyna was unamused. "Some of my associates appear to have decided to turn against me. Naturally, I'm offended."

Lisa widened her eyes. "Naturally."

"But I would be more inclined to strike additional deals if the two of you were open to the same. Assuming, of course, that you're willing to take a few names and excise the filth from the equation."

The dwarf leaned toward his partner and muttered, "Does that mean she wants to cooperate?"

"That's what it sounds like, yeah."

The Atlantean stared intently at them. Her hair-snakes waved

227

around her head and made it look like she sat on an underwater throne.

Starin' at that for too long is gonna make me dizzy.

He cleared his throat. "All right. Here's what we have."

It took him ten minutes to give their hostess a summary of what they wanted and what they were up against, with the occasional clarification from Lisa.

"So." He folded his arms and leaned back on the couch. "Do you have somethin' we can use?"

"That depends." Ameyna raised her chin speculatively. "How many copies of this list exist?"

"Only one," Lisa said quickly. "And we have it."

"Good. I'll help you find the Light Elf and decrypt the rest of the information on that list—for a price."

"Which is?"

The woman ran her hands along the seat cushion of the divan and crossed one leg over the other. "That you remove my name entirely from said list."

"Deal."

"Johnny—"

"It's a damn good offer, darlin'. We oughta take it before she changes her mind."

Lisa grabbed his wrist and forced a smile at their host. "Excuse us for a moment."

Ameyna inclined her head and watched as they left the destroyed living room for a private conversation.

"We can't take her name off that list."

"Why not?" The dwarf glanced at the hounds, who'd made themselves comfortable on any patch of floor they could find that wasn't covered in shards of glass and pottery or rubble from the exploded walls. "She has information. We need that information. Deletin' one name ain't gonna change the fact that we're getting' what we need."

"Johnny, it's evidence-tampering." She glanced into the living room again but Ameyna stared out the wall of shattered windows at the darkening ocean. "Not to mention making a deal with a known criminal. One of the worst."

"Aw, come on. Don't tell me you ain't never used a little extra juice to grease the gears."

"You mean getting into bed with a crime lord to get what I want out of it and calling it a necessary evil?" She folded her arms and shook her head slowly. "No. I've never done that."

"Huh. Well, there's a first time for everythin'."

"Johnny—"

"Look, if she has a way to find Hamish, don't you think it's worth a little smudge on your clean record?"

"And my conscience." Lisa grimaced and stared through the open front door, which no one had bothered to close since they'd arrived. "But you're right. This is for Hamish."

"Yeah." He placed a hand on her shoulder and nodded. "Muddyin' our lines of morality ain't nearly as hard when it's our kids on the line."

She responded with a strained chuckle. "The joys of parenthood."

"It's the right thing, darlin', even if it all feels wrong."

Nodding, she turned away from him and returned to the couch.

Damn. I thought she was rubbin' off on me some, but now it's the other way around. I'd better make this the first and last time.

Johnny rejoined the women in the living room and sat as Lisa said, "Fine, Ameyna. We'll take your name and addresses off the list."

"Addresses?" The Atlantean's green eyes widened. "As in multiple?"

"All four of 'em," the bounty hunter added.

The woman chuckled softly. "Well, that's a relief. There are seven."

Lisa opened her mouth to respond, shook her head furiously, then simply said, "Oh."

"I'll make a call. I have a Wood Elf in my employ who understands far more about information technology than I ever well. He's very good."

"Great."

"I will need reassurances."

"Like what?" Lisa asked.

"Watching you remove my name is a good start. Followed by you sending the updated information to whoever you send it to at the FBI."

"I…" The agent frowned. "How do you know I'm with the FBI?"

"I have a long memory, Agent Breyer. If I hadn't heard you identifying yourself at the Monsters Ball last year, I most certainly would have been reminded of it today. You practically screamed it outside too."

Johnny snorted and pressed a fist to his mouth when it earned him a scathing look from his partner.

Ameyna stood and gazed around her destroyed house. "I won't be more than a few minutes. Feel free to make yourselves at home, for what it's worth."

Lisa waited until their hostess disappeared down the hallway before she muttered, "Not much."

"Oh, come on, darlin'. Her whole reputation is at stake here. Not to mention her empire. I can tell when someone ain't bein' straight with me and despite all them wiggly critters on her damn head, Ameyna's as straight as a crooked magical can get."

"This is new for me, so you'll have to excuse me if I'm not in love with the fact that this particular Atlantean knows my real name and what I do and exactly what we're after."

"I ain't in love with it, either. But it brings us one step closer."

An hour later, with the sun fully set and the nippy ocean air howling through the shattered windows and into the house, the investigators stood at the dining room table and scrutinized the work of the Wood Elf specialist the Atlantean had called in for their "favor."

Lisa had brought her laptop in from the car, which the Wood Elf now hooked up to a gadget he had brought before he typed furiously on the clunky device he called his laptop.

"Now what exactly is that there you're doin'?" Johnny pointed at the screen and the elf slapped his hand away with a growl.

"None of your business."

"It is when it's our damn file you're screwin' around with."

The magical snarled but focused on the screen and continued to type. "I wasn't called here to teach Decryption 101, so fuck off."

"All right. It's like that, huh?"

"Maybe we should give him some space," Lisa suggested and gestured for Johnny to step away with her.

"Oh, look." The Wood Elf snorted. "One of you has a brain."

The dwarf leaned toward him. "Listen here, bud—"

"It's time for a break." She seized his hand and dragged him away from the table.

"What? Do you wanna let this asshole walk all over us with his fuckin' mouth—"

"Johnny, you convinced me to strike an unsanctioned deal with one of New England's most dangerous magicals because we're focusing on what matters—Hamish. Please don't screw it up by letting your ego get in the way. Okay?"

He sighed and pulled his hand away before he paced across the dining room.

The Wood Elf typed enthusiastically without pause, even when he glanced at Ameyna standing at the opposite end of the table.

"Speak your mind, Frank."

He shook his head. "It's only an observation but this looks like you're starting to lose your touch."

"Oh, does it?" The Atlantean folded her arms and raised her chin to study her employee's eyes instead of his flying fingers.

"You know who they are, right? The goddamn bounty hunter and his—"

"I'm perfectly aware but thank you for your unsolicited concern."

"Unless you suddenly decided it was better to squeal to the feds, I don't get why the hell you're helping them."

Ameyna slammed her fist on the table and Lisa's laptop jumped and clattered onto the polished wood that had been chipped in the gunfight. "Because I've done more for Devon than half of the alliance combined, and World Nexus tried to kill me! Me! The line stops here, do you understand?"

Frank's fingers had stopped their ceaseless typing on his clunky keyboard and he stared at his boss with a completely blank expression. "Yes, ma'am."

The woman removed her fist slowly from the table, then walked slowly around it with her nostrils flaring. "That was a reminder of who you work for, Frank."

"I know." He looked briefly at her as she paused beside him. "You don't do warnings."

"And it seems I've given you too much leeway with sharing your opinions. Keep them to yourself."

The Wood Elf nodded and Ameyna floated past him before she turned down the hall and disappeared into another room.

Johnny and Lisa watched the whole exchange from the living room and even the hounds had rolled out of their short naps to witness it.

"Huh. And I thought I already knew why they called her the queen." He raised his hand to scratch his cheek and hissed sharply. "Goddammit."

Lisa turned toward him in concern. "What happened?"

"I opened my mug up again savin' the Medusa-wannabe's

hide, is what." He grimaced and pulled his head away when she tried to inspect the open wound. "I'm fine."

"Johnny, you have sand and who knows what else embedded in your flesh."

"And I'll deal with it later, darlin'. I'm fine."

When Frank finally finished with the rest of the decryption, he interlaced his fingers to stretch them, closed his clunky laptop, unplugged everything, and tucked his device under one arm. Then, he turned to face the private investigators seated in his boss' living room and snorted. "It's done. Have a nice life."

He stormed past them and through the front door. They stood and watched the Wood Elf vanish from the courtyard down the pristine driveway.

"That was…anticlimactic."

"No shit."

"Don't mind him," Ameyna called from the entrance to the hall. "What Frank lacks in social skills, he more than makes up for in ability. Shall we take a look?"

They converged at the dining room table to study the now fully decrypted file on Lisa's laptop. She scrolled through the information and nodded. "It looks like he did exactly what he said he would."

Johnny snorted and leaned toward the screen with wide eyes. "And we have ourselves a damn information bomb right here. Are you seein' all this?"

"Yeah." She scrolled lower. "Wow. No wonder they want this back. Look at this. Every single magical who had an invitation to the Monsters Ball."

"And then some."

"Yes, it's all very illuminating." Ameyna sneered at Lisa. "But I'm afraid I won't be able to let you leave the property until your side of our arrangement is fulfilled."

"I know what we agreed to." With a scowl, Lisa searched for the

Atlantean's information and deleted everything when she found it. With that done, she made quite a show of resaving the file on her laptop and permanently erasing previous versions. "There."

"That's one half accomplished."

Lisa gave her a strained grimace of a smile as she took her phone from her pocket. "You're enjoying this, aren't you?"

"Not as much as you enjoy getting what you wanted, I hope."

"Who you callin'?" Johnny asked.

"Nelson." She stepped away from the table to find a semblance of privacy for the call.

Johnny and his hostess exchanged a strained glance and the woman shrugged.

Yeah, she's gettin' a helluva kick outta the whole damn thing.

"Nelson."

"Tommy, it's Lisa."

"Let me guess. Something went wrong and you need a second opinion."

She turned away from the dining room and stepped toward the open door. "More like we need your help. And the department."

The other side of the line was silent for a long moment before Nelson cleared his throat. "I'm listening."

She told him everything she and Johnny knew about the whistle-blower who'd come to them looking for immunity and a way to get this list into the right hands—the exorbitant bounty on the Light Elf's head and the fact that he was in Nexus' clutches, the list itself, and what having this information would mean for the FBI and the department. The only thing she didn't reveal was that the whistle-blower was her son and how close she was to the whole can of worms Hamish had opened.

"Damn. How the hell didn't we know about this?"

"Whoever World Nexus is, they've put considerable resources into keeping it under wraps."

"Yeah, it sounds like it. Who's your CI?"

"I can't tell you that, Tommy."

"You promised him a free pass on your PI firm's reputation, huh?" The agent chuckled wryly. "All right. If we have our hands on that list, I guess it doesn't matter who or where it came from. Send it to me and I'll have a team pulled together and ready for operations in twenty-four hours."

"Yeah, I'll get it to you after the call. Thanks."

"No, thank you. I…uh, I guess you and Johnny are still planning to take the lead on this one?"

"We're already deep in this so might as well keep going."

"Yep." After another long pause, Tommy drew a sharp breath. "Is there anything else you want to tell me? You sound a little off."

"I'm only…" She turned again to meet Johnny's gaze, then sighed. "No. I'm a little surprised by what it took to break this wide open. Look for my email."

"Okay. Hey, tell Johnny hi for me."

"Sure." After she ended the call, she slid her phone into her pocket and returned to the dining room.

"What did he say?"

"They'll get on it." She avoided looking at Ameyna as she pulled her email up and sent Nelson the entire list of what would most likely now be the FBI's most wanted. The Atlantean woman watched intently until she sent the email and the page on the screen was replaced by a confirmation that she'd sent a highly secured email to the FBI's private servers. "Satisfied?"

Ameyna smiled. "Certainly."

"Good." Lisa closed her laptop and tucked it under her arm. "Do you have any idea who would have had access to the Light Elf before we met with him last night?"

"Is this another offer for an exchange?"

"No. I'm asking you a question. Call it on good faith."

"Ha." The Atlantean's lilting laugh made the agent step away. "Good faith. That doesn't regularly surface in my typical conversations."

"This isn't a typical conversation."

"Very true, Agent Breyer. If you're asking who might have overheard your first meeting with the defector or received the last-minute details of your most recent meeting with him, I unfortunately don't have the answer."

"Right. It was worth a try." She nodded at Johnny and headed out of the dining room. "Let's go."

"But I do know who deals in sensitive information in this part of the country," Ameyna added. "An information broker—underground, of course. If she didn't have something to do with the attack herself, she likely knows who was responsible and how they came to have those details in the first place."

Lisa paused in the center of the room, turned halfway, and stared at the Atlantean woman. "A name would go a hell of a long way, Ameyna."

When the woman grinned to reveal razor-sharp teeth, all her snakes stood on end and hissed with renewed force. "Hannah Penton."

"Oh, shit." Johnny glanced at the hounds, who had now stood and were as ready to get out of there as Lisa was.

"Do you know where to find her?" Ameyna asked.

"Yeah, I have an idea." Rolling her eyes, she stormed out of the beach house and didn't slow until she reached their rental.

CHAPTER TWENTY-SEVEN

"You were right." Lisa propped her elbow on the passenger armrest and rubbed a finger over her lips as Johnny drove them away from the beach house in the general direction of Richmond. "And I was too pissed off about seeing her that I didn't pay attention."

"Naw, you paid attention fine. It's harder to put stock in a gut feelin' when it ain't about a case and you have both goin' on at the same time."

"I should have known Hannah was more involved in this."

"Well, we ain't sure she did know about our meetin's with Hamish—or any of the rest of it."

"But we'll find out." She slumped in the seat and gazed out the window at the night sky. "First thing in the morning."

"You mean you been shot at multiple times, crushed by fallin' buildings, and tried to seduce a wizard mob boss all in the last forty-eight hours and you ain't feelin' up to goin' after someone else?"

"Well, when you say it like that…"

Johnny gave her his crooked smile and took the highway exit toward their hotel in Richmond. "Naw, I reckon it's better for both of us if we get some shuteye first and start kickin' ass in the morin'. Do you think Hannah's gonna be around in the mornin'?"

"If she's anything like she was twenty years ago, she's always around."

The next morning as they readied themselves to take another drive to Jackson Ward to start looking for Hannah Penton at Happy's, Lisa's phone rang with an unrecognized number. With a frown, she silenced the call and returned the phone to her pocket.

"Who's that?"

"I have no idea. Which means either a solicitor or a wrong number." The same number called twice in the next three minutes, however, and she finally gave in and answered. "Hello?"

"Lisa?"

"Yeah."

"Hey, kid. It's Jack."

"What?" A surprised laugh escaped her, and she walked absently across the room while Johnny finished gathering all the weapons he wanted to bring with them for a nice shakedown. "How did you get this number?"

"I pulled your file."

"Wow. So twelve years of nothing and you suddenly decide to pull a file and look me up? It doesn't sound like you."

The dwarf scowled as she paced absently with a hand on her hip. "Who is it?"

She turned toward him and mouthed, "I'll tell you later."

"It was sudden, sure, but not random. Listen, I know time's short for you so I'll lay it all out there. I know about Hamish."

"What?" She froze in the center of the hotel room as the blood drained from her face.

"I've worked a few other cases in and around the Virginia area," Jack continued, his voice low. "I heard a few things from a few of my other field agents. When I got the briefing about what Nelson's putting together for you to retrieve this whistle-blower from World Nexus, I put two and two together. I know Hamish is the kidnapping victim and I know you're on this."

A massive, defeated sigh escaped her. "Jack, please don't say anything about it, okay? I'm on this. I have Johnny with me—"

"Johnny Walker?"

"Yeah. And I know I'm close to this, but we're onto something seriously big."

"Oh, I know. Hey, don't worry, kid. I'm not gonna blow the top off your secret. I know how much he means to you and how deep this goes. I called to beg you off this case, Lisa. Drop it. Let those in the department who don't have any skin in this do their jobs with a clear head."

"I have a clear head."

"Yeah, I know you do and always did. But this is different."

Lisa scoffed, glared at Johnny, and only realized she was doing it when he spread his arms and shook his head in confusion. "I'm not taking myself off the case, Jack. It's out of the question. Do you understand?"

"Yeah." The older agent sighed on the other end of the phone. "I hear you loud and clear, kid. And honestly, I expected you to stick to your guns like this, which is why I put in an emergency request to be your point of contact on this instead of Nelson."

She swallowed thickly. "You…"

"Tommy Nelson doesn't give a shit about Hamish and you know it. Probably because he's never met him, but what Nelson doesn't know won't boost his motivation any. So you'll call in to me from now on."

"And the department approved this?"

"A hundred percent. So while Nelson's here putting an ops team together to find your son, here's where you need to start. Hannah Penton."

"Ha." She sat slowly on the couch and stared at the ugly hotel carpet. "Yeah, that was already the plan. We were about to head to Happy's—"

"Well, you won't find her there. Today, the Kilomea's supposed to meet a couple of low-level thugs to broker some kind of protection deal for their bosses."

"And you know this how?"

"I told you I have other cases and other agents, kid. But the source is reliable and you know I can multitask the hell out of anything."

"Right. Okay." She hurried toward the small desk built into the wall, snatched up the blank pad of paper and pen from beside the lamp, and tucked the phone between her ear and shoulder. "Time and location. I'm ready."

When she finished the call and hung up, Johnny stood in the center of the room with his arms folded and scowled at her. "I think right now counts as telling me later."

"What?"

"Who was that?"

"Oh." She tapped the pen against the notepad and tried to move past her lingering surprise. "Jack Brogan. He's switched between multiple departments for as long as I've known him, but I guess he's currently standing in for Monsters and Magicals."

"How many other damn feds have your number?"

"Probably only Jack and Tommy."

"On a first-name basis and everythin', huh?"

"It's not like that." She tore the top sheet of paper off and tossed the pad onto the desk. "I guess you could say Jack was like my mentor when I joined the department. He showed me the ropes and took me on a few ride-alongs with some of his simpler cases."

"And he's callin' you now outta the blue."

Lisa slid the new address into her pocket and retrieved her jacket from where it hung over the back of the chair. "No. He knows about Hamish and he knows Hamish. He put in a request to be our contact point while we finish this."

Johnny stared at her and his scowl deepened. "What the hell does he think he's doin'?"

"Helping us, Johnny. That was his price for keeping Hamish's name and his connection to me out of the equation—that he takes over on the back end."

"I don't trust a single goddamn inch of this."

"Well, you trust me, don't you?"

He cocked his head. "'Course I do. You know that."

"Okay. And I trust Jack completely. He's...I don't know. Like family."

"Uh-huh. Family you ain't seen or talked to in twelve years? Yeah, I was listenin'. Would Hamish consider him family too?"

"It doesn't matter as long as we get my son out of wherever he's being held and destroy World Nexus in the process. Let's go. He gave me a meeting location for Hannah." Without waiting for the bounty hunter to agree—or disagree—she stormed out of the hotel and left the door wide open behind her.

With a growl, Johnny strapped on the upgraded pistol he'd brought—this one with actual bullets—and took the rest of his fighting gear with him to follow her. "Come on, boys. This sure as shit had better be our last stop."

Rex and Luther leapt to their feet. "You don't sound too sure about that, Johnny."

"Yeah, you sound like this isn't gonna work out."

"Oh, you know what it is?" Rex sniffed his master's hand as the dwarf closed the door behind him and headed down the hall. "Yeah, that's it. You smell like this is a trap, Johnny."

He frowned at the hounds and scoffed. "You can smell all that in my hand?"

"Totally."

After a quick scan of the end of the hallway where Lisa had disappeared around the corner and taken the stairwell to the ground floor, he lowered his voice to ask, "What does she smell like?"

Luther sat to scratch vigorously at his ear. "Like she's gonna kill someone."

"Huh. Lemme know if it changes."

The location Jack Brogan had given them was for a little hole-in-the-wall Asian diner west of Short Pump, Virginia. The parking lot was relatively empty, which also didn't necessarily mean anything. Lisa double-checked her magazine before she got out of the car, then stormed across the parking lot toward the low, squat building surrounded by nothing but empty lots.

"Wait—hold on." Johnny scanned the area before he hurried after her. "What are you gonna do, huh? Simply barge in there with guns blazin'?"

"That's the plan. And it's usually your plan."

"Yeah, it's a helluva good plan, but don't you think we should go in there with an actual—"

"Johnny, it's been almost a week since I walked into my apartment and found it ransacked. Hamish has spent the last three days in the hands of World Nexus. Given what we know about assholes like this, we could both make a fairly decent guess about what the hell they're doing to him. I won't waste more time simply to come up with a plan for dealing with a Kilomean information broker I should have bagged during my first year with the department. Are you with me or not?"

"Hey. I'm always with ya, darlin'. No question."

"Good. Then cover me." She stalked across the parking lot and left him to make a split-second decision.

"Stay on her, boys."

"Yeah, Johnny. We got it."

"Stay close to Lisa. That's easy."

"Whatever happens in there, y'all do whatever you gotta do to make sure she walks out again after. Got it?"

"We're your hounds, Johnny."

"Yeah, read you loud and clear." Luther whipped his head up to look at his master as Rex hurried after Lisa. "What about you?"

"Naw, I ain't worried about me. Git on." As the smaller hound caught up to his brother, Johnny strode across the cracked, split asphalt with weeds growing in the spaces and settled his hand over the hilt of his utility knife.

CHAPTER TWENTY-EIGHT

Lisa threw open the front door of the Asian diner and stepped into a dimly lit room. All the tables and chairs had been cleared to rest against the walls except for one. The single large, circular table almost filled the center of the dining area, and Hannah Penton sat at it with four wizards in matching suits of royal blue. They all turned to look at her as she entered, and one of the men snarled in disgust when he saw Rex and Luther sneak through the door behind her. "No dogs allowed."

"If you have a problem with my hounds," Johnny said as he entered the diner and pulled the door shut behind him with a bang, "I don't give a shit."

"What a nice surprise." Hannah's beady eyes widened as she studied the newcomers almost dismissively. "Usually, I'm the one who finds those who don't want to be found. Maybe you have improved your game since we were all drinking our sorrows away in Happy's twenty years ago."

"We were drinking," Lisa said. "You were merely gathering information to use against whoever seemed like the most desperate target."

The Kilomea spread her thick arms as if in response to a compliment and leaned back in the chair. "It's what I do, honey."

"And now you're done. Who—"

"Oh." The giant woman—whose human illusion remained mostly intact—responded with deep, rumbling laughter. "You came here to ask who knows about Hamish, right?"

"I—"

"At this point, Lisa, I'd say that's most of at least four different crime rings on the east coast. Have a seat." Hannah gestured to the open chairs around the table and two of the wizards she'd been meeting with looked remarkably offended.

"I won't sit down with you." Lisa's hand twitched in her effort to not draw her pistol and put two bullets between the dark, beady eyes in the ginormous face.

"Aw… I thought we could catch up for old time's sake. No?" The woman sniggered. "Fine. You can tell me what I want to know and then you can be on your way." Her smile vanished instantly and a low growl escaped her as her upper lip peeled away from her teeth to reveal the half-illusion of her longer-than-normal canines. "Where's the list?"

"What?"

"Playing the gorgeous but aggravatingly dumb federal agent doesn't do you any favors, Lisa." Hannah pounded a fist on the table. "We know you have it—that Hamish gave it to you before the northern chapter knocked him out cold and hauled him away. You know, I'm curious as to which hurt more. Watching your son being hauled off by the organization he betrayed or having your leg crushed by a piece of building. It was your leg, wasn't it—"

Lisa drew her pistol and aimed it at the Kilomea with both hands. "You stop talking."

"Why? We're getting down to the good stuff." The woman didn't even blink. "Who else have you told, hmm? Your friends at the FBI? Or—wait. I suppose they aren't your friends anymore if you've all but turned in your federal ID to play private eye and house with the dwarf and his overly inflated ego."

Johnny stepped forward to put himself between his partner and the table—not because he was trying to protect her but because the gun in her hands shook visibly. *She ain't gonna shoot right the first time and then we're all screwed.*

"We're the one askin' questions here," he snapped as he approached slowly. He thumped both hands down beside the massive woman—who miraculously didn't need more than one chair to hold her giant form—and snarled in her face. "Who took the Light Elf?"

Hannah hissed at him. "We're all in this together now, dwarf. If one of us makes a move, we all do. And you made the wrong one."

The four wizards at the table shoved their chairs back and stood to draw their weapons. In the blink of an eye, Lisa and Johnny both had a barrel each aimed at their chests and heads and the Kilomea had another hearty laugh over the situation.

"You're so close but you're only two magicals against an entire organization spanning two worlds. Tell me what you did with that list and we can talk about a trade."

Johnny still leaned over her with his hands planted firmly on the table, but he studied the wizards furtively from the corner of his eye. "Lisa?"

"What?"

"How do you feel about makin' a deal?"

Her pistol lowered slightly before she remembered herself and re-centered her aim on the closest wizard. "Are you fucking kidding me right now, Johnny?"

"Yeah, I didn't think so." He launched himself back and thrust his elbow into the gut of the man behind him before he spun to knock the gun from the magical's hand. Two other wizards fired shots at him as he ducked beneath the table. The bullets whined past less than an inch away from Hannah's head before they drilled into the restaurant wall.

"Don't shoot at me, you morons!" the Kilomea roared as she heaved herself out of the chair. "Get—"

Johnny thrust both hands against the underside of the round table and shoved it sideways on top of the two wizards across from the huge information broker. One of them fired another round that struck the ceiling before they were both buried beneath the heavy wood.

Lisa whipped her firearm toward the fourth wizard and squeezed off two shots—one in each of the guy's thighs above the knee. He fell with a scream and his gun clattered noisily. She stepped toward him to kick his weapon away and trained her pistol on Hannah again.

An agonized scream came from the front door, where the wizard Johnny had disarmed failed to retrieve his tossed weapon. He suddenly found himself with one coonhound on his back who snarled and snapped at the back of his neck and another with his jaws clamped around his calf.

"Fucking dogs! Get 'em off me!"

The dwarf glanced at his partner. "You got her?"

"Oh, yeah." She seethed as she held her weapon trained on Hannah Penton's chest and this time, her hands didn't shake at all.

He stalked toward the wizard who flailed wildly and tried to punch and kick Rex and Luther off him. The bounty hunter stooped to grasp the discarded firearm and uttered a piercing whistle. Both hounds leapt off the man before Johnny swung the pistol butt against the magical's temple. The wizard grunted and slumped into unconsciousness.

Hannah sneered at them both as they regrouped to corner her. "You have no idea how deep this rabbit hole goes, Lisa. You're choosing a much harder road than one I can offer you."

"I don't want anything you have you to offer," Lisa retorted. "I want my son—"

The back door into the diner's kitchen exploded off its hinges before two massive Kilomea stormed into the dining room. The one who'd damaged the heavy swinging door stooped to pick it up and hurled it across the restaurant like a frisbee. Lisa leapt back barely in time to avoid having her head taken off. Johnny ducked into a slide toward the kitchen, drew an exploding disk from his belt, and activated the top button.

Hannah, on the other hand, had enough time to see the door careen toward her and tried to stagger out of the way. She was bigger than it, however, and made an excellent target. The bottom edge caught her in the thighs and the top half swung up on impact to smack her in the face with a metallic gong.

The dwarf's explosive disk detonated between the Kilomeas as the woman's large body landed heavily. The explosion rippled and shuddered through the restaurant and flung the other two attackers into the kitchen amidst the clatter of pots and pans and dishes raining around them. When he stood, he turned to check on Lisa and the huge information broker and laughed. "That's one hell of an aim."

Lisa stared in surprise but didn't lower her weapon.

Rex sniggered as he trotted toward the completely unconscious Hannah to give her a quick sniff. "Oh-ho, shit! Did you see that?"

Luther lifted a leg over the fallen wizard at the front door and gave him a final wet canine salute. "That was awesome. Hey, Johnny, it's like that time you stepped on that shovel behind the shed—"

Johnny snapped his fingers. "That's enough. And it ain't nothin' like that."

Lisa pressed her lips together and turned slowly to meet the bounty hunter's gaze. She burst out laughing despite how hard she tried to suck it down. The effect was a chaotic sputter of chokes and shrieks of laughter before she finally reined it in.

He raised an eyebrow. "Are you gonna make it?"

"What? Yeah. I only… Sorry." She cleared her throat and trained her pistol on Hannah's unconscious form again. "This whole situation is so weird."

"Hey, if anyone knows how well stormin' in and startin' a fight can work, it's us. Hell of a plan, huh?"

"Yeah… I should call this in, right?"

"You do that. I'll go check the rest of the place and make sure there ain't more idiots comin' in to break the party up. Hell, if there was ever a time to make themselves useful—"

Another crazed laugh escaped his partner but she forced it aside and shook her head. "Yeah. Good idea."

There were no other magicals on the premises working for or with Hannah Penton. By the time he returned through the kitchen and entered the dining room, Lisa had zip-tied three of the four wizards and handed Johnny another pair before she nodded toward the groaning wizard at the front door.

"Aw, that's sweet, darlin'. But you didn't have to save one for me to make me feel included or nothin'.'"

She grinned. "I didn't. But one of your hounds peed on wizard number four. There's a social contract about cleaning up after your pets, especially in public."

With a disappointed glance at Luther, Johnny snatched the zip-ties from her and stalked toward the stinking wizard. "A social contract ain't a goddamn contract."

"It's close enough." Lisa approached Hannah slowly and crouched beside the huge woman. The information broker's human illusion had disappeared completely now that she was out cold, and her full Kilomea appearance made the agent pause. Even through the dark hair covering almost every inch of the magical's face, the massive knot growing in the center of her forehead was unmistakable. "Damn. No wonder you work so hard to keep appearances up."

Rex trotted up beside her and snorted. "Holy shit, lady. That's the ugliest two-legs I've ever seen!"

She chuckled. "Inside matches the outside, right?"

Lisa couldn't roll Hannah on her own to get another pair of zip-ties on her, so she settled for searching through the pockets of the woman's expensive peacoat. The first turned up two burner phones. The second, however, produced a long, slim box. She opened it immediately to find a silver pen nestled in a foam cushion. Instead of ink inside the pen, there was a thin orange glow that couldn't have possibly been ink. "Johnny."

"Yeah." He grunted and stood, took a tentative sniff at his hands, then scowled and walked toward the only fully conscious wizard with both legs shot above the knees. The magical jerked away from him but he'd only approached to use his shirt as a cloth to wipe his hands. "What did ya find?"

"I don't know but I've seen one of these before."

"Oh, yeah?"

Lisa stood to show him the glowing pen. "I'd completely forgotten about it with everything we had going on at the time—you know, the borgs, Amanda, and trying to decide which case came next. But I took something exactly like this from Marcel Calloway."

"The arms dealer?"

She handed him the pen and nodded. "Yeah. What do you want to bet we'd find Marcel's name on the list too?"

"It wouldn't surprise me in the least. But we dealt with him at his damn ranch in Texas."

"I know. I have no idea what that is but it's certainly not a pen."

"No, it ain't." Johnny handed it to her. "Do you have the other one?"

"No. It's back at the cabin. But if—"

The front door of the restaurant opened with a bang, and half a dozen men stormed inside with their hands on their weapons.

"Well." Lisa shoved the non-pen into her pocket and shrugged. "It looks like the clean-up crew's here." She pointed at Hannah and addressed the response team. "This is the one you want to question out of all of them. It might take extra gear to get her out of here."

The closest man studied the huge prone form and raised his eyebrows. "Yeah, no kidding."

"Agent Breyer."

She and Johnny both looked at the front door and a man in a dark-gray suit with salt-and-pepper hair and a finely trimmed goatee who stood against the mid-morning light. Lisa stared in surprise before her face broke into a wide grin. "Jack."

He surveyed the mess inside the restaurant and nodded toward the parking lot. "Come join me outside."

Turning toward Johnny, she muttered, "Don't make a big deal out of it."

"I thought he was supposed to be point of contact, not in the field with us."

"I know. But there must be a good reason for it so let's go see why he's here."

They skirted the unconscious wizards and the response team that had already begun to clear the mess they'd made. Agent Jack Brogan waited for them in the parking lot with his arms folded. When they reached him, he extended a hand toward Johnny and gave the dwarf a weak smile. "Johnny Walker, I'm guessing."

"Uh-huh."

"Jack Brogan. Nice to finally meet you."

The bounty hunter stared at the man's hand, then sniffed and finally clasped it for a quick shake. "Yep."

Jack turned his attention to Lisa and his smile widened. "You haven't changed a bit in the last twelve years."

"And you're going gray."

Lisa and Jack both chuckled and embraced each other for a quick, terse hug before he slapped a hand on her back. "Listen, I know you're wondering why I came out here with the crew."

"We sure are," Johnny interjected.

"I heard you call in and was in the area, so I thought I'd come past and see things in person."

Lisa raised an eyebrow. "You think I need a babysitter. Thanks."

"No, that's not it at all." He scanned the front of the restaurant, then leaned toward her. "But I wanted to get ahead of this before it got out of control. Do you have the list on you?"

She shook her head. "Not here, no. But it's somewhere safe."

"Good. Okay. Hey, my agents on their other cases in the area threw a few more golden nuggets of intel my way."

"Great." Johnny hooked his thumbs through his belt loops. "Now's a good time to share."

Jack chuckled. "Not out here in the open, Johnny. But since you apprehended one of the slipperiest criminals in the state, why don't you take a breather? You can follow me to my hotel in South Richmond and I'll give you everything I have there. It's a little more secure, yeah?"

"We're good—"

"Yeah, okay," Lisa said over the bounty hunter, who scowled at her with his upper lip curled in disgust and surprise. "We'll follow you."

"Great." Jack nodded at Johnny. "Hey, good work in there."

"Well, you know me. Approval's all I live for."

"Ha. Funny dwarf." The middle-aged Agent Brogan pointed at Johnny, then turned toward his car in the lot and slid inside.

Lisa pursed her lips. "Do you always have to be so abrasive with everyone you meet for the first time?"

Johnny scowled at Jack's car and headed toward their rental. "We can talk about it in the car."

CHAPTER TWENTY-NINE

"Okay, so talk." Lisa turned in the passenger seat to face Johnny as he maintained a cozy six-foot distance behind Agent Brogan's vehicle.

"I don't like this one bit, darlin'. Goin' with him to his hotel."

"Oh, come on. It's not a seedy motel for a drug deal or…whatever else. I know Jack. And if he says he has information, he can help us."

"Point of contact ain't supposed to be out in the field."

"Johnny—"

"And the thing that gets me most?" He glanced at her for a split-second before he looked through the windshield and inched their rental a little closer behind Jack's car. "He asked about the list."

"Yeah, everyone's asking about the list."

"Except that a fed ain't got reason to want that list. You already sent it to Nelson."

"Okay. And?"

"Darlin', how well do you know this guy?"

"This again?" She sighed and slumped in her seat to look out the window. "I know him, Johnny. Hamish knows him. We used to have dinner at his house on Wednesday nights when I was still a rookie."

"That's what I thought." Johnny let out a heavy sigh. "You ain't gonna like what I gotta say."

"It's par for the course. Just say it."

"A department handler who got both sides of the story from Nelson's team and his agents in the field ain't gonna get an emergency transfer to any case without gettin' all the facts."

"Johnny, he has the facts. That's why we're following him."

The stoplight at the intersection turned yellow and then red. Jack's vehicle slowed smoothly and the dwarf waited until the last second to brake sharply. Their rental lurched, the hounds yelped in protest, and he turned to look at Lisa. "If he had all the facts, he'd already know we sent the list to Nelson. And he wouldn't be askin' about it after we bagged the one magical he sent us to after callin' it a brokerage deal."

Lisa's eyes widened and she straightened in her seat. "Well, I'm sure there's an explanation for it."

"Sure. The explanation is your old friend's a dirty fed."

"That's—"

"It ain't ridiculous, darlin'. You got caught up between a rock and a hard place."

She didn't say anything else as they followed Jack's car across town but he could hear her grinding her teeth the whole way.

It turned out Jack Brogan was staying at a seedy motel, and when Johnny turned to Lisa and opened his mouth to comment, she pointed at him. "Don't say anything."

They left the vehicle and joined the agent at the room door on the ground floor. He unlocked it, glanced around, and gestured for them to step inside. A look of distaste crossed his features when the hounds trotted in after their master and each of them uttered a short growl as they entered.

"Better watch it, pal," Rex muttered.

"Yeah, we know what you're up to. Make any sudden moves and you're dead."

Of course, he couldn't hear a word of it but Lisa clenched her jaw even tighter when he shut the door and went to flip the lamp beside the bed on. The room filled with muted yellow light.

"They aren't the friendliest dogs, huh, Johnny?"

"Naw. They're sensitive, is all."

"To what?"

"The smell of shit."

Lisa glared furiously at him and he sniffed as he leaned against the dresser.

Jack seemed completely oblivious to the jibe and opened the mini-fridge instead to pull three beers out. "Want one?"

She took it without saying anything but the dwarf didn't reply at all.

The agent shrugged. "All right."

"So what's this new intel you have," she muttered, took the bottle opener from her old mentor, and popped the cap off without looking down. She didn't drink it, however.

"Well, it's sensitive, you know?" Jack took a huge swig of his beer and sat on the bed. "And I know this is hard for you, kid, but I also don't want to let you in on anything else that'll simply put you more at risk."

"At risk?"

"Sure. These World Nexus bastards? They know about you now. That a half-Light Elf and her dwarf sidekick are still hunting the whistle-blower even though he's already been caught. And that they have the master list."

"Hold up." Johnny stood from against the dresser. "Who are you callin' sidekick?"

Jack ignored him. "So I want to make sure everything's squared away first, right? You do have the list, don't you?"

Lisa closed her eyes briefly and the bounty hunter watched her intently.

There it is. She's puttin' the pieces together and now, we gotta deal with what happens when it's all out in the open.

"Yeah, Jack." She nodded. "We have the list."

"Good. Is it close?"

"I said it's safe."

The agent sighed. "I know you're being cautious about this, Lisa, and you should be. There's so much riding on the line here but I'm here to help. You trust me, don't you?"

She plastered a thin smile on her face and shrugged. "I always have."

"I know. You and I go back a while, don't we?" He paused to take another huge gulp of beer, then nodded. "So how long do you think it'll take to get me that list?"

"What about Hamish?"

"Yeah. The list will help us get him. Your son got himself into more than enough trouble as it is but he'll be all right. He's tough."

"Sure." Lisa glanced at Johnny and the look she gave him said absolutely everything he needed to know—*you were right.* "It won't take us too long to get it but I have one question first."

"Go for it."

"What do they have on you?"

Jack chuckled. "What?"

"I sent Nelson a copy of that list last night—which you would have known if you'd been approved for the emergency assignment to handle us on this case."

"Lisa…" The man's smile widened. "Do you honestly think I'd do anything to put Hamish in danger?"

"I didn't until about half an hour ago."

The motel room fell instantly silent. Jack looked from her to Johnny before he stood with incredible speed and drew his service pistol from its hip holster. His half-empty beer bottle toppled to the floor and he aimed the barrel of his gun squarely at her chest.

Johnny whipped his knife out and stepped toward him.

"Don't move, Johnny. I love this woman but take another step closer, and I'll do what I have to do."

"You lyin' piece of shit. You don't love her. You're usin' her."

"I don't have a choice!" The agent glared at Lisa, his hands steady on his weapon. "World Nexus know about Margery and about what I've done."

"Jack—"

He grimaced to reveal two rows of perfectly straight teeth. "That's what they have on me. I've been chasing Hamish and that list like every other deadbeat criminal because if I don't turn something up, they'll rat me out. You know what that means?"

"It doesn't mean you have to do this—"

"It means I lose everything, Lisa. Everything—no pension and no paycheck. I couldn't give a damn about my reputation. I'm washed up as it is. But if I can't afford her medication and her treatment, it's all over for both of us. No one wants to hire a dirty fed. So tell me where the list is."

"I already told you." She stepped toward him and he drew a sharp breath. Amazingly, the bounty hunter complied when she held her hand out to stop him from doing anything rash. "I sent the list to Tommy. He has it. That's why he's putting a team together. And you still have a chance to walk away from this because World Nexus and everyone on that list is finished. You don't have to do this."

Jack laughed and it sounded like an insane cackle. "You have no idea how much they can do to ruin your life faster than you can blink."

"Truly? They have Hamish and you think I don't know." She stepped toward him again and paused, both hands raised in surrender now. "Put down the gun, Jack."

Sweat beaded on the man's brow and dripped into his graying eyebrows. He blinked it away with a hiss. "I have to do this."

"Then do it!"

"Lisa—"

"Johnny, shut up." She didn't break away from her mentor's gaze as she crossed the distance between them and raised her chin. "If that's the kind of man you want to be—if you can live with justifying this because there's a chance to help your wife—then do it. I've already crossed my lines in the sand to find Hamish and have no regrets. So do what you have to do."

"Stop. Just…" He growled harshly and scowled at her. "Stop talking and back the hell up."

"No compromises, right? Exactly like you taught me."

Jack might have lowered the gun on his own but before he had the chance, a mouse darted out from beneath the nightstand and crossed the room. Luther uttered a sharp bark and shouted, "Rex! Get it!"

Startled, the agent swung his weapon toward the hounds. He fired one shot, but the bullet struck the ceiling instead when Lisa lunged toward him and knocked his aim off when she drove both arms against the underside of his. The pistol arced from his hand and clattered into the tiny attached bathroom and he turned toward her with wide eyes. "Lisa—"

She delivered a wicked right hook into his jaw and powered it with a small burst of light energy that flared inside her clenched fist. He reeled from the blow, staggered back, and tripped on the edge of the bed before he thumped awkwardly onto it.

"Ah! Fuck!" Lisa shook her hand out and stared at her quickly reddening knuckles.

"Whoa, whoa, whoa, lady!" Rex barked and his tail wagged furiously. "That's what I call a knockout! How many times did you do that, Johnny?"

The bounty hunter froze where he stood and stared at the unconscious form on the bed. "Not many."

"Yeah, well…" Lisa winced, stretched her fingers, and crouched beside the mini-bar. "He taught me how to do that too. I don't think either one of us ever expected me to use it on him."

"Shit, darlin'. Are you all right?"

"I will be when I find some ice." She rummaged in the tiny freezer and stopped when Johnny placed a hand on her shoulder.

"I ain't talkin' about your hand."

She sat back on her heels and stared at the open freezer door. "I don't know what I am right now, Johnny. The only thing that matters is Jack is off the table and we still have no idea where Hamish is. So let's focus on getting to the bottom of that before we talk about our feelings, okay?"

"Huh." He removed his hand and stepped away. "That's fine."

With a handful of ice, she stood and went to the dresser to sift through the clothes shoved into the top drawer. "Jesus. He must have been here for weeks."

"And he got close to what he wanted. His wife's sick, is that it?"

"Yeah. Lung cancer." Lisa whipped a shirt out of the drawer, dropped the ice into it, and wrapped the makeshift icepack around her hand. "The last time we talked, she was in remission. I guess that changed."

"But she's still fightin' the fight so he had a reason to do what he did."

"Johnny, you don't need to convince me that he isn't a complete shithead. I know. But the fact that he'd try this when he knows Hamish is part of it? I don't think I can..." She paused at the open drawer with wide eyes.

"Don't think you can what?"

"Shit."

Luther sniggered. "Yeah, I got that problem sometimes too, lady. The trick is—"

Johnny snapped his fingers. "Hush."

Lisa reached into the drawer and pulled out another long silver pen that could pass for any kind of regular pen if one didn't look too closely. A faint orange glow came from its center, however, and she turned to hold it up in front of Johnny. "We need to find out what this is."

"I guess we do." He glanced at Jack and rubbed his mouth. "Do you have any more of them zip-ties?"

"Yeah."

"Good. Mentor or not, good ol' Jack ain't goin' nowhere until we find out why the hell he has one of those pens in his shirt drawer."

CHAPTER THIRTY

The zip-ties proved to be unnecessary. When Jack regained consciousness, it was only partially and he groaned once on the bed before his cheek slumped onto the stained comforter again. Rex and Luther had taken it upon themselves to sit at the head of the bed so they could loom over the unconscious man and watch for sudden movement. There was none.

The two partners stood beside the dresser and studied the two pens they'd taken from Hannah Penton and Agent Brogan.

"We've now found three of these." Lisa turned one in her left hand, her right fingers stiff and sore even with the ice pack tied around them. "And something tells me they aren't souvenirs."

"Do you think they're actual pens?" Johnny's crooked smile faded when she glanced disapprovingly at him but he shrugged and clicked the end of the pen he held. Neither of them expected the tip to open in tiny segmented pieces to reveal what looked like a flash drive small enough to fit inside. "Well, look at that. World Nexus' got a damn tinkerer on the payroll."

"Ameyna had a top-level hacker. Does it surprise you?"

"No. But I liked knowin' I was the only one."

Lisa clicked the end of the pen she held and the tip opened like the first. "So it's not a pen. Okay, so what are they?"

"Wait. Does yours have an extra little hole in there near the drive-lookin' part?"

Lisa smirked. "That sounded super technical."

"Come on. You know what I'm sayin'."

"Yeah. It does."

"It might be it works like a plug."

"You mean like they connect?"

He shrugged and held the tip of his pen toward her. "It's worth a try."

She glanced at the hounds. "Rex. Luther."

They both whipped their heads toward her.

"If this explodes and blows us up, feel free to do whatever you want with the old man on the bed."

"Ooh, cool."

"Yeah, we'll handle it, Lisa."

"Wait. Why would you blow up?"

Lisa met Johnny's gaze and grimaced. "Nothing makes sense anymore."

When she plugged the end of her pen into his, the pieces fit perfectly with a soft click. The orange light inside glowed even brighter before a tiny panel on the side of each pen opened and projected a thick orange light above the connection.

"It's a goddamn GPS system," the dwarf muttered, his eyes wide.

"Oh, my God." Lisa scanned the image floating in the air, and words scrolled across the projection. "Johnny. There he is. It's all right here. We found him!"

"Hold on, darlin'." His gaze raced across the feed and he tried to store all the information in his mind. "Damn. They have some very sophisticated networkin' to share this kinda info."

"Well, it's not like they could simply put up a bulletin board." Lisa released her pen and left Johnny standing in front of the projection. She took her phone out to snap pictures of the information about World Nexus' next big function, including the confirmation that Hamish Breyer would be there "for anyone who wants a crack at the traitor."

"Johnny, we have to get there."

"Yeah, that's one way to do it." When the image disappeared, the bounty hunter disconnected the devices and a click of the ends returned the segmented panels to their place until they looked like normal pens again. "And I ain't happy with it, but I think this is somethin' we oughtta call Nelson about too."

"Yeah. Yeah, shit. You're right." Lisa spun frantically, pulled Nelson's number up, and made the call. "Oh, my God. We found him."

He slid both pens into his pocket before he snapped his fingers. "Come on, boys. I need air."

"Yeah, good idea, Johnny. Smells like mouse turds in here."

"And desperation." Rex leapt off the bed after his brother. "Like worse than the kind in that weird bar."

The dwarf opened the door and stepped into the parking lot. "Do you wanna join us, darlin'?"

"Nelson."

"Tommy." Lisa nodded and hurried after her partner. She slammed the door shut behind her and didn't bother to waste her energy thinking about Jack.

"Look, Lisa, I know you're invested in this—"

"Yeah, listen. We found something."

He paused. "Okay."

"You haven't sent your team out anywhere yet, right?"

"No. I'm putting the final pieces together—"

"Good. Listen, we have new information. We found Ha—we found the whistle-blower. World Nexus has some kind of gala tomorrow night in Roanoke. Nine o'clock start time in the ball-room of the Wells Fargo building. The Light Elf will be there. We need to pull him out."

"Wow. Okay. Uh…where did this information come from?"

"Well…" She glanced at the motel room door and wrinkled her nose. "We got it from Jack Brogan."

"What? What the hell does he have to do with this?"

"That's a long story. And I honestly don't want anything to do with what happens on that end, so you might want to come down here and see for yourself. With backup. Or send someone."

"No, I can be there in a few hours."

"Okay. I'll text you the address. And I'll send screenshots of the information we found. This one should be in the bag, Tommy. But Johnny and I need that team to already be in there when we arrive at that gala—"

"Hold on, Lisa. Slow down for a second. I'm glad you called 'cause there's something else you need to know."

She stiffened and swallowed as she stared at the asphalt of the parking lot. "What?"

"We got some intel about the whistle-blower. Hamish Breyer."

"Fuck," she whispered.

"I'd ask if he's any relation but that one word says it all." Nelson cleared his throat and the sound of a door closing softly came over the line. "Lisa, how close are you to this?"

"I'm…" She closed her eyes and shook her head. "That doesn't matter."

"It does. Especially since I have a team briefed and ready to go at the drop of a hat. I've managed to keep his name under wraps for now, but there's no guarantee how long it'll last. And you know how the department will handle this if they find out you and Johnny took the lead on this op without being completely transparent—"

"He's my son, Tommy, okay? My son. And I need to get him out of there." The agent paused for so long she had to check to make sure she hadn't dropped the call. "Are you there?"

"Yeah. Lisa, I'm so sorry—"

"Don't apologize. Help me."

"Yeah, I am. Which is why I'm calling you off the case."

"Don't."

"Lisa, you're a good agent. As weird as it is that you've technically been on paid leave for months to do…whatever you're doing with Johnny, you're still one of our best. And I can't help you if you go into this without considering the liability. You know I have to file my reports."

"I can't, Tommy."

"Let me talk to Johnny."

She rolled her eyes and held the phone out to her partner with a grimace. "He wants to talk to you."

"What the hell for? It sounds like he already said everythin' he had to say."

"Take the phone."

He complied and pressed the device against his ear with a grunt. "Nelson."

"I know you don't want to talk to me or probably see me ever again, which is fine. We had our run, Johnny and you milked the department for everything it's worth. Christ, you could've gotten a hell of a lot more out of that deal but I need you to hear me out, okay? For her sake."

The dwarf watched his partner pace across the parking lot. The makeshift icepack dangled against her hand as she chewed her fingernails. "Talk."

"I know it's her son we're looking for and my team will do everything they can to get Hamish out of that gala. They will get him out. But I can't promise anything if she can't pull back and let us do what we do. The two of you got farther than anyone else and honestly, at this point, I would have pulled you out of the case by now anyway. What happens next is below your pay grade."

"It ain't about the money, Nelson."

"No shit. Which is why I'm asking you to keep her out of this. She deserves that. And we'll handle the rest."

He sniffed and scratched the side of his head. "Yeah, I hear ya."

"Okay. Have her send me the details. You know, she wouldn't say what happened with Brogan."

"I think that's best for now. I ain't sayin' I'm comin' to work with the damn department again but if I ever do, Nelson, your ugly mug is the only one I ever wanna see. Understand?"

"Wow. That's very touching, Johnny."

"I'll only say it once. I'm trustin' you get this thing done, ya hear?"

"And I'll let you know when it is."

The bounty hunter hung up without another word and handed Lisa her phone. "Go ahead and send him what you said you would."

"What did he say?"

"Send it first. We'll wait for whoever Nelson sends here for Jack, then we'll talk."

"Johnny—"

He cupped her cheek and nodded. "One step at a time, darlin'."

With a sigh, she sent the motel's address and the screenshots of the information they'd pulled off World Nexus' connecting intel pens. With that done, they sat on the curb of the sidewalk in front of the ground-floor motel rooms and waited.

Tommy didn't come out himself but the agents he sent to pick Jack Brogan up and take him into questioning didn't stay to ask what happened. Lisa gave them a brief rundown with a simple, "You'll have to ask him about the rest of it. And take these to Nelson."

She gestured for Johnny to give the pens up and he complied reluctantly.

"Click the ends. They fit together."

The agents nodded and escorted a staggering, mumbling Agent Brogan into their car before they drove away.

"I coulda done a hell of a job on those pens with a few hours in my workshop."

"We have another one at home, Johnny."

"Oh, yeah. Uh…speakin' of home—"

"Now you can tell me what Tommy said."

He clicked his tongue and gazed across the parking lot. "That's the thing, darlin'. We ain't stayin' in Virginia."

"What? That gala's tomorrow night. We need to—"

"The only thing we need to do is to go home. Let Nelson's team handle the extraction tomorrow. His guys know what they're doin'."

"Like hell they do! They wouldn't know where to start if we hadn't found the intel for them in the first place!"

"All right, calm down for a second—"

"Don't tell me to calm down, Johnny. I am calm!"

The hounds snuck slowly away from the couple arguing in the motel parking lot and cast wary glances over their shoulders.

Johnny sniffed. "Yeah. I shoulda said somethin' else."

"Like why Tommy wanted to talk to you."

"You ain't gonna like it, darlin'. I don't care for it either, but Nelson and I agree on one thing at least. You're too close."

"Fuck off." She stormed away from him toward their rental and shook her head.

"Lisa, this ain't about doin' the work no one else can do. We did that part and you handled it better than I ever would have if our places were switched."

She jerked the passenger door open and turned to glare at him. "I helped you with the Red Boar to the end, Johnny. Even when I thought you were insane to go after someone fifteen years later."

"Wait, you thought I was crazy?"

Her only answer was to scramble into the car and slam the door shut behind her.

The bounty hunter squinted, then turned to find the hounds. "Hey. Do y'all think I'm crazy?"

"Uh, yeah." Luther trotted toward his master and his tail wagged. "Batshit insane, Johnny."

"But only in the best way."

"Yeah. Like, the kind you want in your two-legs."

He grunted and headed to the car. "Y'all are killin' me."

"Hey, it's not a bad thing."

"No, it's the best thing, Johnny. You're our kind of crazy."

"So are we."

The hounds leapt into the vehicle, smiled their canine smiles, and thumped their tails against the back seat in anticipation of another trip. Johnny slid behind the wheel and paused for a long, tense silence before he turned toward Lisa. She stared directly ahead through the windshield and her jaw worked furiously beneath her reddened cheeks.

"Lisa."

"I don't want to hear it. You and Tommy Nelson think you know what's best for me and what I can handle, and it seems I don't have a choice. It's typical, I guess."

"Now hold on." He shifted in his seat to face her. "Don't go thinkin' this is about control, darlin', 'cause it ain't."

"Oh, isn't it?" Fury burned behind her eyes when she met his gaze. "The department's tried to control magical agents and contractors since the very beginning. That's part of why they exist. And out of everyone, I thought you would have understood that. But now you're playing their game. For what?"

"Somethin' that matters a helluva lot more, that's what."

She rolled her eyes and jerked the seatbelt down to shove it into the buckle. "Drive, Johnny."

"No, I have somethin' to say and you're gonna hear me out 'cause this shit matters." She didn't look at him again but he continued regardless. "Nelson's put up with my bullshit for years 'cause he knows what I can do. That I get the job done."

Lisa scoffed.

"And sure, it might be he's crackin' down a little harder

on you than he ever did on me but the situation's a little different. Me getting too close didn't have my kid hangin' on the line 'cause Dawn was already—" He grimaced and cleared his throat. "All that aside, darlin', Nelson ain't doin' this to cut you off and cause you more hurt than you're already feelin'."

"Wow." A humorless laugh escaped her. "That's a hell of a way to say this is for my good."

"Naw, that ain't what I'm sayin'. It's as weird as hell, but Nelson wanted to talk to me 'cause he don't wanna see you hurt. It's as simple as that."

"Johnny, this is what we do. We go into dangerous situations with every single case and we don't back down. This isn't any different."

"Sure it is. Hell, I knew it the second you stepped through my front door with that know-it-all smirk and tried to convince me you'd make the best partner by disassemblin' my rifles. And I told you then."

Lisa drew a deep breath and slowly turned toward him. "That you don't do partners."

"Darlin', you ain't listenin'." He couldn't help but chuckle. "Nelson's goin' out on a limb to keep you outta this one 'cause he's head-over-heels in love with you. It's as weird as shit but it's true."

"And what? You're taking his side out of some kind of male solidarity?"

"Damnit. No. I'm—" The dwarf turned slightly to look at both hounds, who leaned forward at the edge of the back seat. Their tongues lolled from their mouths as they panted and watched the conversation with rapt attention. He frowned at them, shook his head, and focused on Lisa's intense glare instead. "I'm sayin' I agree with the sorry bastard 'cause I know exactly how he feels. And it ain't a male whatever-the-hell, neither. It's 'cause I… You know."

She leaned away from him and her anger faded quickly although she still frowned. "You what?"

"I get it. I know. It's the same for me."

"Johnny. If you're trying to tell me something, just tell me."

"I…Christ. I fuckin' love you, Lisa. That's why."

"Yes!" Luther shouted, pushed himself back onto the seat, and panted with excitement.

"Finally!" Rex giggled. "Man, Johnny. It took you long enough."

The bounty hunter cranked the ignition with a wild jerk and shifted into drive. "I shoulda never made those damn collars."

"Aw, don't say that, Johnny."

"Yeah, how are we supposed to give you moral support if you can't hear it, huh?"

Lisa watched him bluster as he clenched the steering wheel, then leaned toward him and covered one of his hands with hers. "Hey."

"What?"

A small, weak laugh escaped her. "You have to look at me for this one, Johnny."

He raised his eyebrows and when he turned toward her, his head jerked like a rusty gear finally used after being neglected for way too long. He finally met her gaze with wide eyes and tears shimmered in hers.

"That was hard for you to say."

"Christ, this ain't supposed to be a therapy session—"

"I love you too."

The car fell silent except for the rumble of the engine, and when she slid her fingers between his to take his hand, he couldn't for the life of him think of what to say. Instead, he simply said, "Oh. Good."

Rex and Luther broke into wild howls in the back seat, which made the two partners jump in surprise.

She spun to swat at them. "Not in the car!"

"Why not, lady?"

"Yeah, this is one of the best things that's ever happened. Wait, Rex. Is it supposed to be that weird and awkward when two-legs get into all the mushy stuff?"

Rex's laughter was the only response, and she slumped into her seat. "You can drive now, Johnny."

"Yep." He cleared his throat, accelerated, and spun out of the motel parking lot with a squeal of tires and the acrid smell of burning rubber.

CHAPTER THIRTY-ONE

Four days later.

Johnny stood at the kitchen sink in his cabin and scrubbed the dishes from lunch vigorously as he gazed out the window onto the back yard. Lisa and Hamish had been seated out there in the Adirondack chairs all morning and through lunch, talking while he tossed a stick occasionally for the hounds.

First the borgs and now her kid. Who'd have thought stayin' in the houseboat and playin' fetch with hounds who don't fetch was a package deal?

But he couldn't honestly be upset with setting Hamish up in the refinished houseboat as it gave him and his mom as much time as they needed to catch up after nine years.

Gettin' pulled outta that damn gala and strikin' a deal with the feds for that list ain't all there is to this. He has some things to resolve for himself.

He only realized he'd scrubbed the same plate far beyond the point of clean when she stood from her chair and looked into the kitchen window. The smile she gave him was dazzling, and he momentarily forgot why he stood at the sink at all.

When the back door opened, he dropped the sponge quickly

into the sink and put the plate into the dishwasher.

"Whoa. Is everything okay in here?"

"What? 'Course it is. I've finished the dishes."

"Okay." She gave him a quick peck on the cheek and chuckled when he hissed. "Oh, sorry. I keep forgetting which side of your face is off-limits."

"It ain't off-limits and simply ain't done givin' me hell yet."

"Hey, I ran into Ronnie this morning at the corner grocery. Your Wood Elf friend with the shotgun."

"Do you think I don't know my friends?"

"Right. Well, he asked me when you would go past his crab spot again to check the traps. He said you'd promised to be out there this week and he thought maybe you'd forgotten about it."

"Huh?" Johnny dried his hands on the towel and frowned. "I never said a thing about goin' to check the traps. Ronnie's losin' his damn mind."

"Well…I kind of promised him you'd go down there after lunch and take a look."

"Aw, hell. Didn't you think to ask me about it first?"

"Well, you weren't at the corner grocery, Johnny. And I wasn't about to call you in the middle of the conversation to corroborate his story."

"Fine. Fine. I'll go."

"Okay." She covered her smile with her hand as he strode through the kitchen and flung the back door open. Through the window, she met her son's gaze and nodded.

Johnny stopped beside the Light Elf who lounged in the back yard. "Have you ever been crabbin'?"

"Not that I know of." Hamish smirked and finished the last of his beer from lunch. "I'm not a fishing or boating kinda guy."

"Sure. I guess that runs in the family." With a grunt, the bounty hunter continued toward the dock.

"Hey, Johnny."

"Yeah."

"Listen, I want to thank you for letting me crash in your giant…yacht or whatever."

The dwarf snorted.

"I know you don't want anyone else staying on your property for a long time. My mom told me about what's been going on around here lately."

"Naw, don't mention it. It's only temporary."

"Yeah. I wanted you to know I'm working on something so I can get back on my feet and out of your hair, yeah? I won't go back to Oriceran anytime soon but it looks like something's about to open up for me in London in the next couple of weeks so it won't be long."

"Sure. I gotta…pull some traps up." The bounty hunter turned stiffly and hurried toward the dock.

If he's tryin' to pull some male-bondin' shit, he's doin' a piss-poor job.

He untied the rope on the airboat and cranked the throttle control stick to steer the craft into the swamp.

Rex and Luther raced to the dock's edge as the airboat pulled away.

"Don't you want us with you, Johnny?"

"Yeah, we'll fight the crabs for you!"

"Naw, y'all keep fetchin' that damn stick. I won't be long."

The hounds stayed at the dock for a moment, then bounded into the yard and barked and shouted for Hamish to throw the stick again despite knowing he couldn't hear a word of it.

Johnny accelerated as he moved downriver with the rising tide and drew a deep breath of the cool morning air. *I guess this is all the peace and quiet I'm gettin' for now. I gotta make the most of it.*

Fifteen minutes later, he pulled up beside the bank in front of Ronnie's trap buoys and cut the airboat's fan off.

I know I didn't tell Ronnie a damn thing about checkin' his traps this week. I haven't seen the guy in months. 'Course, he goes through Lisa simply to screw with me.

He reached down for the first line but stopped when a rustle of ferns on the opposite bank of the river caught his attention. Something large moved through the reeds.

He recognized the white fourteen-foot 'gator he'd set out to bring home on his airboat almost a year before. As soon as the massive reptile slithered into the water with an alarmingly loud hiss, he also spotted the 'gator nest on his side of the river not twenty feet away.

"Shit."

With a grunt, he reeled away from the bow of the airboat and hurried toward the harpoon gun mounted on the deck. The swiveling mount clicked as he spun it toward the predator's tail as it lashed through the water. The dwarf took aim, exhaled a breath, and fired.

Nothing happened.

"What the hell?"

Instead of the harpoon and the rope attached to the end, the gun had expelled a frayed piece of cloth dangling from the barrel. He ripped it off and read the words printed in black Sharpie—
Time to enjoy yourself, don't you think?

"Goddammit. This ain't a cartoon!"

The 'gator hissed again and raced through the water.

Johnny snatched his hunting rifle from beside the fan's mount at the stern and checked the chamber. There was no bullet but worse than that, the bolt was missing.

"Fuck!"

Frustrated, he dropped to one knee in front of the utility box bolted to the deck and jerked the lid open. The damn box had been emptied too, and in place of all his tools was another stupid note in black Sharpie—*Take a break. Put the weapons down.*

Who the fuck's handwritin' is this—

As the dwarf stood, the massive reptile rammed into the side of the airboat with jolting force and knocked him off balance.

With a growl of protest, he toppled overboard into the water and the territorial 'gator thrashed after him.

He drew his utility knife—the only thing some asshole didn't have the opportunity to tamper with—and got his feet under him in the swamp. The water reached his collarbones but at least the sandbar beneath him was solid.

The beast hissed again and opened its jaws as it sliced through the swamp. Johnny hissed in response and waited until the last second before he slashed upward with his knife. Blood and water sprayed away from them and he managed to retrieve an exploding disk from his belt before the 'gator returned to try another attack. He splashed as loudly as he could and roared at the top of his lungs in an attempt to scare it away as he pressed the top button of the disk and hurled it at the gray-white snout.

The device detonated with a boom and another spray of water and the monster hissed again before it turned tail and swam toward the opposite bank. Johnny yanked another disk free in case and waited.

And Lisa thought I was an idiot for keepin' the damn belt on me. Dammit.

Winded and with his heart thumping in his chest, Johnny slogged through the swamp toward the bank beside the airboat, his knife clenched in one hand and a disk raised at the ready. The 'gator didn't bother with anything more than opening its mouth wide and letting out hiss after warning hiss.

When the dwarf finally crawled onto the shore, he sat in the mud and propped his elbow on his bent knees. The slice he'd left along the side of his attacker's neck left a trail of bright-red blood down the creature's side. He'd hurt it but not enough to kill it.

It ain't an it, neither. How the hell did I not know a mama gator when I saw her first?

For a long while, Johnny and the albino alligator stared at each other across the river until he chuckled. "Look at you, huh? Scarred and as ugly as hell. A giant-ass prize everyone wants to get their hands on but can't. I bet you been around the block a time or two before this."

The 'gator took two steps down the muddy bank but stopped at the water's edge.

"Yeah. I feel ya. I ain't washed up yet neither, darlin', and I think you ain't reached the end of your days just the same. I ain't sayin' this is over. I might come back when I find out who the fuck tampered with my weapons so you'd best make use of the time, girl."

Soaking wet and covered in mud, the bounty hunter climbed onto the airboat and thrust his knife into his belt. The spare disk clattered to the deck and he cranked the throttle control stick before he steered the airboat in a wide U upriver toward his property.

After he'd docked the craft and tied it off, he stormed up the dock with his fists clenched at his sides and left a trail of soggy, muddy footprints behind him. The hounds didn't race toward him as they usually did. The Adirondack chairs were empty. Seething, he reached the end of the dock and the rest of his yard came into view when he passed the row of tall grasses.

"Surprise!"

The shout from a dozen voices was almost deafening.

Johnny froze.

Locals streamed out of their hiding places as they clapped and laughed. Arthur reached him first and released a deep belly laugh as he slapped the dwarf on the back. "You didn't see that comin', did ya?"

"What the fuck?"

Darlene stood in front of a banquet table spread with her cooking. The old-timers from her diner had set chairs up beside the table to be closest to the food when the woman said it was time to eat. Even Ronnie had come and he hobbled along in his bowlegged walk and wheezed with laughter. Lisa and Hamish stood in the center of it all and grinned from ear to ear.

"What happened to you, brother?" Arthur asked and examined his hand with a grimace. "Did you decide to take a swim?"

"I didn't have a choice." Johnny glared at Lisa and headed toward her muttering, "Excuse me."

The laughter and cheering died when the guests at the backyard surprise party noticed the state he was in. Rex and Luther raced across the yard howling. "It's a birthday party, Johnny!"

"Yeah, get it? Surprise!"

"Johnny?"

They skidded to a stop when he reached Lisa, still dripping clumps of mud and swamp water.

Luther whined. "Uh-oh."

"Um…" She spread her arms. "Happy Birthday."

"Who the hell took my guns apart?"

"Yeah, that was me," Hamish said with a crooked smile.

"You? Goddammit, I said you could stay in the houseboat, not fuck around with my boat."

"I'm sorry." Hamish chuckled and shared a sheepish glance with his mom. "I just thought it would be a funny prank, that's all. You know, get you to lighten up on your birthday."

"I don't need to lighten up."

"Well…Mom said you've spent too much time focusing on your weapons, so I thought—"

Lisa clicked her tongue and smacked her son's arm with the back of a hand. "Don't put words in my mouth. This was all your idea."

"I thought I'd get rid of the distractions," Hamish finished and fought back a laugh.

Johnny stepped toward the Light Elf who stood a good six inches taller than him and thrust a finger at the man's face. "You cost me a twelve-foot 'gator, son. I'd shoot you right now if you hadn't dismantled my damn rifle."

"Sorry. I guess we don't share the same sense of humor."

"Damn straight we don't. And don't touch my shit again, understand?"

"Yeah, Johnny. Yeah." Hamish raised both hands in surrender and nodded. "My bad. Is there any way I can make it up to you?"

Before the dwarf could spout another angry reply, the Light Elf moved an unopened bottle of Johnny Walker Black from behind his back and raised his eyebrows.

"Do you think a goddamn bottle of whiskey is gonna make this whole thing blow over?"

Hamish shrugged. "It couldn't hurt."

Johnny glowered at him for a long moment, glanced at Lisa, then scraped a glob of mud from the front of his shirt and flung it into the grass. "I guess it never does. Pour me a damn drink and maybe I'll forget how your prank almost cost me my good arm."

"Yeah, okay." With a grin, the Light Elf left to take two red plastic cups from the banquet table.

Lisa gave the bounty hunter a sympathetic smile and wrapped her arms around him for a long kiss. The locals cheered and laughed. "He's right, you know."

"About our completely opposite ideas of what makes a thing entertainin'?"

She laughed. "No. I did say you need to relax more. And… well, I did help plan this."

"Yeah, I guessed."

"It's your birthday, Johnny. It's time to unwind a little with family, right?"

"Ha. Some family." He looked around at all the Everglades locals who knew him almost as well as Lisa Breyer did and snorted.

"It's the only one you have, right?"

Johnny pulled her close against his soaking body and kissed her again. She was laughing even before he released her, and the bounty hunter responded with a wide grin.

"Sure. I guess it's better than nothin'."

Johnny, Lisa and their friends might have just celebrated Dwarf Bounty Hunter's birthday, but that doesn't mean the bad guys are going to give him a break. Continue the adventures with Johnny, Lisa and the coonhounds in *Big Bad Mother Dwarf'er*, coming June 6, 2021.

Get sneak peeks, exclusive giveaways, behind the scenes content, and more. PLUS you'll be notified of special **one day only fan pricing** on new releases.

Sign up today to get free stories.

Visit: https://marthacarr.com/read-free-stories/

I've been working with Michael Anderle for four years now. Feels more like ten but for all the right reasons. So many books have been packed into four short years that it feels like it has to be more.

But even better in some ways, I've changed a lot. Often because of one short sentence Anderle has occasionally said to me. "Why are you still doing that?" That's usually followed by the shaking of his head or well… laughter.

At first, I was doing way too much because I was living by the rule, *if I can do it, then I should do it.* Those *shoulds* in life are like sharp thorns. I had learned how to endure, which means to suffer patiently. Time to rewrite that script.

But to ask for help meant I had become lazy or was skirting my responsibilities. Layered on top of that was my amazement to be co-creating the Oriceran Universe and my joy at being a part of it. Didn't I have to continually re-earn my spot?

Turns out that's a nope. And, that behavior was actually getting in my way. Instead of rising to new challenges that would enrich my life, and even add to the bottom line, I was still doing all the detailed work.

That first time Anderle asked the question, it was a head shaker. He seemed incredulous that I was trying to balance everything and grow the Universe at the same time. *Why* was his next question. That was followed by laughter.

So, I took a leap and hired an admin – the wonderful Grace who keeps the wheels on the bus – and that side of the business – like the newsletter, or doing more promotions, or a hundred other details – actually get the attention they deserve. My business was able to grow. That left time for me to write and enjoy doing it. There weren't fifty things running through my head. I was down to about ten.

The pressure was greatly relieved, and life was so much better, but there were still stress points. Is it possible to get rid of them all?

Here was the next lesson on this path that I again learned from Anderle. Figure out what you love to do and separate it from what you don't want to do. Then come up with a plan. By then, the books were selling well, and I was in a position to give more tasks to Grace to do and really get down to the one thing I love to do. Write urban fantasy and throw a few fireballs. (Maybe swear some. Come on, it's me. Have you met the troll?)

And come up with ideas to connect with fans like Pizza Fan Fridays or my upcoming road trip with Craig Martelle complete with road trip t-shirts. May be brilliant, may be crazy. I'll let you know. First task with that adventure though is to get him to upgrade from the Buick. Maybe I'll ask him, *why*.

Anyway, all of this clearing away of the mind clutter has also made it possible to dream more and dream bigger. Maybe I'll also get back to doing some cartoon drawing again and maybe that will evolve into a children's book. Who knows? But, the bottom line is I have stopped enduring and instead, I find myself looking for solutions.

Now, let me pass on the favor that Anderle did for me and

give it to you. What are you still doing that you really don't like? How can you get help? Write me and let me know what you come up with. See you on the road. More adventures to follow.

Thank you for reading this story, and my author notes where I speak about Martha and her …issues.

Martha has a fantastic way of writing that just pulls you in, wraps you in a blanket, and (if it is winter) hands you a cup of hot chocolate or drink of choice. Then, she speaks naturally and you just follow the story without asking any questions, just taking it all in.

Or perhaps that is just me since I've spoken with her so many times I hear her voice in my head every time I read any of her author notes.

Huh, that means if someone else wrote her author notes and I didn't know, I would hear Martha in my head. That's kinda spooky. I mean, someone has the power to 'put' Martha in my head, and I hear her?

<<Shaking my head… trying to get back on track here.>>

Anyway, my comment is about WHAT Martha was doing when I would say something like 'why are you doing that?'

I'll provide my introspection about life and from there make your own conclusions (very Buddha of me*.)

My thought, which spurred my comments to Martha, was I

feel we work hard with long hours seven days a week. We should enjoy in the present some of the joy of the results of our work, and then we can save the rest for later.

If I were to work only for the future, I'd lose the desire to work in the now. Unless I taste the fruit of the results in the now, my imagination is without raw material to imagine what the fruit I have canned for the future will taste like.

So, I was encouraging her to use some of the results of her present work (income) and hire a person to help release her from some of the work. Then, she could fill this time with something else bringing her joy. She would then continue to work without as much danger of burning out.

Some other benefits include meeting more people that join you on this road of success, providing someone an income that helps them, and lowering one's stress and hopefully increasing their lifespan.

Figure out not only what do you like to do but what are you good at doing?

There is usually where you can make the most impact.

I spent over three years working seven days a week. I took two days off. One of those was one of the Christmas days.

I paid my dues, invested the time, and wanted to not die from the exertion early in life. I went to the hospital in September of 2020 due to heart issues.

Going a bit slower was a good choice.

We don't take money, fame, pride, homes, cars, ego, or any other 'things' with us when we close our eyes the final time. I do wish to provide our sons with a few things for their generation.

Some things. I hope to have enjoyed a large part of what I've made and shared with others while I'm here.

And not only 'when I retire.' I'm not really into this idea of retirement. I'm happy to continue futzing around with new creative endeavors. Perhaps I won't be CEO of a Publishing company, and that will be ok.

I'll have allowed others to challenge and be challenged by continuing to grow a company of stories and connecting those stories with those who love to hear, read or watch them.

Hopefully, that is a few years away.

One thing I will never regret is taking the time to slow down now that LMBPN is larger. I don't need to be 'the man' anymore.

Now, having said all of that? I'm off to go work on another Skharr DeathEater book!

HAHAHAHAHA....

Ad Aeternitatem,

Michael Anderle

Buddha saying I am referencing here is: *Believe nothing, no matter where you read it, or who said it, no matter if I have said it, unless it agrees with your own reason and your own common sense.*

Yes, I just watched a show on the history of the Buddha just two days ago. I had no idea about the history at all. However, this saying above is a personal belief in that I'll listen, but don't ever assume I will take someone's advice just because they said it. I will always think about it (sometimes not long enough) before accepting it, and I suggest others do the same. - Mike

Solve a murder, save her mother, and stop the apocalypse?

What would you do when elves ask you to investigate a prince's murder and you didn't even know elves, or magic, was real?

Meet Leira Berens, Austin homicide detective who's good at what she does – track down the bad guys and lock them away.

Which is why the elves want her to solve this murder – fast. It's not just about tracking down the killer and bringing them to justice. It's about saving the world!

If you're looking for a heroine who prefers fighting to flirting, check out The Leira Chronicles today!

<u>AVAILABLE ON AMAZON AND IN KINDLE UNLIMITED!</u>

CONNECT WITH THE AUTHORS

Martha Carr Social
Website:
http://www.marthacarr.com
Facebook:
https://www.facebook.com/groups/MarthaCarrFans/

Michael Anderle

Website: http://lmbpn.com

Email List: http://lmbpn.com/email/

Social Media:

https://www.facebook.com/LMBPNPublishing

https://twitter.com/MichaelAnderle

https://www.instagram.com/lmbpn_publishing/

https://www.bookbub.com/authors/michael-anderle

www.ingramcontent.com/pod-product-compliance
Lightning Source LLC
Chambersburg PA
CBHW020352110726
47899CB00006B/1692